D1039565

desire and its shadow

desire and its shadow

ana clavel

translated from the spanish by
jay miskowiec

aliform publishing
minneapolis, oaxaca

ALIFORM PUBLISHING
is part of The Aliform Group
117 Warwick Street SE/Minneapolis, MN USA 55414
information@aliformgroup.com www.aliformgroup.com

Originally published in Mexico as *Los deseos y su sombra*
by Alfaguara
Copyright © Aguilar, Altea, Taurus, Alfaguara, SA de CV, 1999

English translation copyright © Aliform Publishing, 2006

First published in the United States of America by
Aliform Publishing, 2006

Library of Congress Control Number
2006922003

ISBN 0-9707652-5-8

Set in Times New Roman

Cover photograph by Ricardo Vinós
Cover design by Carolyn M. Fox

First Edition of the English Translation
All Rights Reserved

CONTENTS

Part One: Chance in the Tail of Desire   3

Part Two: Notes for a Poetics of Shadows   47

Part Three: Of Subterranean Dreams
             and Other Choices   97

Part Four: Shadows that Dance Alone   143

Part One

Chance in the Tail of Desire

I

When Soledad came out of the vase and discovered that no one could see her, she had two absurd thoughts: she immediately went to the Librería Francesa and took a book of photographs she'd wanted for years, and she stood before a fat cop directing traffic on Paseo de la Reforma and began insulting him. The officer looked all around; he stared suspiciously at the stop lights, the cars, the clouds, but not finding the source of the voice, he finally asked his partner for help: "The devil is screwing with my mind. Get me to the hospital."

While the two cops took off in their patrol car, Soledad looked at herself standing there on the median in Reforma. Not even a sliver of a shadow escaped her. Then she thought about Lucía and her words when she'd invited Soledad to follow her into the vase: "It's a matter of your most secret desires. Come on, we'll go together." And as Soledad had a long history of desire, longing shone before her. But she hesitated: desires were strange coins that once tossed in the air fulfilled themselves according to secret designs, unknown even to those for whom they were formulated. And so she was curious to know what Lucía meant by her most secret desires. She had only decide to jump: after all, what was there to lose? It might all be so simple: jump inside a huge Chinese vase, just like when she and Lucía were girls, pass through the red-walled labyrinth and catch up with her before she fell into the dream of the dragon sleeping at its center.

And so when she emerged from the vase and discovered that no one could see her, not even a sliver of a shadow escaping her, she thought she was living through one of those stories that since she was a little girl she'd liked to tell herself. Or maybe it was just the sun, now at its highest point, that left all bodies shadowless. But no, a slanting sun fell over Mexico City on one of those transparently luminous afternoons that were becoming rarer and rarer. Soledad looked around; Reforma lethargically paused during a stoplight. To her left the Angel's golden column, like a stalk touching the sky; to her right, atop a hill, Chapultepec Castle. Before her, luxury hotels and the most modern buildings in the area. But however inaccessible those places were, while the dream lasted it was enough to wander through forbidden zones, to move aside the cordons, the barricades, the cloistered doors or simply extend her hand and take whatever she wanted. A feeling of plenitude enveloped her. She remembered that she was still carrying the book of photographs. A book full of clouds…She began paging through it when the stoplight changed and the traffic and pedestrians started moving again. A boy wearing glasses bumped into her and the book flew out of Soledad's hands and fell into the stream of traffic.

One after the other cars driving down Reforma ran over the first thing Soledad had ever shoplifted. When the traffic finally let up, the girl ran out and picked the book up. She put it down all battered on a cement bench, trying to understand what had happened. She didn't have much time to think, for a man in a dirty tattered trench coat and a red and white scarf wrapped around his neck sat down on the bench. He picked up the remains of the book with his hands tipped by long grimy fingernails.

"I told you to shut up, Francisca," he suddenly said. "This book doesn't belong to anybody and much less you. I found it first."

"Take it," responded Soledad to see what the man would do. "I'm giving it to you."

"Thanks," he replied, wetting his fingers and leafing through it. All at once he slammed it shut and turned toward the young woman. "Yes, I know you're hungry but you could at least wait until I was finished, don't you think?"

"I'm not hungry," she said.

"Don't try to fool me, you're hungry and that's why your stomach is growling like you're full of cats. But I'm not getting up until you say so. If our Lord Jesus Christ could admit 'I'm thirsty' when he was up there nailed to the cross, I don't see why you can't just say you're hungry."

"All right," accepted Soledad, not recalling the last time she'd eaten anything.

The man raised his nose with dignity. His gaze turned to a youth coming by pushing an ice cream cart.

"That's how I like it, Francisca…these photos are exquisite," he said, pointing to a page in the book, "but of course, you wouldn't understand. I can already see you telling me, 'Exquisite, you're crazy, they're just pictures of clouds…' You who like hearing about the Evening Adoration, but other obsessions, never. Cotton candy clouds, ice cream clouds, ices flavored with clouds…But remember clouds are also the Lord's work."

And not waiting another moment the man ran at the ice cream cart. The boy pushing it reacted too late. By the time he did the man had lifted the lid, grabbed a fistful of ice creams and gone running full speed through the passers-by and office workers. Soledad almost cried out, "Come back, I'm here," but the man had already disappeared in the other direction.

She wandered around for a while. As night fell the torrent of people on the street grew. As usual Soledad ran away from them, despite moments when she had to confront them face to face. Then something unusual began: people started bumping into and pushing her, they hit and jostled her as if the space she occupied in the air wasn't hers. She had to jump onto the steps of some store so she wouldn't get dragged along by the crowd and she didn't dare move until it thinned. While waiting she looked at a group of beggars sitting in the middle of the sidewalk before her. Most people walked by without looking and very few stopped to offer any money: or rather they walked around so not to step on them or just plain avoided them; but in any case it was clear they gave the beggars their space.

Confused, barely aware of what was going on, she began walking. She soon found the open doors of a movie theater. The man taking tickets didn't even flinch when she walked by. The movie had already started. In the darkness she took a seat in the first row far from everyone else and sprawled out. But the film didn't interest her. After resting a few minutes she began looking at people.

She tried to discern the way in which the silent audience observed and concentrated on a scene. Perhaps if she stood on the stage they couldn't avoid seeing her. She walked up a few steps and stopped in the middle of the screen; she waited a few seconds thinking the dream would end. But there were no whistles or shouts or boos. Was this really happening? She looked at her hands and her body, disbelieving they could see through her. She couldn't help but feel unprotected, as if the dozens of gazes that passed through her had the capacity to move her, to penetrate the intimacy that she now realized protected her skin. She looked at the screen and a cascade of images streamed over her. Soledad felt she was drowning in them, was being dragged toward that fall where her feet suddenly found the edge.

She must have fainted because when she opened her eyes the movie theater was empty. She ran out, not caring that pushing open the door she knocked an old cleaning woman to the ground. She ran all the way to Reforma; in a daze she turned her face east. At that moment she discovered Chapultepec Castle illuminated and at the top of the watch tower the memory of that *niño héroe*, the child hero who had thrown himself off wrapped in the nation's flag. Soledad also remembered hearing it was all just a story, the need of a country to invent for itself an admirable and prodigious history. Whatever the case, the tower at Chapultepec Castle looked like a lighthouse in the darkness that began to frighten her.

II

She took the path and ran all the way up to the castle. In that way, with the speed, she stopped thinking and feeling, turned into another gust of wind. About to cross through the outer gardens she was stopped by a penetrating odor of burning herb. A couple of soldiers hid between the columns of the arbor smoking a joint, the glow illuminating each of their faces in turn. Soledad began coughing.

"Hey, man," said one of the soldiers. "What are you, some beginner?"

"Fuck you, I didn't say anything," responded the other.

"Yeah, sure, but your cough?

"What cough?"

Soledad hoarsely cleared her throat.

"That. Don't you hear it?"

"What I think is you're already pretty stoned."

"You don't know shit. I heard a cough right close by. Put that out and let's take a look around."

They walked over near Soledad, peering closely from place to place without seeing anything.

"See? Just a fucking hallucination," said the soldier who hadn't heard the girl cough. "If that's what happens with pot, what do mushrooms do to you?"

In the light of the stone arches that surrounded the castle, Soledad made out the young half-Indian faces of the recruits. She went up to the one who'd just spoken and without thinking put her hand on his shoulder. The boy instinctively turned his head, but finding nothing but air he froze. After a few seconds, he ventured, "Where'd you get that pot, man? It kicks ass. Now I'm hallucinating, too."

Soledad observed that beneath the shadow of the boy's helmet a drop of sweat ran down his face. She took her hand from his shoulder and glided her index finger over that visage of nervous sweat. The boy trembled feeling the caress.

"You're not going to believe me," he said in a low voice.

The other soldier looked at him with interest.

"I must be going crazy," he finally admitted, "because I'm imagining some girl's touching me."

III

He was called the Elevated Knight and guarded the castle. There lived an Aztec king, a mad empress, and a female wolf. High up in his watchtower, the Elevated Knight protected them from the inclement city, from the skies and the scant faith of the visitors who thought the place was a museum…No, no.

The Elevated Knight was a stone giant that guarded the dreams of a princess who had turned into a mountain…No, not that either, and besides, that's another story.

9

The Elevated Knight was the name of the castle's tower...Much less.

The Elevated Knight was a man who had been had granted a marvelous gift: to see all his wishes come true...Only his desires were strange seeds that secretly and inexplicably germinated; perhaps for that reason they carried chance tangled up in their tails.

IV

By the time she managed to climb up the Elevated Knight, that raised noble horseman, the city was lazily awakening in the valley: its factories stretched out their smoky arms, the legs of its avenues wobbled along, the cupolas of its churches huddled together again. Soledad rubbed her eyes in wonder so that the play of mirrors wouldn't vanish. She discerned the air shimmering with a transparency that erased all distance: the Hill of the Star, the Cathedral, the Rectory Tower, the Hillock of the Eagles could be touched just by stretching out her hand. She inhaled deeply: the city filled her lungs. How far away seemed everything she had carried around that made her wish to erase herself, disappear, have someone else take the reins of her life and make decisions for her. But these feelings weren't new, nor recent the desires inspired: in reality she'd been hoarding them since the death of her father, or even before.

Now she was walking on the cornices of the Elevated Knight without fearing to fall, she hung from the pole where the flag of the fatherland fluttered on every important date, and she felt light and immune because no one could see her. It was as if Sol (that's what her father used to call her, my Sun) was a girl again, when the world was created with her own steps and she could travel with life hanging like a little hat down her back, climbing inside armoires or jumping over neon signs. Or sitting on the haunches of Javier García and galloping through endless stories. In one of her favorites they got off the horse to take a train to Oaxaca, Javier García's birthplace. On the way there her father remembered it was Soledad's birthday and asked the engineer to stop at the first toy store he came across. They were just about to pass by a big well-stocked store when the engineer pulled the emergency break, at the risk of causing all the wagons to crash into each other. The sudden halt didn't have any great consequences: the passengers only tumbled atop those in front of them, a few ladies in veiled hats left little square kisses on the jackets of their companions, a boy cried because his ice cream flew all the way into a girl in the next car. Soledad smiled as the scoop of ice cream filled her cheeks while Javier García took her by the hand to go look at toys. They entered the store and a wall covered with all sorts of dolls rose before Soledad as he pressed her, "Quick, choose one." She picked a doll dressed like an Asian girl. Cradling it in her arms, Sol boarded the train to continue a journey forever etched in her memory.

And so she began to construct her own myth: her father was able to stop the world in order to make her wishes come true. And when he had to die—because he could stop the world but not hold back death—he left her the stories and that gift of desire she had yet completely come to know.

"I want you to realize," Javier told her before they took him to the hospital, "that desires are always fulfilled. They animate life or destroy it. They're a kind of flame we carry within ourselves. Don't ever let it go out."

Desire. What could that be? Later she learned: around the source of her desires they wrapped a white sheet and buried it six feet under ground.

Soledad turned pale. After the burial she returned with her mother and her brother to the house of the portals. But Carmen cried all day and when Soledad came to check on her, her mother came right to the point: pay attention to your brother, he's the man of the house now, girls don't speak when they're around adults, be still as a porcelain doll: if it moves it breaks. Sol remained still: she didn't want to move anymore either. But within her the flame still sparked, refusing to go out. One afternoon—her mother was crying less, her brother Luis had gone out to play soccer with some boys on their street—she came across the doll her father had given her hidden in that Chinese vase found under the stair landing. Then the flame brought her back to the train trip and her father telling her like a little angel, "Quick, choose one."

V

They spoke little among themselves. They believed that if they came near each other the entire fort might come tumbling down, like the house that fell apart in one of the stories that Soledad had begun reading. There were lots of books in her father's study. Carmen, wishing to see her at peace, let her take a couple. That's how Soledad stumbled across stories and myths like those Javier García used to tell her at night. Then she remembered the words her father had said before dying, that desires are always fulfilled, and she asked herself if she hadn't ever wished for his death.

On the other hand her mother neither read nor left the house unless it was absolutely necessary. It took her years to forgive Javier García for dying. She looked closely at her son Luis, she looked at Soledad and there came to mind the list of fifteen suitors she'd had before choosing him. Soledad recalled the look of fascination on her mother's face each time she saw how Javier smiled as he recited his own list, which he did all the time. "You're so clever," joked Carmen when she saw him pay the same attention to the chief of the cane cutters union as the wife of the Minister of Agriculture. Perhaps because at the end he kept his list to himself and death defeated him in an act she interpreted as betrayal (a renal deficiency that had been incubating since before they even met), or perhaps because she repented having loved him, having let herself be seduced by his image of a fort that would contain the little crystal cup she was, threatening to shatter from the most insignificant rumor, perhaps for all this and because of the list of fifteen suitors Carmen García took refuge in anger. For her, all the bad of the world crept like dust into the objects, furniture and people who inhabited the house of the portals. At least Luis got away for awhile from the ashes in which Carmen and Soledad immersed themselves daily, when the one made pastries because she couldn't get by on her pension and the other finished her homework, each heading off to submerge herself in sadness. Luis, on the other hand, was friends with all the older kids on the block and often played soccer with them. Carmen didn't like him hanging around with such vagabonds (as she referred to Miguel Bianco and the other boys who raised a ruckus whether their favorite team won at soccer or one of their uncles lost a radio station contest), but she finally admitted that men were men and now Luis, in some way, was the man of the house. He didn't have his father's smile, but rather boasted a sullen, reserved manner that Carmen interpreted as good judgment and virility. That's the reason she asked Luis which pastries would sell better, the milk or the mocha; if it would make sense to introduce to the neighborhood market the "sighs" which had made her so famous in Pinotepa (not only because those she used to make in her home town brought a growing clientele to her bakery, the window of the family's living room, but for the good those dainties did her); she also asked him if she should give Soledad cabbage and *epazote* syrup to make her stop being scared because she always wore a frightened look on her face, or if it wouldn't be more prudent to recluse her in a parochial school where the nuns could keep her locked up. Fortunately, Luis wasn't so wrong in his advice: he suggested the mocha pastries because they were the ones he preferred (and the truth is they sold much better); he discarded the ideas of the "sighs" of Pinotepa because he would have to be the one to peddle them from shop to shop (and of course they did a survey and found they were too cloyingly sweet and homemade for the taste of the capital); he also recommended the syrup because he wasn't the one who would have to take it (which didn't rid Soledad at all of her fear but did make her vomit up a foot-long worm that according to Carmen had been sucking out her soul); and finally he counseled Carmen to keep Soledad at home. But they still visited the nuns' school. The mother superior gave Soledad a piece of candy and asked her to wait in the garden. Outside, time didn't seem to go by; in reality the minutes turned into slavering, viscous hours that went on and on in the same place. Some girls asked her to play on the swings. Soledad went along and forgot why she was there. Going higher and higher, the swing and her happiness rose to the heavens. She suddenly looked down. Her mother and Luis were approaching the exit. She leapt off in full flight and fell and rolled upon the ground, getting some bumps and scratches, but she caught up to them.

"Silly, what are the tears for?" asked her mother in the taxi on the way home. "Haven't I told you that girls need to be calm, quiet and obedient? I should enroll you in that school so those saints of obedience can straighten you out."

Soledad looked at Luis. Her brother was reading a Spiderman comic book the cab driver had lent him. She envied his aplomb, his reserve, that air of an older person with which he crossed his legs and concentrated on what he was doing. She thanked him from the bottom of her heart when he put down the comic book to intercede on her behalf: "I told you, mom. Boarding schools are very expensive."

VI

Soledad liked to tell stories. On the floor of the living room, in every two or three mosaics appeared a tile with a drawing. She walked upon the seams of the mosaic as if they were a tight rope, she'd come across a tile, invent a story and thus pass from a singing windmill to a couple watching a river flow by to the faces of a woman and a little boy to the face of a man with a Luciferian beard she always tried avoiding. They didn't have a television and they didn't buy the newspaper; only when Luchita began to clean and turned on the radio with its commercials and soap operas did Soledad learn to some confusion that *Martín Cadena gave an Ariel to his girlfriend to wash the Olympiads that would arrive like whitish swallows from the northern countryside.* But Luchita wasn't always there. When in some indolent moment Soledad came across a mosaic of a bearded man, she made up the story of Lucía, a little girl punished by being shut up in the dark depths of a vase; as they gave her nothing to eat, she scraped its sides and ate the clay that came off in dust. "Ask forgiveness or I won't let you out," someone shouted at her. The voice bounced off the curved walls and the echo made the girl run about lost in the labyrinthine vase. Then words crashed into each other and spoke to her in confusing messages: *Oedipus doesn't drain I'll knowhere you out of here, for a home ask for fortgiveness, quick and abrupt hiccups, ask for an order of cesar gives you hearth, you marry and ere I won't sbreak where beat.* Exhausted and approaching the center of the labyrinth, Lucía didn't hesitate to go on. The open gullet of a Chinese dragon appeared before her as the only way out. Lucía let herself be eaten by the beast. Far from doing her any harm, she smiled triumphantly from within its guts. Facing the impossibility of inflicting punishment, her pursuers furiously gnashed their teeth.

Lucía's story could leave Soledad alone for hours in the dark living room of the house of the portals. Once she'd fallen under her influence, a salesman peddling housewares could ring the doorbell, her brother's friends knock a ball over the roof of the garden shed, or Luchita arrive to make dinner when Carmen didn't get back until evening without her even able to get out of the vase.

The stories of the tiles changed and became more complicated. Out of the shadows of those hours emerged the portraits of Carmen hanging on the walls. Seldom was seen a woman so sublimely crowned by a natural diadem of bougainvilleas. Soledad knew they were photos of her mother before she married, but she'd never seen her like that. Memories of her somber gestures returned, as if an opaque veil covered her face, and the portraits in the drawing room only depicted a bad copy of all that remained of that beauty. One day, while Carmen was coming back from selling her pastries, the man with the Luciferian beard revealed to Soledad that her real mother was trapped behind the glass of those photographs (in reality the windows of a castle). But that wasn't all, added the man, the person trying to pass herself off as her mother was responsible for Lucía having to take refuge in the guts of the dragon.

"I believe you, I don't believe you," said Soledad as she jumped on one foot over the tile of the bearded man. Finally she decided: I don't believe you. "You have seen the proof on the nightstand," responded the man. Soledad ran upstairs to Carmen's bedroom, searching for a vase with a petrifying non-desire. Once in the room she took a few steps in the darkness and turned on the light. Instinctively she closed her eyes. A rain of reddish sand flooded the insides of her eyelids. When she opened them to look for the nightstand, guilty white teeth glistening with water emerged before her.

She began to tremble all over, and so the bearded man was right. Soledad had always had doubts about her mother, but now…Now the bearded man burst out in a hammering cackle and she was all alone in a house that was a jail, where they'd hidden her so that her father (who was still alive) couldn't find her. She felt like she was choking, now aware of the truth with which the walls of her prison closed in and cornered her. Lucía was certainly freer in her vase.

A reddish glow, like that which emerges when we try to see the inside of our eyelids, showed her the way. Soledad entered those narrow passages and amazement swallowed up her steps and sadness. And so desires were fulfilled. One had only to examine them by the right path.

"What were you getting into?" asked her brother as soon as Soledad opened her eyes.

"And Lucía?" she asked, realizing she was no longer in the vase. Luis furrowed his brow.

"You were playing hide-and-seek with one of your friends...What a scare you gave us. Mama called the police and they've just shown up."

Soledad heard voices downstairs. And to think all this revolved around her. Luis ended up helping her out of the vase, offering his hand so she could jump out. She couldn't believe a simple desire could cause such an uproar.

"And we'd already given you up for dead and disappeared," Luis said. "The bad thing is the police have already come and will have to arrest you for filing a false report."

VII

She sleeps with a candle burning. Your light illuminates the clarities of sleep. I'm here, but I don't know where. I hear footsteps coming towards me. Then I flee. An overflowing garden hides me among violets and lilies and spear-like iris leaves. The gardener's room emits a faint light. I want to enter but a lock prevents me. A side window forces me to stand on tiptoe to reach it. I watch the gardener from behind greasing a mower. His fingers glide over the blades without being cut. An earthquake shakes my legs while the man moves the tool's inner mechanism. He takes out the ball bearings, he tightens screws, a few small springs jump free and finally the mower spurts oil everywhere. The man casts a glance before leaving: I have to squat down so he doesn't see me. Finally he comes to the door. His head grazes the frame: that's how big and tall he is. I follow him inside an immense house. He's got grease spots on his pants and from one of his hands hangs a drop of oil. I climb the stairs after him; in silence I blur into the shadow of his tracks. On the stair landing a Chinese vase has trapped a dragon. Its mouth is as dark as my room when I'm alone at night with crocodiles creeping beneath my bed. Or they're probably little dragons, lizards or salamanders doubly cursed: if you touch their transparency they will pursue you during the day as well as while you sleep. I haven't touched any with my hands. But their eyes are also tactile, like the eyes of the dragon that swims in a sea of blood where it finds itself imprisoned. They say you don't have to feed it, but I know it's alive. For that reason I throw pieces of meat from my meal into its dark stomach. And that's also why I'm here, unable to move, in this darkness which my eyes feed upon and from where I can see the gardener come upstairs. He didn't try to, but he has abandoned me to the prying eyes of the dragon. I want to escape, jump down the stairs before it's too late. Futile. In vain. The dragon's pupils open like the eyes of a lock and inspect the room where the man's steps have directed him to. Luminous nights of bodies that grope in the dark and perceive and creep and waste away implacably. Now I know where I am. I can see with my hands the remains of digested meat and dark, transparent salamanders. Here, imprisoned in the lecherous guts of the dragon.

VIII

As the minutes passed, Soledad appeared more and more like the clouds: as soon as she saw that city of mirrors at her feet, she became illuminated with a full and subtle happiness, as if she had crossed some memory with her soul and were becoming enveloped in a deep shadow burdened with damp and sadness.

Or it might appear a blessing to challenge the emptiness of the castle tower, feeling more than ever how her life and desires belonged to her.

But it was enough that a couple passed through the inner gardens at the foot of the Elevated Knight, that the boy looked into the girl's eyes with that passion of someone who wants to wake up in order to continue dreaming, and in turn Soledad should have asked herself if in truth what had happened to her, becoming invisible, was a gift. She felt alone and lost. She looked at the sky and then the forest surrounding the castle, cloaking it in some autumnal dream. Farther away, the triangular tower of Tlatelolco and the train station reminded her again of her father, and then of Miguel Bianco, conqueror of epic poems and soldiers. But to get to Tlatelolco she would first have to make a stop at her friend Rosa Bianco's. She boarded the train of memory because something akin to strangeness or melancholy made her think she'd perhaps find an answer in the past.

IX

Soledad couldn't understand why her and nobody else. Cruel, torturous, difficult lives abound so that there's always someone worse off than you, someone more torn than the one whose seams are ripped, a thought which ties together that life is a labor of undoing threads. Though it's true, as they say, that you draw the outline of your own shadow with every kind of loose and tight weave. But Soledad's past, the sum and total, the multiplication and the division of fractions, she didn't invent, or at least not everything. For this reason to know which path her stepless tracks would follow, she returns to the past and pokes among her memories—true photographic moments—before they, just like her, end up becoming veiled. The prodigious thing about those moments is that despite the dust and yellowness, it's enough for them to settle in that special eye of memory for the fixed images to follow one after the other. Frame by frame a scene now creates its own atmosphere. There is a brick building where Soledad's friend Rosa Bianco used to live, a half block from her house; long hallways connect one apartment to another, numerous staircases go from floor to floor. Soledad focuses the frame: a staircase, the one leading to Rosa's apartment. But this scene, in which appears a girl who is Soledad herself and a man who will always be the Unknown Man, originated in exterior, miscellaneous things, on the street a glance exchanged between two people who recognize each other, a rapid history of seduction

18

and turbulence that led the man and the girl to the shadowy cube of the staircase leading to Rosa's apartment, where the girls played in a language of lips and hands that almost always led to a dark corner of a closet where it was easier to take refuge from guilt.

But the point of departure was the staircase. In the dim light, Sol focuses on the disparate silhouettes of this girl and this man who leans forward to whisper something in her ear and at the same time kiss her on the cheek, who lifts the hem of her rather short dress, and puts his hand up it (in reality, not as damp as the soft little cushion guarded by the girl's panties).

Before going on (the excited look on the man's face, the girl's shining eyes, the silvery coins he offers her all rush together), Soledad resists believing everything which will be determined by this scene. All right, she asks alone with her shadow, how many people have desperately gaped into the caverns of sex? For whom does the anguish of one's own unknowns prove easy? Who isn't a plaything of another's desire? And above all, who doesn't enjoy being so? Wasn't that what happened to Soledad and the Unknown Man, when beyond any judgment based on the difference in their ages which would incriminate him, she was the one who signaled for him to follow her, so that later, facing his legs, and then later he facing hers, he initiated her into the pleasure of her body, foretold from that gaze in some store?

Fine, as well weighed the coins that one after the other the man handed to the girl as if to keep up appearances, his pervert's honor in complete peril. And the coins weighed even more heavily because the girl desired to buy a gift for her friend Rosa Bianco who had lately preferred playing with her neighbors. What sort of gift?

Rosa Bianco wanted some ballet slippers that she ended up getting, and two pairs of them. The coins Soledad got from the Unknown Man would be added to the coins from her allowance she avoided spending and those Sola, as her friend called her, surreptitiously extracted from her mama's own funds.

But the story of the slippers would occur later with its inevitable dose of disillusion. Before that were the snapshots of the staircase and the Ángeles sisters.

Cloud Lesson 1

I don't know how the skin of secrets is made. In front of me an old man turns to verify my submission. I follow him to a cube of darkness in an abandoned building. Before entering the penumbra I stop: someone screams my name with foreboding anguish. The man's eyes then shine in the darkness that buries him. A coin invitingly blazes in one of his hands. I take a step and hear my name again. The man shows me a bigger, shinier coin that turns him into a silvery specter. I discover what I knew from the first complicit gaze: the same smile that conquers everything, not the original, but it looks like it with the imprecision of an old sepia photograph. Spider threads inexorably draw me in. Behind, in the light, my shadow remains listening to a name already far from me, shouted for the last time.

Both coins confer a benefit upon me. In my hands radiates the obscure light of a secret. The man looks at me but doesn't see me: he sees only his own desire. The whiskers of his moustache tickle me but the coins in my hands are part of a pact. He touches me for the first time. On my silky skin will remain the trace of a sobbing earthquake. Quiet, very quiet while the man takes off my clothes—the little red dress, the little cambric panties he lowers to my calves—in order to play out a desire. I'm not a duck but I swim in the humidity, I don't have glass eyes but I'm next to a window where everything has become memory. The rain falling outside doesn't refresh me. The man's lips search me out again, his hairy mouth searches for my shortened breath and makes it even more labored. I don't know why his hands have so many pin-shaped fingers, and why the pain of feeling myself go beyond myself is something that has little in common with pain. I'm just a doll. Immobile, waiting in a dark station for the man to finish constructing a tunnel in me. He approaches with a resplendent smile that breaks the darkness like the coins in my hands did before. But the train no longer moves forward: an indispensable stop has turned it into a postcard image. Once again they've said my name. Not that it's been shouted: someone simply appears out of the passageway of light and threatens to become present. Then I run. I climb the stairs that lead to closed rooms. One of them is my own bedroom. Before I enter, something gets tangled in my feet. Then I get dressed. But my body is still all a beating heart. I crawl to my bed before the dragon smells my steaming blood. The coins remain in my hands. They've lost their splendor. Now they only cast their rays upon the flaming darkness of guilt.

Cloud Lesson 2

Rosa and I were playing in the patio of her apartment building when a pair of angels arrived. There are angels of varying sizes, sexes, and hierarchies but these were almost old. They invited us to their house and we couldn't refuse— who could resist such an offer? They took us by the hand and sat us down on their bare legs, they fed our mouths a pap of clouds and grated air, they patted us on the back to burp us. And amidst all those things (combing our hair because we were dolls, rubbing noses because these were Eskimo angels), was a delicious friction, that tickling absence left behind by fingers or tongue.

They decided to bathe Rosa: their angel mouths slipped beneath her dress, the t-shirt, the panties, sipping the grime and stains from my filthy, piggish, dirty friend. I felt hungry. I looked around and found a plate of pears in the middle of the flower-strewn mantle. I reached out my hand and brought the fruit to my mouth. One of the angels approached and looked at me with her crystalline gaze while I sucked out the pulp and gnashed its rigid peel. The other angel left Rosa to see how the pear disappeared inside my mouth. I thought as they were angels that such a simple act of magic was impossible for them. Then they surrounded me.

"You shouldn't have eaten it. We were only playing," said one. "Aha," said the other, "now what will we tell our mother when she comes home?" I wanted to say it was no big deal, it was just a piece of fruit, but they menaced me from above with their sword of mortal sins. I cringed in terror and the pear fell from my hand, bitten forever more. They threw me out of their house. I begged them forgiveness, I suggested we arrange the pear on the plate to hide the mark of my teeth. But they still flew resolutely across the patio, brushing their wings against the cube of the staircase leading to Rosa's home. They were going to accuse us.

The frowning brows of the angels were fixed in wrinkles.

Rosa insisted, "I'm going to tell you something, a secret."

The angels stretched out their necks and ruffled their wings a bit.

The silence extended like a taut cord. They waited.

Rosa said in almost a whisper, "God punishes bad girls."

The angels rose upright as if a bolt from God had really struck them.

"That's it?" And they laughed with a hollow, sonorous laugh that revealed to me their true essence.

"Let's get going. They're so...stupid."

And they marched away arm in arm. Rosa and I watched from the landing: they were still laughing. I looked for their sharp, pointed tails, but to no avail: their wings covered their talons.

"Rosa, what is the heart of an angel made of? Is it like our own?" I asked to say something.

"I don't know. Instead answer this riddle: What are the lions at the entrance to Chapultepec Castle made of?"

"Bronze?"

"No."

"Marble."

"No."

"Then clouds."

Rosa let out a sigh and rested her head upon my shoulder. "We won't play with them again," she said, referring to the angels, her eyes glistening with tears.

I promised her no, I caressed the sleeve of her sweater and we stayed there holding each other while we watched the afternoon change in color. When we parted (her mother had just shouted it was already dark), Rosa carried off my pubis and one of my legs and me her heart and left arm. I knew then my promise had been in vain. Rosa would go tomorrow for our ration of clouds.

With the coins the Unknown Man had given her, plus those she'd managed to hoard, Soledad bought some pink ballet slippers. She seemed more clever than ever when she asked her brother to go downtown with her to buy them, telling him she needed them for the end-of-the-year festival, but Carmen couldn't know because she wanted to surprise her. For the couple weeks the trick lasted, Luis would come up to his sister making butterfly movements with his hands and feet to the confusion of his mother, who ended up thinking it was just another adolescent phase her son was going through. For her part Soledad had to act like a little branch of spikenard, svelte and delicate as she imagined were the world's *prima ballerinas*. Firm and reticent more than anything else after her frustrated attempt to ingratiate herself with her friend, the slippers she bought her still shone beautifully with her ribbons and satin skirt, but they'd arrived too late: the day before, the Ángeles sisters had given Rosa slippers adorned with little bouquets of silk roses. It didn't seem strange, then, that Rosa should like them better and decide to wear them in a private performance for the sisters. Sol returned home with the slippers under her arm. Now that she'd gone up to her room and looked at their satin fabric, she imagined her friend fluttering among the Ángeles. Perhaps if Rosa had suddenly died Soledad might have cried less, but to imagine her in the company of others, enjoying herself so far away, inexplicably gave her the perception of her own death, a cutting dimension in which the adverb "never" incarnated the horizon of every verb and name possible. ("Will that be the reason," Soledad thinks now, mounted on the shoulders of the Elevated Knight, "will that be the reason why really serious events, like death and betrayal, leave us outside the battle, like me now, in this limbo where my steps are lost?")

And while those other limbos arrived, sitting in the darkness of her room Soledad ran to the farthest corner of herself to find Lucía: she jumped into the vase, crossed the labyrinth and reached the center. The reddish glow surrounding the dragon let her see she'd found it asleep. She silently approached with the slippers in her hands and set them to one side of the enormous head. The dragon's eyelids stirred but it didn't awake. Finding the slippers, Lucía broke into a smile between its two gleaming fangs. Then she carefully separated the scales on the dragon's throat to form a hollow where she nestled her body.

"They're pretty," she said, trying them on. Then she took a couple leaps. "And they fit me perfectly. Next time bring me a velvet ribbon for my throat."

Soledad nodded yes and Lucía responded in turn with a curtsy, then stood on her toes and arced her arms like a professional dancer. It was strange to see her dance in the kimono, but it didn't seem to hinder her. With each leap she rose a little higher and when she began to fly, Soledad couldn't tell if her legs propelled her through those rarified airs or if the slippers were magic. Suddenly Lucía held her hand out for Soledad to come along. She hesitated a moment but the slits of Lucía's eyes were smiling and what could she do but accept. Her hands split through the red clouds that the sleeping dragon exhaled with an unusual calm. To untangle herself so, to go after Lucía just to touch her neck and have her burst out laughing, to do pirouettes together as if the one were the reflection of the other…Sol glittered but still lay in wait for the dragon. Contemplating his unchanging sleep, she and Lucía laughed together.

Finally the dragon began to move. Carmen's voice woke it as soon as the sound entered the vase. Soledad couldn't fly anymore and she fell on her butt against the clay surface; Lucía ran to take refuge in the dragon, which devoured her in one bite. Now Carmen's shouts crossed the reddish cavern like thundering bolts of lightning. The dragon became enraged: it roared and exhaled a black smoke that covered everything in confusion. Soledad felt afraid and tried to reach her mother's shouts. She jumped without being able to touch any of them and it wasn't until they diminished, until her mother lovingly begged, "Wake up, my child," that she could grab that thread of a voice and emerge from the labyrinth. On the outside, Carmen was hugging a doll the size of Soledad. It didn't take long for her to realize the doll was herself.

XI

Soledad couldn't remember at what moment she told her mother about the ballet slippers, about Rosa and Lucía.

"A punished little girl in a vase. What foolishness you come up with. Well, I suppose it comes from your father. The poor guy was rather ideatic. But if those slippers exist I want to see them and I want to know where you got the money to buy them."

And for a good part of that Saturday morning Soledad immersed herself in the dictionary looking for possible meanings of "ideatic," asking herself if it wasn't a cousin to "maniac" and in consequence half-brother of "sexual"; or if, starting from the premise that lunatics lived in lunar attics, then the ideatics might live in the attic of ideas, a place where surely the slippers had never gone, given that Lucía was rather a member of the dragonatic family and there was no way you could ever get them to leave the vase.

Carmen wouldn't accept that the slippers had disappeared. "Maybe a couple good whacks would make you remember."

"I remember..." said Soledad visibly trying to recollect. "Yes, yes, I remember. At Rosa's house there are some slippers." And she went to look for them. On the way she kept repeating to herself the reasons she'd give her friend for borrowing them. But Rosa wasn't home, she had gone with Doña Cande to pick up the money order her father had sent from New Mexico.

Rosa's older brother Miguel opened the door and told her to come in and wait. Soledad was just about to go home empty-handed. Seeing her hesitate, he said, "What, you scared?"

Soledad looked at her scuffed shoe tips and came in. Miguel closed the door. On the sofa in the little living room rested a newspaper. Soledad sat down next to it.

"You want something to read until my mom and sister get back?"

Soledad wore such an astonished face (they never bought the paper at her house) that Miguel replied, "Sorry, but here we don't buy the funny pages."

Soledad picked up the paper and began to read it with seeming attention. Miguel went into the bathroom. Although he shut the door his stream of urine splashed loudly. Soledad remembered a few weeks earlier when she and Rosa had for a few moments shared that same bathroom with him. The two friends were in the bathtub "swimming" in their t-shirts and panties. They bathed their dolls, told each other stories and were playing with their t-shirts off when Miguel knocked on the door and said he had to come in. Rosa had locked the door and refused to open it.

"Look, Rosa, if my girlfriends leave without me it'll be your fault," begged Miguel with his mouth right up to the hinge, a faint ray of light from the hallway filtering through the crack, so that the girls could watch his face and he could see a piece of the curtain.

"Girlfriends? Why don't you go to a demonstration?" shouted his sister.

"Ah, dumb little Rosa," whispered Miguel again. "If you shout a little more, you'll save me the trouble of having to tell mom."

Rosa looked at her friend and trilled with pleasure a few times.

"Mama, Miguel says..." she pretended to shout.

"OK, OK, Rosa. What do you want in exchange?"

"Well, a little formal gown for my doll you can buy at the stall of doll clothes in the market, two passages down from the Japanese store."

"That's it? You don't want by chance some ballet slippers and a paper parasol for you and another for your friend? Come on, Rosa, I'm peeing in my pants. Let me in."

"First promise me the dress."

"Sure, but open up already."

Rosa asked him to wait until she got back in the tub so her brother wouldn't see her "naked." The door didn't open until she said she was ready. Then Miguel came in. They heard him urgently unzipping his pants; then the stream of urine broke against the ceramic toilet and churned the water's surface with an unknown intensity (at least that's what it seemed like to Soledad, who couldn't ever remember sharing the bathroom with her own brother Luis). Rosa looked slyly at Soledad and signaled for her to take a look. Soledad shook her head no and feeling cold sat down in the tub so the warm water would cover her more. The curtain barely came down to the top of the tub and from there they could see Miguel's pants. An impulse pushed Soledad to move closer and take a look, but she could only see his back. He was wearing a blue suit and not, as usual, a t-shirt and gabardine pants. Still standing, Rosa carefully quickly closed the curtain and peaked out. The stream of urine ebbed and a gaseous burp escaped the lips of Miguel, who was completely absorbed in himself. Rosa burst out laughing.

"It looks like a turkey head," she said.

Miguel shushed her and took a swipe at the curtain that only caused a noise.

"You're going to kill my inspiration. Attend to your friend, it seems she's not even breathing."

The stream trickled like a leaky faucet and finally turned silent. In the meantime, Rose returned to the far end of the tub where she found her friend. They both shivered a little from the water, which was turning cold, and a bit from the silence they heard on the other side of the curtain. Miguel's shadow extended over the plastic surface and the outline of his hand searched at the other hand for the faucet.

"Oh, the little ones are cold, are they?"

And he opened the cold faucet. The spray fell directly on Rosa who without meaning to protected her friend with her body. They screamed with feigned indignation. Rosa quickly reacted, pushed aside the curtain and with her hands like a stick jabbed at her brother. Soledad began to do the same.

"Terrorists," exclaimed Miguel, taking hits so he could get closer. He took off his jacket and stretched out a hand toward his sister's head to dunk her under the water. Rosa flung out her hand trying to scratch him, but her brother finally pushed her down. When Miguel at last let go, she screamed. Suddenly Soledad remembered the time Rosa had interceded on her behalf with the Ángeles and threw water into Miguel's eyes. He pressed his eyelids together while Rosa started laughing. Miguel, too, but now his face turned toward Soledad; as soon as he got the water out of his eyes he came near and took her arm. He pressed so hard that Soledad almost screamed. She fell to her knees, feeling like all of Miguel's strength was concentrated in the hand that grabbed her and in the lower lip he bit distractedly. Despite the pain, Soledad discovered at that moment Miguel had the same lips as Rosa: fleshy and pressed together in a gesture that recalled a child's pout.

Rosa began shouting for her mother. Suddenly Miguel let Soledad go, smoothed back his hair and turned around to put on his jacket before the mirror. It was true: he was going out with his girlfriends.

They didn't realize Doña Cande had arrived until she let out a little laugh.

"This is the big scandal? A water fight?" And she laughed again while taking down a couple towels hanging over the washer to dry off Rosa and Soledad. First she helped her daughter; when she turned to Soledad and ran her fingers through her hair, Soledad thought there was cream on her hands, but then realized that was simply how soft the fingers of Rosa's mama were.

A long silence transpired and finally Miguel decided to break it. "So, the doll store is next to the Japanese?" he said, putting on cologne. "Good. I'll pass by there tomorrow because right now I'm running late."

"And where is this boy going all dressed up? What's he late for?" asked Doña Cande, flicking a couple drops of water hanging from Miguel's hair.

Rosa's brother took a necktie from his jacket pocket and began tying it. "I have a date," he said mysteriously.

"But with members of your high school's Strike Committee," interrupted Rosa out of revenge.

Of course Miguel turned to look hatefully at his sister, but Rosa didn't seem to notice and continued stroking Soledad's arm.

"Miguel," began Doña Cande, standing in front of her son and adjusting the knot in his tie, "you know nobody here is going to stop you from anything."

"Mama, believe me, I have a date with a girl."

"Miguel, I'm the first one to criticize the government. But with your father so far away, us always short of money…You all know you're stirring up a hornet's nest."

"Mama, I'm going to meet a girl at the Museum of Anthropology."

"That's right," joined in Rosa, turning to her mother, "because that's where the demonstration starts."

"She's not my girlfriend, but my pal here is jealous…"

"Who's jealous? You? Soledad?" asked Rosa testily.

"All right kids, enough. No fighting. Rosa, why don't you lend Soledad some underwear and both of you change? And you, Miguel, all dressed up, but you're going to wear this medal," said Doña Cande, taking it from around her neck to put on him.

"But mama, I'm not a believer."

"You don't have to be, the Virgin of Zapopan will still accompany you. If something happens, tell me, who's going to wash the dishes tonight?"

Weeks had gone by since that meeting. Back then Soledad and her friend had shared the watery trench to ambush their enemy Miguel. Now, on the other hand, Rosa was better friends with the Ángeles and Soledad was alone with Miguel who had just come out of the bathroom. Correction: Soledad was alone because the boy had gone to his room as if nobody else was in the apartment. He must have reconsidered the situation because he suddenly shouted for Soledad to go into Rosa's room and play with her dolls. Soledad knew this was her opportunity to look for the slippers but doubted she could do it because she would have to pass by Miguel's room. When she finally made up her mind, she tried not to make any noise: the beating of her heart was enough to blare to everyone a sudden fever, deadly and unusual. While she walked down the hallway she caught Miguel out of the corner of her eye lying on his bed reading. She finally reached Rosa's door and once in her room began quickly looking for the slippers. She thought of borrowing them, although to do so she would have to carry them hidden from Miguel's view. It didn't take long to find them in the drawer with all of Rosa's favorite playthings tucked under her bed. They were ripped at the toe and sole and one of the little bouquets had come off, which Rosa had reattached with a pin. Soledad supposed they had started to fall apart from all the private performances for the Ángeles and decided to leave the slippers where they were.

She scurried back down the hallway. Once again her heart beat as if a stormy sea was about to overflow inside her. Before passing by Miguel's room, she stopped. The scuffed toes of her shoes seemed to await an order. She tensed her body but the sea and her beating heart dragged her towards Miguel's room. She covered her face with her hands. What would she say to him? Would she smile like a fool, tell him that she had jumping shoes that made her leap to the shores of his room before the sea—what sea?—could reach her? Soledad formed a wish out of the shame of finding herself there before him. She asked, "Don't let him know I'm here."

She covered her face with her hands for a few seconds, but Miguel didn't say anything. She opened her eyes and contemplated him while he read, absorbed, not paying any attention to her presence, as if her desire had been achieved. At first Soledad was scared of what she'd done, but a few seconds were enough to consider the advantages. She could near him without danger, smell him, perhaps touch him and inhale his own breath. She cautiously approached until her face was almost touching the spine of the book. No, definitely, Miguel didn't see her. She, in turn, looked at the curve of his eyelids, the exact color of his eyes, the scar in his right eyebrow, those fleshy lips that attracted Soledad's mouth as if the room where they found themselves, the book between them, or even she herself didn't exist and everything was concentrated in that attraction to his lips that erased all else. She kissed him. She had dared. Barely the caress of an angel's wing, a burning and complete happiness. But on the other side of the moment, in that dark face behind all things and time, was unloosed Miguel's reaction, his head jerking backwards with a surprise that almost covered his eyes, as if he'd fallen into a trance. Soledad thought he had rejected her.

She flew from the room; her lips carried the feeling that something had been ripped from them, as if Miguel had bitten her and in the hole from his teeth remained a fiery void.

But Soledad didn't know the rest of the story, what fifteen years later the dead from the Cathedral would have to tell her: those who will die by violence begin to live in a limbo where they are touched by neither pain nor happiness, and at times this limbo prevents them from seeing even their own hands; and thus begins the hurried forgetfulness of a body that once dead will horrify others just to be seen and known as their own. But at that moment Soledad only thought about the story of her desires, how as she fulfilled each one she did so secretly and obscurely, in an imperfect, inconsistent, failed way. Or were the material and character of her desires incomparable?

She moved away ready to leave. Suddenly Miguel's voice called to her. "Sol, are you still here or have mice eaten your tongue?"

"No…yes…I don't know. I mean I'm still here but the mice haven't robbed me."

Suddenly Miguel appeared in the hallway. Seeing the girl near the door, he hurried to add, "My mom and Rosa won't be long. Why don't you come chat a little?"

Soledad looked at her shoes again. What would Lucía do in her place? She imagined her emerging from the vase wearing the ballet slippers and walking self-assuredly down the hallway where Miguel awaited an answer. She remembered the fiery angel's wing that still burned her lips and could only think of fleeing. Lucía, on the other hand, approached Miguel asking, "What are those?" and pointed to a poster of three beautiful women hanging on the wall of Miguel's room near a desk and shelf crammed with papers and books.

"You don't know my girlfriends. Come here, I'll introduce you: Angélica María, Marilyn Monroe...and this one here, who tells secrets to my *comandante* Che, Bridget Bardot. So what do you think? You like them?"

"I'm not a man."

"Well, you look a lot like your brother. If you cut your hair, I could confuse the two of you, even ask you to go look at girls on Insurgentes Avenue."

Soledad lowered her eyes. She knew that her brother Luis, his friend Miguel and other guys on the block made incursions through the neighborhood for nothing more than the pleasure of discovering some nice ass, a pair of dreamy eyes or a head of silky hair. She envied their complicity and that air of experienced hunters with which they attracted their prisoners. No doubt she would have liked to be one of them, to put her arm over Miguel's shoulders and walk together to the men's room and seal that alliance of sex that passes from urinal to urinal, without walls or isolated stalls like women have. But Miguel must have realized he had offended her because he added, "Well, you're not so bad, and when you grow up maybe you'll be a surprise. I can wait for you. Look at them—I'm not so picky."

She knew he was kidding but once again she felt in danger. She stayed there, recalling the time she was a marble doll while an unknown man stirred feelings in her. The memory of that image made her tremble all over because it was one thing to be carried away by her own desires and something else entirely to obey another's and discover in her submission, as had happened with the Unknown Man, our own true nature. She thought of fleeing, but her thoughts somehow turned transparent because Miguel reacted by grabbing her arm.

"All right, tell me, when you grow up which one do you want to look like?"

She knew she had to respond, but her muscles had gone numb, just like her will. "I don't know. Which one do you like best?" she answered.

Miguel squeezed her arm even harder. Soledad remembered the time in the bathroom and she couldn't stand the pain but was still unable to scream or try to escape.

Miguel bit his lip before going on. "What do you think?"

"I don't know," said Soledad, dragging out her words.

"You do, too," affirmed Miguel and squeezed her arm even harder. Soledad bent over in pain, but she couldn't avoid the emotion spilling from all her pores, bringing her to the edge of her body and threatening to overwhelm her. They ended up rolling on the floor, him pinning Soledad's arm down, she with her stubborn "I don't know." A sudden glimmer let Soledad perceive Miguel's near squeamishness, but she was scared what might happen. A "yes" would have sufficed, or a nod of her head, that signal of "you got me" which in reality was "I let myself get trapped." But instead, obstinate, terrified, her skin turned into a whirlwind, she repeated, "I don't know."

Then Miguel let her go and returned to his bed and book. Soledad looked at the trace of his fingers on her skin, vanishing with an ease that had nothing to do with the indelible mark of later days and years when she thought about what could have happened that day. She began to retreat. When she heard Miguel talking, she thought he had decided to give her another chance.

"Close the door all the way when you leave," he said not looking at her.

That's just what she did. Lucía took Soledad's hand as they went down the steps. Suddenly Lucía let her go and said, "You should have left him to me."

Later she jumped back into the vase and didn't come out again until she heard about Miguel's death.

32

Guilt carries its hands bound. I listen to histories, I remember prohibitions. There is an immense garden and a tree at its center. After having tried the fruit, disobedience isn't the most important thing. (Of the three friends, innocence is the one we never get back.) Leaves on the vine hide most of the sins. The serpent is a wingless dragon, a fallen angel that can't get up. In the meantime they pay: the expulsion of a life that is also death: everything in the monodactyl flaming sword and in the vine's leaf with its five bashful fingers.

The man carries a white blindfold in his hand and a branch of flowers for his wife, who has just given birth. (Children are born of sin; that's why they must be baptized.) (How does a man touch a woman? What does he do to her when they're alone? Does he sit her upon his lap like a swing? Aserrín, aserrán, the beams of Don Juan. They ask for bread, they ask for kisses, they choke upon the…penis?) I walk behind the man. His back doesn't keep me from seeing him rocking back and forth in his bed last night. Of course I look at him with the dragon's eyes, from its steaming guts that penetrate the night. The walnut beams creak in the floor upstairs. A squirrel comes out of a hole and climbs over me. Touch it and it will clamp its needle-like fangs into you. I don't touch it, I don't touch it, but it already strikes with its violent little claws, its stinging teeth and it distracts me with a new, resplendent pain. Like that stirred in me by the fangs of the dragon that drank my first blood. Like that lacking to the man who groans and almost cries. He has wounded his hand and now will have to bandage it. He has touched the forbidden fruit. Sharp edges surrounded the fortress and tore at him as he entered. Despite everything he made the fortress his own just like the Cricket King does after crossing the bridge guarded by the dragon's fangs. Now the man's bandaged hand is the sign of guilt.

XIII

Whoever he is, isn't Cain one of her brothers? Or at least, doesn't she desire him so? If God spits on you or strikes you for a single excessive error while he looks with smiling eyes upon the errors of your brother, how can you accept those first slaps in the face? In any case it was a matter of brothers: scratching fingernails, rolling around on the ground, swearing at each other…Carmen had gone to the hospital to have a hernia operation. Her older sister, Aunt Refugio, came to take care of Soledad and Luis. Soledad only remembered having seen her a few times. On the other hand Luis started sending her cards in Pinotepa just as soon as he began learning his abc's. Aunt Refugio, who only had daughters, answered him now and then, and Carmen thankfully read those letters because since her marriage to Javier García, she and her sister had become distanced and not even Javier's death managed to re-establish the familial order that had joined them since long before the death of Grandma Marina. Luis took the first steps, encouraged by his mother: in one letter in his messy fourth-grade handwriting, he asked Doña Refugio to be his communion sponsor; later came in the garish style of his aunt an invitation to spend summer vacation in Pinotepa and Puerto Escondido, where she went each July to soothe her rheumatism. Trying hard to remember her because they clearly had crossed paths, Soledad finally concluded that her aunt could only be that woman whose gloomy face was marked as if two deliberately drawn lines sutured her lips. She also recalled the simple barrette that kept her abundant silvery gray hair in a bun.

And so in one of his letters Luis informed Doña Refugio about Carmen's approaching surgery. And Doña Refugio's decision came in a telegram: "I'll take care of your children while you have your surgery *stop* I'm on a bus tomorrow *stop* Cuca." Mama cried with joy and repeated the last word over and over. Not understanding why, Soledad stood in the door and shouted at Luis, "Did you real-ize Aunt Refugio signed her message 'Cuca'?" Luis came across the improvised soccer field, ruining his team's offense to the whistles of his teammates, and excitedly asked Carmen with a smile, "Really, ma?" Soledad looked at them as if they possessed a trea-sure map whose plan and direction they wanted to keep secret. She didn't know then the etymology that transformed a comforting and protecting word like "Refugio" into "Cuca," the wife of the incommensurable, dark and frightening Cuco. And so she asked, "Is that her name, 'Cuca'?" Carmen was so happy that she forgot to scold the girl for asking a question without first being given permission. "No, girl, don't even think of calling her so. Your aunt only lets people she trusts and appreciates do that. It's been years since she let me, but you see, time erases everything," she answered, winking at Luis.

Before Aunt Refugio came to the house of the portals, mama talked with Luis and Soledad. She put him in charge of the house and gave him money so their aunt wouldn't spend her own. To the girl she said, "Soledad, be on your best behavior and do what you're told. Don't talk back, don't contradict her. Use common sense and do what you're told, and you'll win her over."

The meeting between Carmen and her sister was quite the scene. Doña Refugio welcomed her into her arms, and protection. As a sign of forgiveness, she took a small wooden box from her purse and before the astonished eyes of her niece and nephew opened it. She removed from it Grandma Marina's ring from her marriage to Grandpa Tobías and gave it to Carmen.

"Here," said Doña Refugio. "You should keep it."

Soledad looked at her mother, who almost floated with happiness. Carmen gathered her children around to show them the ring. It was a double band of gold cast in one sole piece, engraved with the initials of her grandmother's maiden name. Carmen put on the ring and embraced her children beneath Refugio's beatific gaze. It was a strange and distant happiness, but Soledad was attracted by the forgiveness that had so reconciled her mother with life.

The first day went by without any change. In the morning they took her mother to the hospital and the rest of the day was like any other. In the afternoon they ate with their aunt, and Luis, contrary to his custom of going out in the evening, went to study in his bedroom. Aunt Refugio returned to the dining room and took out her sewing while Soledad cleared the table and began to do the dishes. When the girl finished, she decided to go to her room. But she paused first: it had been a long time since visiting her father's study. She took from a shelf a luxurious illustrated book from a museum in Europe she had never leafed through before.

Barely had she turned a few pages when the figure of her aunt appeared.

"That's why you were so quiet," she said, taking the book from her hands.

"Yes, Aunt Refugio, I mean, no…" stammered Soledad.

"Merciful god, take a look at this: the Virgin Mary with her boobs showing. This is a sacrilege…Where did you get this?"

"They're my dad's books."

"Ah, that heretic. And who gave you permission to look at them?" Not waiting for a reply, she continued in a suffering tone, "Poor Carmen. As concerned as she is with taking care of you, she doesn't even realize what you're doing. At least your brother is sensible, but you, it's already obvious you take more after your father, of course. And with that face, it's like I'm looking at a female version of him…"

Soledad had always noticed the similarity, and looking at herself alone before the mirror she was proud of it, but something in the tone of Doña Refugio's voice made her feel like she should be ashamed. "Auntie, it's a book about museums. Look," she hurried to say, showing her the cover.

"Be quiet. Do you really think I'm so stupid? And that naked woman there with the little angels you're going to tell me just got out of the bathroom, no? Sinner that you are, get on your knees and pray fifty Our Fathers and fifty Hail Mary's!"

Once Soledad had knelt, Refugio brought her gaze back to the book and continued looking through it carefully, muttering "Jesus" and "Christ Almighty" while she finally headed to the dining room with it. A little later Luis came to put back a thick volume he had apparently been reading. Seeing his sister on her knees, chewing on her forty-second Our Father, he asked, "And what did you do now? Why is she punishing you?"

At first Soledad thought it best not to answer, but then she considered she might need an ally. "Because I was looking at a book. Can you believe it?"

"What book?'

"One with paintings."

"What paintings?"

"Well…the Virgin, saints, other things."

"Really? It wasn't one of papa's art books of women with their tits and asses in the air?"

Soledad blushed. "Don't say that."

"It really makes you embarrassed? That's how you feel, no?" Quickly looking her over, he added, "Not quite, eh?"

Soledad began to pray again, but now aloud. Luis got right down next to his sister with the book in his hands and began to read in her ear, "Then Splendor hugged him between her legs. Hassan felt his member separating from his body, launching itself toward the sky and he tried to satisfy his desire in the arch-shaped fountain from which sprang the precious nectar of his beloved…"

Soledad didn't quite understand what Luis was reading but she pressed her hands against her ears and began to say in a sing-song voice, "I don't hear, I don't hear, I've got codfish ears."

With Soledad resisting, Luis continued to tease her, reading aloud more erotic fragments, emphasizing the words not with the volume of his voice but with exaggerated gestures. In turn Soledad pressed harder on her ears and sang even more loudly the codfish song.

Doña Refugio must have heard all the uproar. Her steps resounded up the staircase as she asked, "Soledad, are you finished?"

"No, Auntie, it's just that Luis…"

"What about your brother? He's reading in his room."

Luis wanted to escape but his room was on the other side of the staircase and his aunt had just come up.

"He's bothering me," said Soledad when Doña Refugio appeared in the doorway.

"I'm just putting this book back," said Luis seriously. "It's from that lower shelf. All I did was ask her to let me by."

"But, my child, don't you see she's being punished?"

"That's not true. He didn't ask me permission for anything. He was reading me dirty things," said Soledad pointing to the book Luis was holding.

Doña Refugio raised her eyebrows and held out her hand, ordering Luis to hand it over.

"*A Thousand and One Nights*," she said, reading the cover. "Are you crazy? That's a very healthy book for children. Your grandmother Marina had a copy and Grandpa Tobías used to read excerpts to us when he came back from work."

Soledad didn't understand. She had also read stories from *A Thousand and One Nights* in an anthology for children with princesses and thieves, sailors and magic lamps, but not things like Luis had read. She understood a couple weeks later when her aunt wasn't home and she could calmly look through the two volumes of that complete version of the thousand and one oriental stories which contained more than one erotic episode. But at that moment of confusion she could only resign herself to Luis having made the whole thing up. She hatefully glanced at him. Her aunt caught that resentful look and decided to punish her.

"All right, boy, go get me a belt," she ordered Luis. "I'm going to settle accounts with this little liar."

It wasn't possible: Luis left feeling all successful and she remained there kneeling. She looked up at her aunt, the Oaxacan Mount Sinai, but with the rancorous eyes that the laborer Cain must have had when he discovered that despite offering the best fruits from his land, Jehovah still preferred his brother's ewes. Luis came back with a thick strap and gave it to his aunt. Sol hated him and wished him dead. She didn't know how the desire was unleashed, but in any case she formulated it out of time: Miguel Bianco had fallen to the maniacal fury of the bayonets a few days earlier in Tlatelolco. Doña Cande still hadn't gotten his body from the municipality. Luis, who had gone to the demonstration to look at girls, saw him killed and was the only witness who could explain his disappearance. Soledad's brother had to hide in some building's garbage-filled basement and didn't come out until hours later. Then he talked about what he had seen, but over the following days, while he was recovering from his fright, Sol pretended that the roles had been reversed and it was Miguel who had the painful task of telling Carmen about the death of Luis.

Instead Luis smiled at his aunt and looked with disdain at his sister. Suddenly Soledad was only the puppet of his desires. Luis was always occupying the place of others. She threw her body against her brother with a fury that knocked him to the floor. The head of Luis hollowly struck against the mosaic—how else, Soledad would think later, could the head of such a hare-brain sound? The response was explosive. From above a flaming hand lit Soledad's cheek on fire. She'd never been slapped in the face before, but more than the pain, the surprise stupefied her. Then from the mountain top thundered, "Where did you ever get such pride if your father was a Mr. Nobody? You have no right…"

Soledad refused to listen to her, and shut the doors of her body and sought refuge with Lucía. But even there the voice repeated again and again, "You have no right, you have no right to anything..." Her friend begged she not listen, urging, "Ask for a wish, that your aunt fall down the stairs or that she get such a bloody nose she bleeds to death..." But Soledad's desires began to frighten her, and so she swallowed her rage. She heard them again saying to her, "You have no right to anything..." Lucía put her hands over Soledad's ears and the voice almost shut up, but very softly it went on and on. Then Soledad discovered it wasn't Aunt Refugio's voice speaking. Lucía spread out her hands defeated: it was Soledad's own.

XIV

The last time Soledad saw her friend Rosa Bianco, they were both in mourning. Sitting on the landing, they were waiting for the movers who would transport the Bianco family's belongings to the village where the bells always rang, Tingüindín. Days earlier Rosa had dressed up her short little body in black and, assuming an adult air that didn't seem at all out of place, became the sole support of her mother, crazy from so many things she'd had to see in hospitals and municipal halls, with the anxiety that her son wasn't there—a cruel paradox—among those with a black cross painted on their chest waiting to be cremated at the Rubén Leñero Hospital. There were piles of cadavers and Doña Cande had planted herself the whole night of October 3 before the hospital doors, watching how the crematorium's chimneys exhaled a constant black smoke stinking of a slaughterhouse.

When the Ángeles learned about the death of her brother, they impatiently waited for Rosa to come out with a message so they could ask her some details.

"Is it true he was a terrorist paid by the Russians?" they asked almost in unison. "That's what our father told us. It was in the paper."

Rosa didn't understand, but she fell like an avalanche upon them with her teeth and fingernails. The sisters escaped to a safe corner of their house, but they still spit out their venom: "Terrorist!

Terrorist!" Of course, neither Rose nor Soledad understood the word (in another situation they would have thought a "teller of terror stories"), but at that moment, said in such a tone, even the word "angelic" would have been an insult.

Once they'd taken off, Rosa let drop her arms as well as her spirit, her pale, inert face making her seem older. Soledad thought she was literally a withered rose, yanked up by the roots by a willful, sinister hand. She went up to her friend. Then Rosa rested her cheek on Soledad's shoulder like she used to back when they were just getting to know the Ángeles. They contemplated that October sky, its clouds full of fury like ships that never manage to leave port. Soledad picked up Rosa's hand and began to play with her fingers.

"This little one went fishing in the sea and caught a cold," she said, touching her pinkie. "This one went to the market and bought the cold at a good price; this one here began nagging that the other loved it and called a soldier and…"

"And this one here," mused Rosa with reddened eyes, "they killed with bayonets."

"No, Rosa, that's what Luis said, but he made that up, Miguel is going to come back. Hey, and in the meantime why don't you tell me already about those lions at the entrance of Chapultepec Forest. You told me when the Olympics started you were going to explain. They're made out of lies, right?"

Rosa Bianco looked at Soledad as if her friend were transparent and she could penetrate deeper than her skin and her flesh, passing through the heart to see the wounds, to know how much Miguel's death pained her and how much she could trust her. She must have looked upon her as quite the little girl, seen from a vast solitude acquired by such an untimely blow, because suddenly she said, "Well, I better go check on mama and see if she's calmed down and awake."

"Sleeping, you mean."

"No, awake. Remember, that's when she's calmer."

"I forgot she remembers more when she closes her eyes."

"Yeah…her tears start to flow and then she forgets everything. You've seen her..like she's in limbo."

"And your papa…why doesn't he come for you, for her, for you both?"

Rosa looked a the sky and swallowed a sigh before adding, "I lied to you. We haven't heard from him in ages."

Lesson in Darkness 1

The epic began October 2, 1968: the smell of blood and gunpowder had barely spread through the streets before the people rose up in arms. Even children took part in the struggle: little girls spilled gasoline on Lerdo Street, down which the tanks had to retreat, and set it on fire; fourteen-year-olds attacked tanks with Molotov cocktails burning in their hands. The people indignantly kept up the struggle. "Why are you fighting?" the reporter Rosa Falaci asked a combatant. The young man puffed his lips into a grimace before answering, "You don't see? Well, for freedom." They were called Freedom Fighters: bureaucrats, nurses, workers, housewives from the neighborhood who declared to the English journalist Soledad Fryer, "You don't do such things to the children of the Nation."

On Brasil and Belisario Domínguez Streets, they discovered the memory of the Palace of the Inquisition preserved beneath it in the secret quarters of the PGR. There were galleries various floors in depth, with walls several feet thick, doors that sealed hermetically, instruments of torture, an entire system of basements going all the way to the National Palace.

Students with cartridge belts, employees from the cantinas and night spots in the area, and part-time construction workers who advertised their services next to the Cathedral emptied trucks of weapons and armed themselves with machine guns and cattle prods.

By the time the government could react the uprising had freed three hundred political prisoners. During those days of freedom, October 2-19, only grocery stores opened, while movie theaters, banks, theaters and restaurants remained closed. New political parties appeared, as well as new journals. Young people brought poems, articles and descriptions of the revolution to the daily papers.

At the Hotel Diplomático, where most of the international reporters were staying, came rumors about United States military intervention saying that six hundred tanks and thirty thousands soldiers and marines were advancing. The dawn of day 14-Eagle, from the hills of Tepeyac and Chapultepec American cannons bombed the City of Palaces until it was turned into the Valley of Rubble. The US message endlessly repeated by the loudspeakers declared, "American troops are reestablishing order. US soldiers and diplomats are your neutral friends."

At the end of the military attack that day hundreds of dead bodies sprawled in the downtown streets next to piles of gravel, bottles, bricks, spent cartridges and empty crates of munitions. Indignant at the enormous losses, the people kept up a desperate and valiant fight. Downtown workers, students, deserting soldiers, fathers and mothers with families all vowed to resist until the end. Each day they told each other, "Tomorrow it will all be over," but in the meantime they furiously assailed the tanks and military forces.

The journalist Soledad Fryer crossed the frontline. She had joined up with an Italian journalist whose daring and impulsiveness had led her to risk her skin in Madagascar, and the two headed toward the Zócalo, the city's main plaza, where combat was still going on. The English journalist would write in an article about the resistance published days later in European newspapers:

> The tanks were marauding everywhere and stray bullets forced us to walk hunched over. We ventured onto Brasil Street, the site of bloody fighting. A Freedom Fighter, a youth of sixteen or so carrying a Molotov cocktail, yelled at us to get out of there.
>
> Minutes later we passed by a destroyed hotel that had been the general quarters of a guerilla detachment on the Plaza de Santo Domingo. With tanks just around the corner, several youths no older than twenty strummed the stocks of their machine guns like they were guitars. As the tanks

came closer, they took up post inside the hotel, where there was a well-stocked cache of arms, as well as workers and students ready to spread out down the canal along Perú Street and continue fighting if the hotel were attacked. Seeing the cameras on our chests, they invited us to meet their commander, a boy just a bit older who wore a cassock stuffed into his military pants. He recognized that the resistance was desperate, but insisted they would resist until the end—to the last person. He confirmed that he was in command and directed the fighting throughout the entire zone. As Rosa seemed disbelieving, he had the boy carrying the Molotov cocktail take us around "his" territory. On the way I took the opportunity to ask the young combatant a few questions. The boy I interviewed was sixteen and born in the state of Michoacán, but as a child emigrated to Mexico City. He had enrolled in the movement by mistake: a date with a girl was at the now disappeared Museum of Anthropology, where he participated in the historic Demonstration of Silence. In fact, Lieutenant Grimace (that's what the comandante called him when he ordered him to accompany us) admitted the meetings were the perfect place to meet girls. From one event to another, the date might be, "See you at the next demonstration." That's how he met Lucía. It was a pity we hadn't arrived two minutes earlier, Lieutenant Grimace told us, because she had gone to flirt with Yankee soldiers in order to lure them into an ambush. Lucía had saved Lieutenant Grimace from the massacre on October 2 by hiding him in a big Chinese vase. Now they were fighting together.

By October 21 it was clear the struggle was over, although the resistance continued in isolated areas. The English journalist concluded her article, "The revolution was defeated, drowned in blood and buried amidst ruins and lies, but...BUT..."

("Shut up! I'm not playing anymore!" shouted Rosa, shaking Soledad. "Understand? No more!"

"But Rosa...It didn't all end there," responded the other girl, filled with anguish, flipping through one of Miguel's books left unpacked from the boxes where they had put their things. "We can provide another ending, compose the story...if you want."

"What story? You don't know what you're talking about! That took place in Hungary in 1956 according to the book. Give it back to me."

And she grabbed it out of her hands to destroy it. When she'd finished ripping it up—in the pieces strewn about one could still read *The Tragedy of Hungary*—she spit out hatefully, "Don't compose the story again. Your stories are good for nothing. People have done nothing here since October 2, no armed uprising or clamor for the truth, and my brother isn't any Freedom Fighter...Instead, there were no dead and no wounded here. There were no bloody bodies. And I never had a brother named Miguel. I'm not here and I don't know you. Even more I don't see you."

And she ran off giving Soledad back neither her pubis nor her leg, and without Soledad being able to return to Rosa her heart and left arm, like when they used to dream of grabbing wisps of clouds and seeking shelter from the Angels because they were still unaware of their true essence.)

XV

Soledad went back several times to the building where her friend Rosa Bianco used to live. She visited the stair landing where an unknown man had initiated her into the pleasure of her body. She stood before the door where Miguel had invited her to wait for his sister. The door, once brown, now shone in a horrendous green.

The last time she had gone there, the school year had just ended and vacation approached with its tedious and melancholic burden. She climbed up to the roof: the cupolas of the church De Los Josefinos and the *art nouveau* points of the Chopo Museum gleamed in the crepuscular brilliancy of that afternoon. The melding of houses and buildings, dissimilar constructions discolored and opaque with few trees about them, extended all the way to the surrounding mountains, spreading in places like some dry weed. Soledad couldn't help but think about the extinct lake they talked so much about in her history and civics classes. She tried to imagine the waters and canoes, the canals and bridges, the ducks and floating gardens. She was about to wish to glimpse that first world but she stopped. She would never wish for anything again.

Soledad didn't know that the most glorious and terrible desires are woven without one realizing it.

Part Two

Notes for a Poetics of Shadows

XVI

What was holding her back? If it were really true that nobody could see her, then they wouldn't know anything about her death either. And if there was something obscene about the most decorous of suicides, it was coming across the body like some painful trace, a bloody vestige, a tabloid photo. Depending on the mode of death chosen, the degree of horror could grow or diminish but in the end it was just like one of those photos that show the ruins of war, hunger, injustice: in a short time people get used to it and then forget. It becomes invisible, like everything that truly touches or wounds us. Soledad reflected that, seen clearly, the desire to disappear without leaving a trace had been a good desire: without stains or traces even if you ended up being dragged through the emptiness. Knowing that comforted her: she didn't feel like she was the master of her life, but in the end she could be the master of her death.

Afternoon was falling over the city when she came down from the watchtower. She walked through the terraces already empty of visitors, peopled only by ghosts and soldiers. Now the castle belonged to her: its Empire-style residences, its furniture of faded brocade and velvet, Carlota's private bathroom with its mosaics of dahlias and peach branches, the elevator that Carmelita Díaz used to ascend to her vestal alcove, Juárez's austere coach, the musical clock that once delighted Eugenia de Montijo, the urns and tables of Russian malachite, the paintings by the artist Cordero and the screen with scenes of the Parián market...Was everything she touched and saw true, or was it all a dream? She probed her luck: she opened the curtains and turned on the lights, but it seemed the castle's security system wasn't working or...didn't exist. It would have been delicious to amuse herself by running from the soldiers when the alarm sounded. She sat down on a small chair in the music hall. Through the window she could see the moon, almost full, casting a silver glow over the high crown of the eucalyptus trees and the "cypresses of Moctezuma." How many times had Carlota Amalia, the second empress of Mexico, sewn dreams of glory seated on that furniture embroidered with the fables of La Fontaine? Perhaps at the very outset it had seemed her life was a fable from that empire of Mexico which had magically emerged. The moon was perhaps clearer, the forest denser and the world, without any doubt, vaster...But her wishes? Carlota Amalia crossed the Atlantic searching for a dream that had become reality. Then Soledad recalled the fate of the empress and felt saddened. If desires were completed, and once thrown into the air there was no going back, what had happened with Peter? At what moment, loving him with a physical hunger, had she desired to lose him? Why were desires so inexplicable? And why did they act against you? She remembered that at her lover's departure, the simple act of touching caused her pain. As if her skin didn't exist and her whole being, having been abandoned, was left laid bare. That had happened once before when Rosa and Miguel left her life, but then the pain disappeared as suddenly as one recovers from a childhood fever; on the other hand when Peter returned to Hungary, the physical feeling grew as she discovered that his absence was an absolute and bottomless emptiness, her soul falling hopelessly with nothing to hang onto. He had left no note at his hotel where Soledad had gone with all her baggage, precisely because they were about to leave on that voyage together. Not even a thought of returning home with her tail between her legs, after weeks earlier showing Carmen a telegram that supposedly notified her that the Hungarian Ministry of Culture had awarded her a scholarship (which Soledad fabricated from photocopies of telegrams and letters Peter had received from his country). Her mother only thought to ask two things: one, that she store all her belongings in the garage because, if Soledad didn't mind, they might rent out her room; two, that she send them post cards: "It doesn't matter if you write on the back or not, but send lots of them, with frozen rivers and tulips in front of the storybook houses. Who knows, maybe I'll save up some money and Luis and I will come visit you in…Holland, no? Or did you say Hungary? Aren't they the same?" Sol told her yes, she packed all her things in a few boxes that she left in the corner of the garage, and she planned her supposed leave for the day after Carmen and Luis were to leave on a weekend excursion. Soledad knew how hard it was for them to give up their trips. Since his break-up with Lorena three days before their marriage, Luis had taken an unpaid leave-of-absence from his work and left his mother's side no more than he had to. Soledad pretended to be magnanimous: "No mama, you needn't go to the airport with me. If these getaways do Luis so much good, it's not worth canceling the trip…to the basalt prisms of San Luis Potosí, no?" Her brother, although distanced from so much going on around him, still asked, "I forgot why you said they gave you the scholarship." "*Puszta* photography," she hurried to reply, drawing on the scant Hungarian she'd picked up during those nights with Peter when he forgot his Spanish learned from a Cuban friend living in Budapest. "And your studies?" her mother suddenly burst out. Soledad was about to say, "My studies? Who the hell would be interested in a degree in Graphic Arts when they can be learning twenty-four hours a day with the maestro Peter Nagy?" Of course Carmen would have answered, "And who is this Don Peter Nagy?" as once before she asked about Cartier Bresson and Casasola. It's just that Soledad couldn't show her the works of Peter guarded in her room as she was indeed able to show her famous photos by the others (a man jumping over a puddle or a woman soldier on the steps of the train; looking at them her mother arched her eyebrows and said, "Well, at least the one of the man with the clock shows something from today"). And not only couldn't she show them to her because of Carmen's rejection of all eroticism (for her, nudity was nothing more than perversion or sin), but because the body photographed in them, that cunt, those breasts, that puckered "o" of the ass, although shaded by light and shadow, were Soledad's. So she limited herself to making up, "I'll get credit at school here for the classes I take there. Besides, when have you ever cared about what I do?" This last comment almost cost her permission to travel with Peter.

Now that she thought about it, it was absurd to expect that with Soledad being twenty Carmen could have stopped her. An absurd dream, but not really: if her mother hadn't finally given her permission, she wouldn't have dared leave home. Making up something like the scholarship to escape with Peter left her so dizzy that to transgress the limits not only of her own existence but of the entire world and take that daring any farther would have made her hesitant to step upon any unknown land. And because of her nature, or that thing she was, that silent, sputtering flame, she felt incapable of great changes or spectacular escapes. Only her love for Peter—or the fascination she thought was so—could make her venture down unknown paths, but always at the risk of getting lost.

For that reason—after inventing a trip to study with a scholarship, inventing that double life she kept up so Peter would know nothing of her family, nor her family anything of that Hungarian professor who after teaching in an exchange program was returning home, after betting that world of values and feats inherited from Carmen against the love of a foreigner, as foreign as his world—for that reason when Peter left without saying goodbye, having made her believe they would go forward together, not only did a dream vanish but Soledad felt stripped of even her skin, as if suddenly she had been flayed and a simple flutter of wind would wound her barren flesh.

Her hands especially felt skinned. She had to wear white cotton gloves and like some ghost (but out of an *opera buffa*, Soledad joked to herself), she remained in that sleepwalker city, witness to her relation with Peter. How could one describe the city in those days after her abandonment? Wherever she cast her gaze, the buildings and streets, the cafés and galleries they frequented where she'd later wander by herself, had taken on a terrifying cloudiness: such was the feeling of unreality, of walking around with no sense of surety and completely apart from herself, she remained in after Peter's absence.

Besides there was a difference in time zones. The seven hours separating Mexico City and Budapest let Soledad pass through a tunnel of space and time where dreams and wakefulness became confused: she would wake up and wander sleepwalking with no more sense of reality than believing herself a ghost that went all the way to the drifting edge of Peter's dreams: she would sleep and then Peter became the fleeing shadow that escaped down unknown streets and suddenly appeared before her eyes with the magic of a wish fulfilled. And on the shore of one world and another, her happiness was volatile until the moment she got out of bed and put her feet down into the hotel room's intractable and carpeted solitude.

She stayed in the hotel where she had spent her last days with Peter. Back then she thought it a way station on the road to paradise. What kind of happiness was she waiting to find in that projected voyage, which only much later did she understand that she herself and not Peter had forged? On those occasions, while Sol was talking about the trip they'd take together, he only listened— or pretended to listen—plucking his dark beard and playing a particular game of his since childhood: to turn things around without touching them, to imagine exactly the part you couldn't see, so fascinated by that dark side hidden from the gaze.

Soledad remembered one day when he had taken some proofs of her in this same hotel. They'd been given a room with a street view, but Peter asked for that dark room whose two circular windows reminded one of the portholes on a ship. As soon as they were alone, Peter indicated with a gesture she take off her clothes. He took the camera and light meter out of their cases, and Sol saw him arrange things with that air of lord and master with which he set himself down anywhere in the world. From there, from that mount where he stood to contemplate the world, Peter quickly discovered that his indifferent will worked its effects, which surprised him: he observed the frame before him, the skylight's cutting light scratching the deep shadows, violating with little crashes that berth suddenly transformed by his gaze into the center of the world, and a bit beyond it, a naked woman in turn observing him. Soledad perceived for the first time the game of shadow and manipulation Peter so much enjoyed playing without having to lift a finger, but just exert his gaze. It was as if his view didn't rest on the visible parts of her body, but caressed as well those zones hidden from his eyes. A bit uneasy, she dared ask, "Peter, what's the light like in Hungary?"

Surprised, he stopped those fingers that without touching ran over her neck, her shoulders, her back, her ass. "What?" Peter threw out, irritated.

Instead of being silent again, which obviously would have been for the best, Soledad just modified the question: "Does your house in Hungary have a lot of light?"

Peter grabbed her by the arm and brought her into the stream of light. "Smart girls only speak when they have something to say," he said, the rays through the skylight crossing Soledad's face. He took a reading of the light and walked off to take the picture. His anger was obvious and the girl couldn't help feeling guilty. She lowered her eyes and shoulders and then the surface of light fell on the nape of her neck.

"Like that, like that…don't move," Peter directed with a voice that was also a supplication.

After taking several photos he changed her place. Now the light cut across Soledad's stomach. Peter was just about to step back when he turned to adjust a strand of her hair; then he passed that same hand down the slit of her ass. The pleasure was so abrupt that Soledad gasped. She heard the click of the meter behind her. Peter was measuring the light on her shadowed half. He decided to take the picture from behind. He moved back several steps and finished the roll before coming up to her again, then he put a chair in front of Soledad and indicated she lean upon it. The light struck her now in the face and passed across her like a flaming arrow. Peter's hands hovered right above her back and then caressed her. Soledad thought she knew what it was like to touch light.

"I love your skin, *csillagom*. Luminous and transparent," said Peter before he bent her over.

Hungarian Rhapsody 1

I'm writing this in Hungarian. Once when I was a child I went with my parents to Balaton. They had some things to take care of with Grandpa Gyula. As soon as we arrived, papa gave me a few florins so I'd go take a walk by the "sea." I didn't feel like swimming and I took off kicking stones and sand out of my way on the road. I was so angry I only stopped when I heard laughter. I lifted my eyes and saw her. She was pretty and irreverent, carrying a shoebox that guarded secrets she later refused to share. Suddenly another girl came up and whispered something in her ear. They started laughing again and pointed at my shoes. I looked down: they were on backwards. I was getting ready to leave (they were only a couple of silly girls), when she asked me to help her look for treasure. I agreed. She took her hand from her friend and began to run. She went along the edge of the Balaton "sea" and disappeared behind the "shifting dunes," a bend in the beach where, according to Grandpa Gyula, more than one bather had died drowning in the sand. Those were stories invented by my grandfather, but I quickened my step. I couldn't find her. I ran from one place to another. My side hurt. Finally I spied the shoebox abandoned on a little hill. I was going to open it when her laughter quivered on the nape of my neck. I turned around. For a moment she was there before me, just about as tall. She asked, "We're going to look for treasure, right?" She flashed a flirtatious half-smile. I replied no. Then she said, "At least put your shoes on the right feet." And she took the long way to her shoebox. She picked it up and began to wander off as if the world and I had ceased to exist as soon as her eyes were filled with other images. I took off my shoes and followed her barefoot.

We didn't find any treasure and ended up going in the water. She didn't want to show me the box and left it with her friend. I asked her what it was she guarded so jealously. She answered "sighs" and jumped in the water. We raced and got farther and farther away from shore. While we were resting she asked, "Do you like Estela?" I was treading water. "Estela? Who's Estela?" "My cousin," she said, pointing her finger at the beach. (Now that I think about it, that girl I met in Mexico, Soledad, looked a bit like those two. The cousin and the other one whose name I never knew.) Estela saw us looking at her and covered her face with the shoebox. "Let's go farther out," said my companion and started swimming again. We didn't stop until her cousin on the beach almost disappeared. I floated on my back to rest. The sky was clear, the sun high in the sky. The day had suddenly turned perfect. Then I felt something brush against my ear. Then on my forehead, my cheeks, my lips. I burst out laughing. "How do you do that?" She took some water in her mouth and pointed her lips at me like she was going to give me a kiss. Out of the hole burst a spout of water that struck me in the face. "They're water darts," she said and continued shooting them at me until I was able to lance one that struck her right in the forehead. In the middle of the battle, she exclaimed, "I have to go," and started to swim right back. I looked at the shore. A woman was signaling to us. As soon as she got to the beach my friend turned to wave goodbye. I, too, moved my hand. I stayed floating there a little longer. The sun had moved but the sky was still brilliant. I was happy to think I still had another week of vacation left in Balaton.

But she didn't come back the next day and I never saw her again. On the other hand, her cousin followed me everywhere: as soon as I turned around or tried talking to her, she ran away and didn't stop until she disappeared. I resigned myself to her silent presence. The day before I returned to Budapest someone knocked on the door. I thought it was one of the cats that used to come begging scraps from my grandfather. It was Estela. She didn't cross the threshold. Through the metal screen her face was even more undefined. Her voice, in turn, had become tremendously clear: "She asked me to give you this...it's a bit crumpled...I'll leave it here." She bent over to push it under the door and then fled. It was a postcard from the Basilica of St. Peter's in Rome, as it said on the back. There was also a message that had been blotted out with a pen. Of course I hated the cousin. I sought her out to make her tell me what it said but she too had gone. I sat in front of the Balaton "sea" holding the postcard. St. Peter...like my name. I looked at it through the counter-light of the setting sun. In any case she hadn't written down an address: that part of the paper was blank. I let the sea carry it off to St. Peter's. It floated in the water until it disappeared with the last splendor of the Golden Bridge.

XVII

After Peter's departure, she stayed in a hotel with the money she had planned on taking to Hungary, savings she had gathered taking photos here and there, helping Peter's friends develop and print film, and doing a few small jobs for an advertising agency. If she had saved it up to realize a dream, why not squander it now that Peter had decided she shouldn't spend it with him in Hungary?

That first night in the hotel room Lucía paid her a visit. She had been sprawled on the bed for hours, wearing the same clothes she had on when she left the house of the portals, observing now in the darkness her suitcase left without a destiny, when she saw her friend. She knew it was her though it had been a while since they'd seen each other and Lucía had changed her kimono for jeans. Soledad was pleased to recognize they still resembled each other, despite her friend's pallor that reminded her of a Chinese porcelain figurine. Moreover, Lucía had thin lips. Soledad tried to remember if they'd always been like that or if they changed after that occasion when Soledad was becoming a teenager and Carmen had surprised her in the astonishment and seduction of contemplating herself in the mirror. Sol was observing herself ravishingly, looking at her big eyes, her well-defined eyebrows, the sharp oval of her face, the fleshy lips that looked like her father's…Soledad liked her lips so much that she tried caressing them with her fingertip and tongue, which left them shining like a plum just bitten into. Suffice it to say she was fascinated by the reflected image and was about to cover it with kisses, to kiss that fleshy fruit and consecrate herself into the cult of those faithful to themselves, when she heard her mother's voice and however strange it seems she felt herself naked, uncovered, discovered. The fruit fell from her hands, rotten, although it had looked tasty. Carmen said, "If you suck in your upper lip, you can still correct it." With barely a line to begin with for a mouth, she accompanied her words with a demonstration that left her lipless, like the mouth of an ape or fish. Soledad could have laughed at how absurd her mother looked. But instead she looked at the mirror and from its depths a new Soledad with a small little mouth gazed back.

Of course the lip never was corrected because she got tired of trying and then it puffed up even more inflamed and indignant from

so many minutes of abuse. And perhaps because of this rebellious-
ness she didn't become a complete ghost, although she was looking
more and more opaque and blotted according to what pictures
from the period bear witness, where one had to dig her image
out with a magnifying glass from among the dominant bodies
and faces like that of her brother Luis, which caught the eye at
first glance.

But it wasn't always like that. Now that no one could see her
climbing atop the Elevated Knight, that observation point once used
to examine the movement of the stars, where she contemplates
equally her life and the tumult of the dizzying, ever more distant
city, what else can she fasten on to (like her hand to the tower's
flagpole so not to fall) but the truth of a confession that seeks only
to seize her ghostly condition? Things being so, Soledad admits that
at times she used to act forcefully and attract people. They were
situations so strange—other people coming around her—that she
became kind of mad from pleasing them, but in those fleeting
instances she thought it was Lucía who enchanted them with her
graceful walk, that timid but flirtatious air with which she turned
away her eyes and meekly resisted before singing or reciting a
poem at family gatherings. Then Soledad would take advantage of
those occasions to stand before a mirror or window and understand
that her reflection faded away no matter how much her finger
followed her shadow on the mercurial, glassy surface. At those
moments, looking at Lucía take her bows while Carmen and Aunt
Refugio applauded with her remaining on the outskirts of everything, Sol felt powerful, so powerful that she could pass alone through
the labyrinth and visit the sleeping dragon.

XVIII

Two fears are sprouting on my chest. I walk bent over to
disguise them and hide from everybody that I'm sick and
going to die. I know because they ache with just the simple
touch of a gaze that feels in them a missed deadline. And so
I flee and hide among the weeds. I should have wanted the
knowledge of some little bug that can curl up into a ball
each time someone comes near and looks at me out of the

corner of some suspicion. I lower my head, I crook my back but disapproval finally lets fall its sword. Then I flee to the room of recognized solitude. There I carry out my labor of a scared little centipede that barely lets one see its antennas and flexes its little legs. I persevere, resisting until cramps began to stretch out my legs and change my posture. I lift my gaze and discover the silence lurking for me in the astonished surface of the mirror. Jailed in that daze, the image of someone hurls itself upon my mercurial breath. Now I only wait, quietly, quietly, for his hands to reach out and unbutton my blouse and uncover my tumors. Every finger that brushes against them tests my state of being a marble statue. One…two…three…a seed has just come out. Or better yet, a little louse rolled into a ball trembles scared on the point of each tumor. Unexpectedly now experts, his fingers knead with the will of a crumb that in the end drags from me a groan. Before the thread of my scissor voice the mirror trembles and shakes in unusual waves. Someone is about to leave. Only then do I bend my neck forward. I can only let my clothes drop. Slender men in the air, shame as well. Then I implore: Saint Olaya, allow neither pain nor fear. Someone is already coming near. He places his kiss on the tip of my fears. Now it is I the image in the mirror that moves in waves of watery pleasure. His red ribbon tongue entangles them in feverish circles. More…more…On a silver tray, pared, shiver the suspicions. But he can't kiss me, lick me, suck me. He hasn't left. Jailed. Someone is still behind the crystal glass. I hurry to touch him. His extended palms and my hands, his mouth and my lips, his tongue and my saliva, his chest on my breasts. I swear his metal breath burns.

XIX

Lucía always helped her overcome difficult situations: class exhibits in junior high, a role in a high school play, meetings with classmates at the university, the first time she smoked marihuana, and when they returned to be together in company of the dragon…On that occasion Soledad asked her if she liked the outside world so much, then why didn't they change places? Instead of responding, Lucía began to run through the labyrinth and became lost from sight. Inexplicably (or perhaps it was the effects of the marihuana), a surge of waves began to beat against the walls of the vase. Strong, and with each wave stronger, while Soledad followed Lucía's steps. It was as if someone had thrown the Chinese vase into a roaring sea, as if the damsel that lived in it had said, "If I can't get out, if my soul has to remain here imprisoned, at least grant that I may visit the seven seas," but she didn't count on the storms or the shipwrecks, and with each assault, far from being able to get up and discern the horizons and the heavens, the damsel had more and more to take refuge deeper within the vase. Suddenly the waves changed. Instead of furious waves it sounded now like they were nailing a column or a beam in the center of the labyrinth, as if they were attaching it with a clean blow of a hammer. When Sol thought she'd lost track of her, Lucía touched her on the shoulder and led her to the dragon. Soledad asked, "What's that noise?" Lucía gestured to be quiet and said, "You're going to wake the dragon." "But isn't that pounding going to wake it?" "Come, curl up in its stomach. Here its skin is so soft that once you put your hand in, everything follows right after." Lucía took her hand and led her to the beast. Her caress made the dragon stir and exhale a moan. But not even that awoke it. The pounding became lighter. At first when they were playing with the dragon's skin, Soledad thought those sounds were its breathing. But little by little she discovered the beating came from her own heart. When she no longer heard it, Lucía told her, "It's better to stay here. Anyways, you're already dead."

Nevertheless, when she woke up Sol didn't see reddish walls, nor the dragon, nor Lucía at her side. She was no longer a girl, she was recuperating the body of a...she hesitated a few moments—of a nineteen-year-old stretched out upon the carpet of an unknown apartment. On one of the walls a Chagall poster shone this Sunday in flaming reds and yellows. She finally recognized the place: Juan Carlos's new apartment, and then she remembered the little shipwreck from the night before. One of her buddies, Manuel, rested his head upon her stomach. She got up carefully so not to wake him, stepped around other bodies sprawled throughout the apartment and went to the kitchen where Guadalupe, Juan Carlos's girlfriend, was making coffee that smelled delicious. As soon as she saw Soledad, she said, "Hey, Solitary, so you didn't know his tricks." "Who'd you say is a dick?" she responded without thinking, not quite hearing. "Don't. You're going to tell me you didn't know Manuel is going out with Lucía?"

"Lucía?" Soledad was confused: since when had the others known Lucía by name? "Yes," replied Guadalupe. "Lucía Cervantes, the sculptor. Wasn't she your friend in high school?"

Lucía, no, Lucila; friends no, but they knew each other…But Soledad knew nothing about her going out with Manuel, whom apart from that one-night stand she'd never had anything more to do with. Guadalupe looked at her disbelievingly. "Yeah, I think her name was Lucila Cervantes," she said. Manuel suddenly came into the kitchen. The smell of the coffee had woken him, but instead of pouring himself a cup he hugged Soledad around the waist. "So," he asked, "are we going to the movies this afternoon?"

And so began her reputation for being two-faced. Soledad didn't possess a spectacular aura like Lucila or other girls who were hit on all through school, but a frightened, fragile air that made her seek refuge in corners and shadows. She didn't know that the darkness she preferred to hide in could also be attractive to other people. The case of Manuel was repeated several more times before Peter appeared, but already circulated the rumor—at least among the women in the group—that she shouldn't be trusted. When Soledad finally learned of it, she began to go out less and withdraw into herself. It almost always worked: people quickly got bored and fastened their attention on other things. And Soledad would relax again and then could concentrate on her design classes and the books of poetry she had begun to read. Lucía drew well and resumed illustrating a poster for a poem by a writer of cold and desolate dreams—Soledad could never remember if his name was Gilberto or Xorge Villaurrutia—which she handed in as her typography assignment. On the other hand Soledad preferred photography: its duality of light and shadow spoke to her obscurely of an internal tapestry, the texture of a live moment detained in the heartbeat of death…something she had already seen in the belly of the vase.

XX

When they met again in that hotel room, Lucía seemed to realize where the memories of Soledad were heading. And so when she asked about the dragon, Lucía laughed that the other still remembered. "No," she said. "Instead you tell me about your Hungarian." "'My' Hungarian," repeated Soledad in a muted voice. "How do you not know everything?" "No," responded Lucía, "you no longer tell me everything." "It's that you and the dragon disappeared," replied Soledad. "We didn't go," answered Lucía. "You forgot us." Soledad was silent a few moments. Then she decided to tell her friend about that double life she began to lead when she met Peter, about Genet and Montero, and also about Lola…And finally they agreed that Soledad would bet everything she had, she would stick to her plan to travel to Hungary and look for Peter. "And if he has a family, you know, a wife…children?" asked Lucía. Soledad was so enthralled with the idea of seeing him again that she didn't want to listen anymore. She fell asleep believing that the next day, in just a few hours, she would start her trip.

But when she awoke her strength failed her. How could she think of imposing her presence when it was clear he didn't want to see her? How could she suddenly arrive at his apartment in Emör and say, "Here I am. I've come to stay with you"? Soledad could imagine the surprised and disgusted look on his face, that unequivocal gesture of raising his eyebrows while his gaze flitted from side to side like an animal looking for a way to escape. "My grandfather used to say neither tight clothes nor a horse that can't be ridden," Peter could only lecture when she would ask him to stay a little longer. No, the best thing to do was write him. To say she loved him and understood his leaving but ask that he give her another chance. Lucía wore a disenchanted smile. "That is, not only do you forgive him but you want him to forgive you…" she said, continuing, "All there's left is for you to ask his permission to go visit." But Soledad wasn't listening, stirred by the idea of re-establishing contact with Peter. Certainly he'd reply and say he missed her, too, certainly everything had been a mix-up; perhaps Peter had even told her he was leaving earlier to get the apartment in Emör ready, but she hadn't understood. She went to the reception desk for a pen and paper while Lucía jumped back into the vase. "First the trip, now the letter. I wouldn't be surprised if you ended up not mailing it," she said from inside. "Of course I'm going to send it," said Soledad while she took the paper from the man at the reception desk who held it out to her. "And if he doesn't answer me…" Lucía thought she heard a brave tone in the girl's voice and stuck her head out again. Soledad looked at her directly and firmly went on, "I'll write to him again and again until he writes to me and says…" But Lucía didn't want to listen anymore and so let Soledad go on dreaming by herself.

XXI

The day Soledad met Peter she had arrived late to his class. Carmen had asked her to go with to her gynecologist appointment, so Soledad could be present during the examination. Carmen made so many disgusted faces and acted so stubbornly that it took quite a while before the doctor could do the pap smear. The poor man examined closely the panorama between the legs of the lady, he gave her space, he asked her to relax, he put on a new glove, the nurse moved the lamp around, Carmen said the light was burning her, the doctor tried again to insert the "duck," as the forceps was called that tried to separate the narrow vaginal walls of Soledad's mother. Finally, after two attempts and a local anesthetic given amidst it all, the doctor left the examination room with the little piece of gauze in a glass container to await his patient in his office wearing a fed-up look on his face that Soledad had seen on other gynecologists treating her mother. Carmen argued that it was best to change doctors because to stay with the same one way could even become sinful. And Sol thought the doctors must thank her mother for such a Good Samaritan attitude. Anyways, while Carmen got dressed behind a screen, she heard the nurse say in a low voice to another who'd come to get the used instrument, "More than half an hour for such a silly little thing…Imagine if it'd hurt like that when she had her kids…she would have screamed like crazy."

Carmen pretended that her pride was so great she could wrap it around her shoulders and neck and cover her ears with it. But when she and Soledad were out on the street, she looked at her before adding, "The good thing is until you're married you don't have to see these perverted doctors and their insolent nurses."

Soledad kept silent. It was useless to discuss with her mother that gynecology was a profession like any other.

"Aha. I can guess what you're thinking but really, tell me, don't you have to have something rotten in your head to choose among all the other specializations in medicine looking at the intimate places only a husband should know?"

"Well," her daughter responded, growing testy, "why don't you look for a woman gynecologist? I could…" She was just about to let slip that she'd seen one when she thought she was pregnant after having sex with Manuel. "I could ask a friend of mine to give you her sister's number."

"And you think I'd let a woman touch me? No, a thousand times no…"

"But mama, if she's a professional, are you going to tell me she does it because she has homosexual tendencies?"

"Shut your mouth. There you go. One can't have a decent conversation with you. Always your disgusting topics. I was just saying that, in the final analysis, a woman is a woman. What's she going to know, the poor thing? Look, Soledad, here comes your brother. Let's just get going."

And there was Luis's red Volkswagen double-parked waiting for them.

As she was in a little pain, Carmen asked her son to drive slowly. Luis looked at her with pity and slowed down. After a couple blocks, Soledad told them to let her out at the next subway station.

Luckily the school was on Tacuba, but even so she didn't arrive on time. Added to being late was the train that passed outside her school. Soledad was resigned to leaning against a light post to wait while thirty-three cars rolled by one after the other.

But "resign herself" wasn't really the right phrase. Soledad had been taking the subway forever and it was precisely the presence of this train which passed in front of the Design School that made her choose that school on Tacuba Street. She had wanted to attend the Academy of San Carlos ever since she was a little girl and heard that was where artists studied, but the sole mention of the train tracks in front of the old building, once occupied by the former School of Chemical Sciences and now destined for the newly created department of Graphic Communications, made her hesitate.

One of her classmates (Lucía Cervantes, Soledad recalled) got fed up with her indecision at the registration window and convinced her, "Go on, you can take pictures of trains." Soledad agreed and momentarily forgot the Academy of San Carlos, with all its court of haloed painters and sculptors, and registered for that unknown field of study. When she finally realized what she'd done, she couldn't defend her old desire, for nobody wanted to exchange places with her. But at least that first day of class she was comforted there was a train, although she had to wait more than twenty minutes to cross the street, for on that occasion she found herself on the wrong side of the tracks with other people who couldn't get across first.

And so there was Soledad, watching her life pass by, with no one inviting her to the land of fulfilled desires. Train car after train car, the minutes passed. Soledad didn't realize she was crying until another girl waiting held out a piece of toilet paper to her.

"Does it bring back a lot of memories?" she asked, searching her eyes.

"No," replied Soledad, not looking at her. "It brings me a lot of non-memories."

Of course the girl didn't understand, nor did Soledad want to try explaining. All the cars had gone by. She dried her tears and crossed the train tracks without adding a word.

She was running to the classroom when she went by the registration office and saw the clock on the wall: too late to risk Professor Bonfil using her as a target for that mental effervescence that so easily made him relate the commitment to be on time with the instant of divine creation and from there, brimming over, pass on to the "decisive moment" of photography and the *objet trouvé* that gave him a unique opportunity to shoot his rifle of ideas so that his prompt students might join the Revolution and not Utopia which, as ubiquitous as it was, would fill their skulls with smoke.

Whatever the case, Soledad went to the classroom. Through the little window in the door she peered at a bearded man sitting on the desk that Bonfil used to occupy. She hadn't yet heard his voice, but it was enough to see him for the dragon sleeping in the depths of the labyrinth to stir in its sleep. Soledad felt it awakening as if an earthquake rumbled in a deep unknown place and was spreading through her entire body and running through her hands with her completely unable to resist. She turned the handle, opened the door and suddenly the lights went out. For the briefest instant, the eternal dimension of the blink of an eye, Soledad believed she was back in the depths of the labyrinth. Suddenly blinded, she felt the dragon stepping violently toward her. She was scared and looked for Lucía, but Lucía wasn't in the vase. Upon the initial terror of not finding her was superimposed something else disconcerting: a stream of light poured out, a horizontal cascade that struck the blank wall and suddenly was transformed into a screen. There surged forth the image of some brilliant palm trees, adorned with a blinding light, contrasting with a dark enveloping sky they seemed to hold up like columns.

Then Soledad heard his voice and discovered that she wasn't in the vase, but outside it. The bearded man was speaking from the other side of a shadow created by the light from a slide projector and began to explain, "The effect is created with infrared film. That darkness was captured by my friend Javier Hinojosa in the middle of the day. The palm trees shine because they reflect a light the eye can't see. Other photographers speak of light, I will speak of the nature of darkness. It isn't light that defines objects, but the lack of it. Blind light, shadows create the range of colors. Volumes, textures, feelings emerge from cutting off light. Da Vinci said that shadows are more powerful than light…"

Soledad finally discovered where he was. That penumbra had confused her to the point of thinking she was in the dragon's labyrinth, but it must have seemed strange to her classmates to see her just standing there. She walked towards an empty desk in the front row.

"Miss, please, stay in the shadow," the voice of Bonfil's substitute said, interrupting her steps. Soledad noticed he lengthened his vowels, as if trying to accommodate the syllables in their exact place. "Like that…Now, submerge your arm in the light."

Submerge her arm? Yes, it was a river of light. Soledad obeyed. What else could she do? She suddenly started to feel ill, as if she were being bled and didn't have the strength to resist. She vigilantly peered at the haloed silhouettes of her classmates, but she was no longer concerned about them.

"Do the rest of you see? The direct light on the arm hides volumes…In turn the range of grays increases the shades of the colors. It's not the light that illuminates, but rather by extinguishing it…"

When the class was over and the lights came back on, Soledad remained at the front of the room. Nagy Péter—that's how the new professor of photography asked to be called—was gathering some papers on his desk. One of the students shut off the projector and gave it to him. Two smiling girls came up, eager to help him put away the slides. Sol was about to leave, but the man's voice stopped her.

"Excuse me...I haven't thanked you yet." The new photography teacher walked towards her and held out his hand.

She couldn't help shrinking back: the transparency of his eyes, that intense and persistent gaze, made her feel naked. He must have perceived her reaction of covering herself because immediately his gaze sharpened in a gleam that Soledad couldn't interpret right at the moment but only much later, when after nocturnal ramblings, hours of interminable silence, uninterrupted lovemaking, the stridency of his friends, photo sessions to find the design of a shadow, was it too late and she saw and felt with Peter's eyes and skin. But as well Soledad would only then obscurely understand his poetics of shadows and experience it in her own flesh.

But that first moment in the classroom, Peter's gaze insistently continued, as if at Soledad's need to recoil and cover herself he had responded with another instinct: to stir things up. Soledad looked at him out of the corner of her eye and although she responded to his greeting, she made a circular movement to flee. He'd already held out his hand and then took hers so hard that she almost shrieked. "Soledad, my name is Soledad," she said. He still held onto her hand a few moments. The girls at his desk began to whisper. And not for nothing: that unknown man was grasping her hand as if they had met long ago and he had finally found her again.

Hearing the girls murmuring, the new photography teacher turned to shush them. Then a curious scene took place: the man forgot that Soledad's hand was between his own and he tugged her brusquely. Lucía, who loved sudden movements, jumped out of the vase and helped Soledad gather herself together in the air. She freed herself of the man's hand with a jerk and looked sidewise at the girls laughing, and then she ended up laughing, too. They left while the new teacher picked up his slide case and jacket.

Soledad went to sit on a bench in the garden. From there she saw Nagy Péter (afterwards she learned that Hungarians are accustomed to introducing themselves by their surname) come out of the classroom building and look from one place to the other searching for something or someone. It frightened her to think he was looking for her. But more than her own fear, Sol felt the joy of Lucía leaping down among the walls of the labyrinth.

"We'll lose him if he wants to hunt us!" shouted Lucía while she zigzagged inside the vase.

Peter would later claim she hid because she wanted to play hard to get. But what's certain is that he passed near Soledad and whether by distraction or chance—at least, that's what she thought later—he couldn't see her.

Perhaps nothing else would have happened (Peter with his eternal court of admirers, both female and male, her in a corner of the classroom) if he hadn't arranged a visit to an exhibit he was having. One of his artist friends had arranged a show for him at the Design School and the opening coincided with class hour. He canceled it ahead of time and invited his students to go with him to the Ciudadela.

XXII

Who says an amorous passion can't suck out your soul, sip your will and pare you down to nothing? Soledad at least thought so before knowing Peter, or thought that stage was an appearance, a disguise the impassioned wore to consecrate themselves all the more in the rites of love. That is, she thought it like a rose of the will that one could prune at any moment. She should have recalled the moment she met Peter, that restlessness, that sudden blindness that made her stumble within herself and discover—perhaps with more pleasure than terror—the dragon's deep, lumbering movements.

She should have remembered that after that first class with the slides when she met the new photography teacher she wasn't the same, that barely having seen his presence she entered into a kind of forgetfulness that often led her not to know where she was going, what she was doing or even (but this only happened twice) who she was. It's not that she was always thinking about the bearded man, strange in his way of looking around and being among others, but rather it felt like some kind of internal compass had spun around and now she found herself inhabiting a space and time that didn't recognize her.

Her appearance was strange, even sick or run down to some. Carmen suggested she get a vitamin injection and finding her lost in a subway station one of her classmates went out of his way to take her home. On the street they went the wrong direction several times before they found the house of the portals, with its flower pots of elegant leaves and cascading ferns, the neglected garden surrounding it that gave the structure the look of an abandoned aristocratic house.

The experience taught her a lesson and so she started taking notes in a small book she always carried in her bag. Anyways, as nothing guaranteed that by looking in her book she would remember, she asked Lucía to look for her. Lucía lifted her head out of the vase and answered, "I've had it with looking out for you and lulling the dragon. And all for a Hungarian sorcerer who uses silver halogens in his love potions."

What was Lucía talking about? Why did she make up those ridiculous fairy tales at her expense? What did the chemistry of photo paper have to do with the alchemical act in which Peter, like any other professional photographer, transformed a handful of silver salt sensitive to light into a little seed of the human soul? Soledad asked her to shut up.

"So!" Lucía began to say, snorting, the bangs on her forehead moving to the rhythm of her words. "So not only do you want to play the stupid but you want me to as well! I already said it: I've had it, really had it. But I'll stop being Lucía if the more you try to get away, the more he doesn't try to come closer."

And she went back into the vase to cast shadows by the reddish glow the dragon's nose exhaled. Soledad hadn't realized all this at that moment, but her friend confessed it the night in the hotel when, after Peter's departure, they met up again. But right then in the belly of the vase, Lucía's delicate fingers cast on the walls of the labyrinth a story of shadows and eclipses that later Soledad would come to know quite well.

What soon she could indeed corroborate is that her friend was right about Peter not taking long to look for her. And he did so, blatantly, at the opening at the Ciudadela. While the rest of the group went into the gallery, Soledad stayed looking at the poster outside announcing the photography exhibit:

Peter Nagy
Photographer of Shadows

She should have fled, escaped before Peter came to see why she hadn't come in. Instead, it flattered her to know he'd come out just to look for her. As soon as she saw him beside her, she couldn't help smiling again. He took her hand and didn't let go the whole evening.

XXIII

Luckily a few weeks earlier Carmen had started having trouble falling asleep and was now taking sleeping pills. They made her rest so deeply that barely was her last soap opera over did she say a Magnificat for Luis, a resident at the General Hospital, and a Shadow of St. Peter for Soledad, who studied in the afternoons at the Design School, and went to sleep. And it was a real sleep because starting with that exhibit, Soledad could share with Peter a life of cocktail parties, openings, performances, walks, visits to bars and cantinas as well as to the studios and houses of his artist friends, without worrying too much that her mother would realize what time she came home.

The first occasion the party continued at the apartment Peter shared with his friend, the painter Montero. It was in one of those old buildings that abound in the Juárez neighborhood, with dirty walls and rundown staircases, but as soon as they walked through the door the visitors were amazed, as if they'd entered a black and white photo or painting: the shadows of men and women appeared frozen on the white walls and black ceiling. On one window was even seen the silhouette of a motionless bird in the act of landing. The tiles on the floor, alternating as well between black and white, projected the spatial perspectives and accentuated the sensation of emptiness that runs through some dreams. And in the middle of everything was a camera on a tripod. Besides a little white table with plates of hors d'oeuvres, plastic glasses and bottles of Egri Bikavér, whiskey and tequila, and a few stools and benches, there was no other furniture. Later Soledad would see the room Montero used for a studio and, of course, Peter's bedroom.

It was after three in the morning and the party was still going on when Soledad told Peter she had to go. Without saying another word, he took his overcoat and put it over the girl's shoulders, then grabbed his Leica before they left. "Gentlemen, *érezzétek magatokat otthon*," shouted Peter to the gathering of friends, students and a few reporters. "*Auf Wiedersehen!*" answered Montero, at that moment with both hands firmly against the ample bosom of a blond woman who, he would later tell his pregnant wife, had been after him since the exhibit.

The street was dark except for a single arc of a streetlight. As they neared it, Peter asked his companion to approach the lamppost's luminous fountain as he took out the camera. Soledad would later see the print and had to recognize that Peter was an expert in matters of light and darkness: the photo of a body converted into the shadow of itself.

As they lived in nearby neighborhoods, Peter said he'd walk her home. They did so in silence, taking Reforma with its bronze heroes and plant beds sewn with poplars. Soledad didn't know if it was the intense lights on the avenue or the vertiginous rhythm of the few cars out at that hour, or her own nervousness of knowing that desires invade you, rush at you, overtake you until you're turned into a wanting, trembling, fragile body…The thing is she stumbled. Peter, who had stayed close without touching her since taking the photo outside his apartment, grabbed her by the waist. He must have believed he was helping her but the truth is that as soon as she felt his contact, Soledad lost her footing again and tripped. Then Peter stopped her to say, "*Ha egy ló egyszer megbotlik, meggyógyítjuk, ha kétszer megbotlik megöljük.*"

He accompanied his words with a gesture pointing to her temple. Then he translated, "In my country, if a horse trips once we heal it, if it does so again…"

He kept pointing his index finger at Soledad's left temple as he finished the sentence. They laughed. But before Sol could formulate a desire, Peter's hand-pistol touched her cheek, went around her lips and slid down her neck, breasts, stomach and, over her clothes, his forceps hand pressed against Soledad's sex. She felt like a fiery path leveled the places he'd marked and she held out her hand to feel Peter's beard and convince herself he wasn't going to harm her. Lucía and the dragon remained silent. Soledad knew that in some way they were leaving her alone. She trembled to think they could abandon her to fate, and she would have fallen to the ground if Peter's hands hadn't held her, and he searched for her mouth to help her start breathing again.

XXIV

Look, our death is already beginning to murmur. All that must be put aside. The dragon's stomach and the mirror of water have finally shattered. We have to change houses as soon as possible. The vase on the staircase is completely in pieces. The mirror in the bedroom has shattered to bits. I'm still on the tip of the branch. Arms welcome me.

XXIV bis

Soledad still trembles to remember. The city would be the proper haunt for her cry. He called her: Princess, Mistress, Little Girl, *Csillagom*, Cloud of Attila, Heart, *Szüz*, Virgin's Bower, Iris, Angel, Sweetcakes, Gala, Tender Ilka, Cocoon, Almond, Earthen Bowl, Corrupted Tongue, *Tündérkém*, Grain of Rice, Swan, Beatrice, Damsel, *Tisza*, Quetzal Feather, Moon…and she fell— what can you do?—with the empty words they are, in love.

XXV

On several occasions she was able to spend the whole weekend with Peter. Luis disappeared for days at a time due to the residencies of the last year of his medical studies and Carmen left to travel to Pinotepa, whether to take care of her sister Refugio, who had broken her hip, or to attend the ever more frequent burials of friends and family.

The first time it was Peter who brought her breakfast in bed, a steaming cup of coffee and a plate of fresh cherries. Sol had never eaten them before except in preserves, and had barely tasted one when she began devouring them all. But Peter held back her hand and put them into her mouth one by one, observing her with that crystalline gaze that seemed to penetrate everything. He watched her eating, watched her breathe, took notice of the reflective movement of her eyelashes. Soledad felt frightened to be observed so closely and she hid in the empty vase. Peter wanted to follow her but no matter how hard he tried he remained outside. He ended up frustrated and left the room, then came back with his Leica and confronted the girl with the lens. It was already afternoon but the light was dim from the opaque plastic curtains that cast the place in a permanent penumbra. Peter got up to open them a little, letting an arced stream of light slip into the room. Soledad held the plate of cherries, but was no longer eating them. Peter climbed on the bed and began shooting her: standing, squatting over her body, off to the side, cornering her against the wall, but she ran and ran through the labyrinth although no longer with the reddish glow or her friend's hand to guide her. She touched the clay sides and continued descending, going deeper inside without the vase's darkness scaring her as much as the bluish clarity of Peter's eyes, and the giant cold eye of the camera. Then she heard him get off the bed and put the camera back in its case. He poured himself a shot of some clear liquor from a bottle he'd also brought in the brown leather camera case and tossed it down in one gulp.

"Photography places the gaze upon the surface," said Peter as he sat on the edge of the bed, his shoulders slumped, his voice just a whisper. "It hides the secret life breathing within things…"

He turned and looked at Soledad. She appeared just above the lip of the vase. The plate of cherries had spilled over and the little fruits drew an ominous figure on the carpet.

"Those are Kafka's words…You know who he is? Have you read *Az antalkalis, A folyamat*, his conversations with Janouch?"

He took a sip of the coffee he had brought Soledad. And she found a cherry hidden in a fold of the sheet and wanted to throw it.

"I've won awards…After Moholy-Nagy, on the international scene few photographers from Eastern Europe ever get discussed. My work is starting to stir some interest…Still I'm far from doing what I'm after. Sometimes I tiptoe up to the edge of things, but nothing…Eurydice slips from my hands. The myth of eternal fleetingness."

"Eurydice?" she asked interested. Pursued by her fingers, the cherry was hidden in the groove formed between the cushion and Peter's butt. She tried to get it without interrupting him: it had been so long since someone had told her a story that she jumped out of the vase, took the cherry and waited in suspense. Peter carefully observed her transformation and looked at her intrigued.

"What are you waiting for?" he asked.

Sol responded without hesitating, "A story."

"Well, I have a lot of stories to tell you," said Peter, suddenly in better spirits, "but then…"

He brought his lips to the girl's mouth.

"How is it you go touching my ass without permission? Girls who let that happen deserve to be punished. Turn around," he ordered, taking off his belt while Soledad slipped under the sheets.

Hungarian Rhapsody 2
Ilka and Mátyás
(or, humor and the noble's fickle nature)

King Mátyás was used to taking trips incognito throughout the entire country. His statue in the garden of the Buda palace depicted him in the finery of a hunter, accompanied by a falconer and a young village girl. One day while out hunting, the king wandered through the royal forests of Gödöllö. A thrashing rain forced him to take refuge in a guard's house, where the beautiful daughter Ilka offered the young hunter a jug of water and a fresh smile. The sovereign was captivated by the luscious country girl and prolonged his stay, taking long walks with her. When he finally had to go back, before turning his face towards the Duna River he suggested the girl visit him in the city.

"Whom should I ask for?"

"Mátyás, the royal hunter."

The guard's daughter soon traveled to the city. Before the palace portals she saw a reverent multitude proclaiming the name of her hunter, who was sitting in the royal carriage: "Long live Mátyás, our king!"

Ilka returned home without having visited her "hunter." And later, dying of sorrow, she asked her father to bury her beside the path where she had accompanied her friend.

("But how is it then that Mátyás passed into your country's history as a wise and just king?"

"He was. He took what was his. Not because he was kind...but because Ilka wanted to give it to him."

"But...what's the joke?"

"In other stories Ilka is the joker...Here she lacks a sense of grace..."

"So she's supposed to burst out laughing when she discovers who Mátyás is and then go back to her village and get married and end up telling her grandchildren the story of 'Little Red Riding Hood'?"

"OK, dying of love is rather much. But this rhapsody must come to an end, princess. A serf's room isn't worthy of a highness. Return to your palace. This serf has much labor to do."

"Can I help you? Are you going to develop film in the darkroom?"

"No...I'd like to be alone. I'm writing up my notes on how to sketch a shadow."

"You're writing...in Spanish?"

"An article for a magazine here."

"I can help you with the words you don't know how to translate."

"Thanks, I have my Magyar-Spanish dictionary. Although thinking about it, it's not a bad idea you helping me.")

XXVI

Soledad didn't know at what moment the roles became reversed but soon she was the one bringing a *pálinka*—the crystalline liquor he drank in the morning—and an espresso to Peter in bed. Not that from one day to the next she turned into a housewife (she didn't wash his clothes or cook for him, and Dorita come twice a week to clean the house), but she had indeed become his assistant. She helped him develop and print film, she got ready the audiovisuals, slides and lecture materials for his classes at Tacuba and the Academia de San Carlos, she graded his tests, posed as his model, accompanied him to exhibitions and parties of his circle of artist friends in Mexico City. It didn't bother Soledad to let her classes go, nor to submit herself to a rhythm of little sleep, nor to feel the constant anxiety of lies and precautions so that Carmen or Luis wouldn't realize what time she came home late at night, and how at the same time Peter always found her available. From the beginning, seeing that her mother might be suspicious of her wanderings, she told Peter that since she didn't have a phone the best thing would be for her to look for him. Peter seemed at agree, just like when she told him that Carmen was a woman with modern ideas who didn't judge her daughter's acts; it was only that the one man she might have rebuilt her life with had just been killed, and as it was natural to be so sad, she didn't want to see anyone.

This story wasn't completely false, for Elías González had appeared in Carmen García's life two years earlier and had practically been the one responsible for her letting Soledad study at the university after high school (among other changes that surreptitiously began happening to the residents of the house of the portals). They had met at a store where Carmen had gone to buy a bra for her generous bosom. She had just got in line to pay when she felt the presence of a man behind her. Discretely, so he wouldn't think she was flirting with him, she pretended to look through a magazine and glimpsed his big, strong hands holding a can of shaving cream, a box of razor blades, some anti-dandruff shampoo and a couple bars of Heno de Pravia soap. The soap must have captured Carmen's attention because she didn't realize the cashier had taken her merchandise from the shopping basket and was now showing the entire world the ample bra with frilly cups she had chosen. When she finally turned to look at the cashier she found not only her intimates—those scandalous 38-C cups of lace and white lycra—but that her trustworthiness as a customer was being questioned, for the girl was now calling for a price check, making her wait through a long and embarrassing misunderstanding. Carmen felt mortified; she tapped her fingers and heels and fixed her furious eyes on the cashier, but waited stoically while the weight of the truth, like in some Medieval ordeal, restored a lost dignity to her. Meanwhile the bra passed from the hands of the cashier to the boy checking the price, to the woman in charge of the lingerie department who verified the price tag was correct, to the floor manager who handed it back to the cashier so that now, yes, she could ring up the price on the cash register. Carmen was about to pay for her restored honor, but a careless change of attitude in the girl made her stop.

"If I were you," the man with the Heno de Pravia soap said, "for wasting all your time I wouldn't pay. And much less for such an intimate item," and here he paused, "so uselessly handled."

Carmen didn't understand at the time the meaning of that adverb so loosely pronounced by Elías González (but she did later when she made some subtle excuse about the encounter while telling Soledad about it), but in any case she thanked him with a smile for interceding and gathered her forces to refuse to pay, an act Elías seconded by leaving behind everything he carried (except, of course, his new intentions), and offered Señora García his arm so they could leave together with their dignity intact, while the cashier and manager looked at them in confusion. After going to a café for an ice cream and to laugh about the prank they'd just pulled, Elías took Carmen back to the house of the portals and after that they began going to the movies, to the theater, out to eat, always on the "friendly plan" as she liked to emphasize. They would also occasionally spend the afternoon playing cards or dominoes and it was curious to see that man with enormous hands handle the cards and tiles with such unusual delicacy.

Of course Luis, accustomed to monopolizing Carmen's attention, treated Elías with hostility, but after awhile he began to date a nurse and sufficiently forgot about his mother and her new friend. On the other hand Soledad liked Elías from the very beginning. Directing his gaze to one of Lucía's drawings of a lunar labyrinth hanging in the living room alongside the portraits of Carmen, he said, "What a marvelous sense of space, as if you really had been to the moon."

Lucía smiled inside the vase. She came around so often that people confused the two of them. Soledad also smiled: if Elías only knew that she couldn't even draw a round "o."

"But she didn't do it. It must have been one of her friends from school," said Carmen, hanging it beside her portrait of the Tehuana woman. "I asked her once if she could make me a pencil copy of that drawing and, well, she took the pencil and the best she could do was stick herself in the eye and I had to take her to the hospital."

Elías put his hands in his pockets and winked at Sol before adding, "Well, that's because the beauty of the model is difficult to imitate."

Carmen looked at him pleased but preferred to change the subject and so asked him if he'd finally fired the workers at his factory who were threatening to strike.

Elías owned a factory that made paints and dyes for graphics and printing that had prospered while his wife was alive and took charge of running it. But the losses were so heavy now that for the last two years he hadn't given a bonus to his employees. He wasn't worried about closing the factory because the last of his daughters had gotten married and if he wanted he could settle down outside the city with one his brothers, but then Carmen had appeared in some store, mortified by the bra incident and how it unfolded, and now he wasn't so sure about getting rid of the factory. This and other details of his life she had learned about over the months. As for him, he entered the house of the portals with more and more familiarity. When Soledad finished high school, Carmen suggested she get a job in a bank. Soledad had seen her mother while standing in line contemplating the whole time the tellers in their impeccable suits, their nails done and hair all in place. Sol's mother looked at them for a long time: sitting on their high stools in front of the tills, with that marvelous ability to count the bundles of bills while their smiles floated above them and they answered "yes, sir" or "no, ma'am." She contemplated their svelte torsos leaning over the counter, their taste for bracelets and necklaces, that air of an international airline stewardess with a silk scarf tied around the neck…Carmen was almost ecstatic when she walked up to the counter and perceived the fragrance of some designer perfume that surrounded those creatures like a cloud.

"And why do you want such an ordinary future for your daughter?" Elías asked while he helped her put away the groceries they'd bought one afternoon. "Let her study at the university. The best thing one can give their children is education. Look at my daughters—one is a physicist, another a bacteriologist, and Eva María is finishing her specialization in gastrology. If their husbands fail them, they have a career to confront life with."

Carmen became furious. "You talk like my dead husband," she said after a long silence. "Still, you're a man so you must be somewhat right."

But this fresh breeze circulating through the house of the portals, dusting corners and shaking out shadows, quickly ended. After Elías neither phoned nor came around for a week, Carmen got a call from Eva María, his youngest daughter. A bolt of lightening darkened the house: Elías had gone to the factory late one night and the watchman didn't recognize him. Just that simple. A misdirected shot dead on. Months later Carmen would ask Soledad to go with her to visit his gravestone. She prayed, cried and finally before parting in company of her daughter took a handful of dirt and threw it on the grave.

"They're all alike," she said with a sigh. "At least your father had the decency to say goodbye at the hospital."

XXVII

She almost never talked to Peter about her father. When she was with him her feelings went dormant and she found herself as lost from herself as if she were in a labyrinth. At first after running through the empty vase, she missed less Lucía's violent fits and the dragon's deep breaths. She arrived to Peter's with her hands tired of measuring the darkness, thirsty to feel beat that magic skin in which everything became submerged. Soledad had never traveled by boat but at times, when she reflected on what was happening, she thought it was like being shipwrecked, like discovering the sea by horizon and sky and sustenance, seduced by the deep, dark waters that called to one's blood from the echoing abyss. And when she began to feel herself choking, happiness or anguish stuck in her throat and she was capable of doing things she had never imagined. But was that really her? Soledad doubts so when she thinks that right now she doesn't know with any certainty if she is the same person that used to ride upon the shoulders of a gentleman astronomer, erected atop a hill and at whose feet slept a stone grass-hopper. That person who she was and that person whom no one can see, aren't they almost shadows of a dream from which a joking god has awakened? And now what's left? To vanish like an overexposed photo, like those desires failed or betrayed, like the life we leave behind, still with the belief it will always be there awaiting our longing?

Still, memories exist. Soledad can doubt herself, but they loiter inside the labyrinth, they inhabit her like the echo that is no longer a voice but the reflection of a presence: her own, fleeing and volatile. The city's noise rises with its horns and rumbling; it is a trembling ant hill that rends the form of the clouds. Peter maintained that clouds don't exist by themselves. One bright morning they climbed the hill at Tepeyac, but instead of visiting the holy image of the Virgin of Guadalupe or looking at the city laid out in the valley, they devoted themselves to looking at clouds.

For him, their volatile architecture was like that of dreams.

"Years ago, in Arles, I met Philippe Dubois, the photography critic, but not at the international exhibition. Philippe was out hunting clouds and we immediately recognized each other. We didn't attend the press conference, but instead went to the top of the tallest buildings to look at clouds. Clouds, clouds, and clouds. We talked about Stieglitz and his 'Equivalents,' almost a decade recording in photos of clouds what forty years of photography had taught him. Without definite form, without their own body, clouds are there for everyone, they're free…untouchable like memories or dreams. Architects of the impossible. For Philippe they were the essence of photography…the trace of light. The evanes…How do you say?"

"Evanescence?" Soledad looked at the voluminous structures suspended in the air. Palaces, dragons, rocky paths…She couldn't imagine them, as Peter would say, colorless, making themselves visible by the effect of the light that rained, unusually crystalline, over that city more accustomed to skies gray with smog.

"But for me," continued Peter, who liked to hear himself speak and so quite enjoyed teaching, "that theory insists on the purity of light, not the body of light that impedes its rays. But if it was only a matter of light, photos would be white canvases, blind, luminous windows. Photography is the result of an object cutting off light. A body interposes itself…and the photo is a trace of that body. The luminous recording of a shadow…always."

Sol couldn't help thinking about her father in the only photo she had managed to save from Carmen's grasp. In it Javier García is five, wearing a kepis and holding a tin drum in his hands. It's nothing more than a discolored sepia photo, but Soledad has always guarded it like a treasure—a "my father stood here as a child"— even more so since his death, for Carmen insisted on him being forgotten. The drum that shone in his hands, his smile and skin, are as distant as an extinct star and not for this reason have they ceased glimmering to Soledad. She thought Peter was right to define photography as a luminous shadow.

Suddenly she noticed Peter observing her. How long had he been scrutinizing her face? She felt he'd asked her a question because he was stroking his beard impatiently.

"I'll repeat everything. Montero has hepatitis. Mayra, who's pregnant, can't take care of him. He needs a nurse. He'll pay well. Should we go?" At what moment had Peter stopped talking about clouds and shadows and photos? Soledad looked at him in confusion but he'd already started walking away and all she could do was run to catch up with him.

"But…what time will I see you?"

"Montero will be in his studio all day. Besides, friends come first. I had hepatitis as a boy. You?"

"I don't understand," she responded, unsure what he was asking.

"Did you have hepatitis as a child?"

"Yeah, I had it when I was nine."

"Well, there you go. Good," Peter replied before giving her a kiss and lifting her into the air. Then he spun her around a couple times before putting her down on the ground. He took her hand as they began descending the hill. Then Soledad began to experience that happiness the blind must feel when someone assures them, "The second turn on the right and then go straight ahead until you run into the abyss."

XXVIII

Peter thought of throwing a surprise party for his friend. As Montero had to eat sweets, Peter congratulated himself on the idea because, moreover, it had been a long time since he'd celebrated anything. They split the tasks: Soledad took charge of the cake, confetti, and streamers, and he would buy the gift. Later they met back outside the apartment. Peter was waiting for her in the building entrance with his arms full.

"Great, you're finally back," he said, as excited as if the party were for him.

They went up. Montero was lying in Peter's bed talking on the phone to Mayra.

"Of course, dear. Rigorous quarantine from people who haven't already had hepatitis, especially pregnant women. You can't come within ten blocks of here. Yes...yes...we'll be in touch. Peter and Soledad will take care of everything...Don't worry. Of course you can...Uh-huh, you let me know ahead of time and I'll go to the window, but it can't be very often because the draft and direct light don't do me any good."

Montero was thin and yellow. Peter threw streamers and confetti over the bed and shouted, "*Sok boldog születésnapot kívánok. Ezt a Télapó küldi neked.*" Soledad then came in with a cake lit by little birthday candles. Montero blew them out and opened with great interest the gift Peter gave him. His smile turned to astonishment: it was a white nurse's uniform. Peter took it and put it up to Soledad to see how it fit. Then Montero understood. They all three laughed.

Montero was always resting. Soledad attended to his calls, took his temperature, prepared his little dishes with a good dose of sugar, went out and bought him the greatest variety of sweets and the most perfect African daisies for his dresser, played backgammon and checkers, read to him the *Memoirs of Casanova*, the book he had asked his wife for so he wouldn't get bored. And always outside as well as inside the apartment, Soledad went about dressed as a nurse, with a cowl and even white stockings. The first time the cleaning woman Dorita saw her she burst out laughing. "These kiddy artists, the things they come up with."

Soledad also laughed. The truth is she enjoyed going out on the street in that get-up. It was as if the game she shared with Peter and Montero in the apartment extended to the outer world in a complicity that made her feel privileged.

When Peter discovered the sweetshop Celaya with all its variety of exquisite Mexican treats, he asked her to go there every day. Soledad bought "royal morsels," "heavenly glories" and "egg yolks of angels" to make Montero happy. Sometimes she went by foot, taking Juárez Avenue past the Hotel del Prado, passing through the park the Alameda, taking pleasure in this loaned identity with the same fruition that couples held hands or kissed under the ash trees. After a few days, the clerk at Celaya recognized her and without Soledad saying anything offered her new and evermore succulent sweets whose flavor began with the very name.

"You must really be in love," she said one time with a pointed smile while giving her a couple "little love birds," continuing, "The good thing is your man likes sweets…although the bad thing is there's no man who doesn't end up cloying."

And she let out a sigh. But rather than looking into the distance as they say do those who no longer remember (although in this case, the background was one of those buildings on 5 de Mayo whose windows make them seem transparent), the woman looked down and remembered her legs.

"Along that line," she said in a whisper, "I was wondering if I could ask you something in confidence."

Soledad looked at her intrigued. What could this woman want?

"You know, I spend so much time on my feet, my varicose veins swell up. And I thought maybe the young nurse might suggest something."

"Glybenol," responded Soledad without the least hesitation, for it was the medicine her mother took for the same problem, "although it's a bit expensive. I'd recommend you take a few rattlesnake pills that you can buy not far from here, in the passageway off Guatemala Street. Recent studies have shown that extracts from poikilothermic creatures are good for vascular illnesses," she concluded with a doctoral air fully earned from sleepless nights when she helped Luis and his friends studying medicine type up their reports and assignments.

As soon as she left the sweetshop she ate a pineapple halleluiah. She stole a glance at her reflection in the plate glass windows on Juárez. As if it were nothing, a little boy stopped his mother and pointed at her, saying, "Look, mama, a nurse." The delicious texture of the halleluiah that stuck to her palate and dissolved little by little lasted her all afternoon.

XXIX

It was Montero who took the game the next step. He asked her not to wear anything under the uniform. Peter agreed and he took off what was hindering Soledad in front of his friend and asked her to get used to leaving her dress open as soon as she came in the apartment. Occasionally while she was taking care of him, Montero ran his hand over her ass, asking, "Go on, give me my medicine." Other times, as soon as she got back from the sweetshop he would rub her sex with tamarind pastries or a "little taste of nuns," savoring them between Soledad's legs. But he never took it any further. He would suppress his will and ask the girl to leave. Soledad would go out, staggering and crushed by these daring fits of faithfulness to Peter of which she didn't feel quite so capable.

When he arrived Peter would begin anew the siege together with his friend. Soledad let him. On one occasion while she was in Peter's arms, Montero took her from behind. It was night and the lights had gone out due to a storm. They'd lit a candle and the flame flickered in an empty bottle of *pálinka*. While the two men took her, she discovered Peter had turned into a wall. On it their three shadows melded into one. And Peter looked at it as if he were making love to that shadow.

XXX

To appear in the depths of the water with the heart out of place. Hands tied to the shoulder to play at being guilty. I'm not afraid. I've learned that horror is as delectable as beauty. I remember other memories: slithering blades of rough skin brush against my dream; a tree pruner runs through me with neither sound nor pain; transparent little hands brush against my mouth until turning it to foam. I don't know why but I'll always hold my position: the skin stretched out in one bold movement. I only lean my eyes over the edge to touch the tip of a desire.

Before me a silky luminous handkerchief sinks upon the water with a twilight indifference. All lips, I approach and trap the damp fabric that quenches an unsuspected thirst. I begin to pull and a line of tension draws out a handkerchief that abandons its new destiny. At the point of departure everything stops it. I pull even harder, only to recognize the legs of an insect lit with a deceitful luminosity. The insect turns into a butterfly. Now its golden wings beat with agony at the water's edge, rebelling against the death to which it is completely delivered. As well within me an impulse that isn't will but abandonment and obedience leads me to pull again with my lips. Tongues say the dust of a blind butterfly's wings. These maledictions don't reach me: my eyes have disappeared and I am only the fold of my own lips, forcing myself to preserve intact the gold of its wings so that later it can dazzle and blind others. I pull, then, the silky butterfly and when I'm about to lift it from the waters, something pulls back on it again. I continue pulling only to discover the mouth of a fish that imprisons the butterfly's wings. From the depths of the abyss the fish's membraned eyes provoke in me a hypnotizing repulsion. I discover in fascination that the fish's face is my own.

XXXI

Never had Soledad felt so resplendent and fulfilled. Around that time a photo occurred to her. Peter was gone and Montero was sleeping. She put to the side the shadow puppets adorning Peter's installation, took down the screens and white umbrellas, spread on the floor the metallic reflectors and lit all the lights. The light meter read overexposed. She set the shutter and placed herself in the middle of the viewfinder. Some time later Lola Álvarez would look over this series and say to her, "What a highly developed fascination for light. How did you take this evanescent angel and its wings?" Then Soledad looked closely at the photo whose brilliant rays emanated like a fountain of light itself. The almost complete absence of contours transformed it into a veritable luminous shadow. In a few takes, the silhouette unfolded its diffuse wings. It was only a robe wrapped around her arms, but it made Lola smile.

"If you don't want to, don't tell me," said the photographer. "One must have a radiant soul to make something like this. What I also see is that you jump from heaven into hell," she added, pointing to other photos of Soledad that Álvarez had asked to see, "as they say, from clarity into darkness."

The smile stuck on Soledad's lips. All the time in the world had passed since those days she had been quarantined with Montero and Peter, when she had been, beyond a shadow of a doubt, radiant and happy. And now, on the contrary…She felt goose bumps and could barely kiss Lola goodbye. She needed to escape, run, lose her wits. To not confront what had happened. Luckily Peter was at the apartment. A few caresses from him was enough to heal her soul, a spoonful of honey in the mouth before making unlove to him.

To go running from places had become as laborious a task to her as when a child she would run to take refuge in the vase. The difference was that in the past she had tried to escape and now she only wanted for that bearded man to seek her and, in a way she didn't yet understand, rescue her. At first Peter forced showy persecutions in which his friends, people on the street, and in one case the police, had to intervene. But as things got repetitive, Peter became frustrated and more and more put off trying to catch up to her.

And so came the day when not only did he take a long time but it was Soledad who had to return over her steps, go back through the labyrinth of downtown streets (for on that occasion they met at a dingy little cabaret near Plaza Garibaldi), and feverishly run amidst the drunks, mariachi players, prostitutes and pimps, in order, finally, to return to his side.

It was almost 6 in the morning but the place still had that fluorescent light that annulled the passing of the hours. Peter and Montero's group included some other artist friends and a young filmmaker, an assistant director they'd met a few hours earlier at an opening. Deborah, as the woman was called, sat beside Peter and they both broke into laughter at the behavior of somebody else they'd just met, a fat fifty-year-old transvestite named Janet, but whom Montero had baptized Genet. Next to Genet sat an adolescent girl whose name, Razzia, prompted a benevolent smile from Peter. He was telling Deborah that in Hungarian there also existed the word *razzia*, when Soledad came up and asked to leave. Peter kept talking as if he hadn't heard her and Soledad thought the noise in the place had kept him from hearing her words. But then Genet pointed at Soledad with the tip of her fan.

"Hungarian, what kind of manners are those? We ladies should be treated with respect," she said and then made a place beside her. "Come, my dear, sit her with me."

"You don't deserve it, Genet," said Montero from the other side of the table. "You don't know her, but that girl here has a couple tequilas and starts dancing on the table…"

Deborah parted her hair that had fallen over her face and smiled at Peter, then looked Soledad over from head to toe. Montero broke in again. "And well, it's entertaining the first time, but…not all night."

"Come on, Hungarian," Genet said again to Peter, "a little friendliness never hurt anybody," and she smiled flirtatiously while casting her glance over the dance floor. She must have remembered something for she suddenly turned to the adolescent girl she'd arrived with. "As to friendship, go on, Razzia, see if someone at one of the tables will invite you to dance. That's why you asked me to bring you here."

Montero got up just at that moment.

"Genet, if you'll allow me," he said, extending his hand toward the girl.

She stood up to her full height and just then, as she adjusted her green sequinned strapless dress over her smooth body and strutted onto the dance floor, Soledad realized she was a boy. Montero followed and they chose a song together on the jukebox.

Genet let out a sigh when Razzia put her hands on the hips of the young stud and began to dance a *guaguancó* like Ninón Sevilla. Deborah and Peter laughed and got up to dance. One of the artists who'd come with the group asked Soledad but she wanted to stay with Genet. They smiled at each other and Genet opened her fan and waved it at Soledad to cool her off. A landscape of mountains and clouds swirled about. Then Genet brought her face close to Soledad's and gave her a light kiss on the lips.

"No, Genet," said Soledad while she watched Montero embracing the boy and caressing his ass over his clothes. Deborah and Peter barely touched their bodies, but he began to play with her hair and she pretended to move away from him only to end up even closer.

"Well, it's obvious you don't fulfill him," whispered Genet. Her mouth remained behind the open fan and it was impossible to guess her intentions by only looking at the sweet eyes on the other side of the Oriental landscape that covered part of her face.

Soledad looked at Peter. He was a foreigner but he asserted the right to plant himself wherever he was, which granted him an irreducible presence. Now in that dingy cabaret he could talk with a cab driver, a laborer or a prostitute, and the next day have breakfast with the daughter of the Brazilian president or welcome Genet or Razzia to his studio so they could do a private striptease for him. As well there was art and photography, exhibits, Arles, his poetics of shadows and life...Why would Genet ever think Soledad or anyone else could fulfill him? But Genet's words had fallen into a fertile well and they seeded themselves and germinated like magic beans because in some way the waters of that well had risen with dark feelings, forewarnings that eliminated beforehand any possibility to those who only lacked a name, a word where was concentrated the rotted sap that would let it blossom in a flower of evil. It was true. Soledad recognized that she felt unable to fulfill Peter. She could barely admit it, the well rose to the top and then overflowed. It flooded the little cabaret, drowned Genet with everything, with her fan showing mountains and craggy clouds, it dragged along Peter, Deborah and Montero as they took each other's hands to twirl around Razzia. Genet shouted before she was submerged in the waters, "Child, where have you gone?"

Just to amuse herself, Soledad answered, "Here, Genet, I'm still right beside you."

Genet looked from one side to the other for her. "Stop your stupid jokes and come out from wherever you are," she mumbled, looking under the table.

Then Soledad pinched her flabby arm. Genet rubbed it without understanding what happened and Soledad was just about to pinch her again. She could have made her swallow her words about Soledad and Peter, but a sudden happiness—like that which inexplicably erupts in dreams—led her to the dance floor.

A few seconds later Deborah stumbled and put on a face like a fly had bit her on the ass or a mischievous spirit were pulling her hair. She finally asked Peter to take her home. He seemed unsure but not seeing Soledad beside Genet he agreed. They went out to catch a taxi and Soledad hurried to get in with them.

"I feel like I'm being watched," said Deborah, sitting rather stiffly next to Peter. He tried to caress her neck, but she jumped to the edge of the seat as if someone had hit her.

"These Mexican women," said Peter a bit pissed off, not caring that Deborah could hear him, "are so…are so, how do you say, *a francba.*"

Soledad had to bite her tongue not to give him any ideas. It was all a dream but she didn't want to wake up. Deborah lived in Tlatelolco and they headed there. As soon as she got out of the taxi, Peter told the driver to drop him at his apartment. Soledad watched him sprawl on the seat and close his eyes. He must have fallen asleep because when Soledad caressed his lips and chin he barely moved.

When they arrived Peter stretched and quickly got out. Sol had to push on the door so she didn't get left inside. He thought the door had come back open because he hadn't slammed it hard enough and so came back to close it. Then he strode off to the building and Soledad trailed behind. While she watched him take his clothes off and climb into bed, she asked herself what else she could do before the dream ended.

It suddenly occurred to her to look in a mirror. Montero had a full-length one in his bedroom. She was just about to stand before it when she got scared. And what if the mirror were really a door leading to an undesired place? She shut her eyes. When she opened them again she could relax: there was her image, just like every day, perhaps with bags a bit darker than normal under her eyes.

She went back to Peter's bedroom He was fast asleep but as soon as Soledad got under the covers he embraced and kissed her.

"Why did you disappear?" he asked before falling back asleep.

Soledad didn't answer. She thought that if it were all a dream then falling asleep she might awaken. She slipped over to that side of dreams or watchfulness, happy and secure because Peter's arms still held her.

XXXII

But the dream repeated itself: Peter, suddenly blind, groped in the air, unable to touch her. Soledad started sobbing, I'm here, here, turn and look at me. Peter tried a couple more times and finally went on his way. She looked at her hands, but instead of hands she found a hole, a white leprosy devouring her arms and then her body…

She let out a scream. Peter woke and began to calm her down.

"Please, please, don't go," she begged him.

Peter lulled her in his arms until she fell back asleep. But when he tried to move away, she pressed closer against his body.

"Tell me again the story of your grandfather Gyula. The one about the amber deer," she asked.

Peter kissed her hair, moved by Soledad's fascination for stories.

After that she managed to stay right by Peter's side. She felt that if she were touching him all the time, no bad could overcome her. At first, after that dream in which she woke him screaming, Peter proved understanding to that almost animal need he discovered in his lover of having to stay near him and his body, but after awhile he got fed up.

Soledad felt his reticence, but far from letting him go she chained herself even closer. Perhaps she thought that if she pressed against him she could avoid catastrophe. Naturally, she interpreted distrustfully anything Peter did. She knew in advance the subtle reasons he thought up with Montero to avoid her, but her rage-filled reactions only convinced Peter to flee. When he proposed she put together her own portfolio of photos, Soledad couldn't believe he was telling her she should work by herself. She needed to see him alone more and more, and he, on the contrary, needed to be more and more among other people.

After his last class at the school on Tacuba he had to return to Hungary at the end of the year. Soledad brought up the idea he had made early on about her following him to Budapest and finishing her studies there, and she began to embellish the trip they would undertake together, not seeing in Peter's silence something other than her obsession with imagining that secret life, that play of shadows she scrutinized in things and people.

One morning they met in the darkroom. The photos of the series "Shadows and Light" that Peter wanted to show Lola Álvarez began to emerge in the plastic basins. Among them were a few he had taken of Soledad in the studio bathroom, in the shower with all that vertical light flowing down, erasing the contours of her body. In a few places the grain of the film had opened as if huge liquid drops still flowed across the paper.

"Look," said Peter examining the print under the red light. "The pore is open. Almost sweating."

"The pore," she repeated, fascinated by the magic of the image, "or rather its granularity?"

"No," said Peter with an edge in his voice. "I'm talking about the pore. Here," he pointed at the photo paper, "there's skin: feel it."

Lately Soledad had felt Peter getting annoyed, and so she wanted to touch him, extend a hand toward him. But Peter thought the girl was going to touch the photo with her fingers and furiously added, "Fuck! It's skin for the eyes. Learn to touch it with your eyes or forget about photography."

And he turned to use the enlarger. Soledad still had in her hands a few sheets of paper in the developing solution. She had to make up with Peter. In that darkness barely illuminated by the red light, she remembered the story of the man who had left the kingdom of the dead to recover his beloved. In the end the gods had granted him his desire: he could take her back to the land of the living if and when he resisted the temptation to look at her following behind. She imagined those caverns in which Orpheus had wandered followed by that beloved shadow. He mustn't turn to look at her even when he no longer heard her steps; of course, they were those of a shadow. As he walked along, the man began to have doubts: Was Eurydice's shadow really following him or were the gods mocking him? Was he walking alone and would he never again possess that lost happiness? The only answer to his questions was silence. Finally the man could no longer resist and turned his impatient gaze to look for his beloved. Something like a stream of direct light struck an image in the process of being formed. Perhaps for that reason the ghost of Eurydice had been overexposed like a photograph too quickly exposed to light.

Soledad thought the coincidence between the darkroom and the story of Orpheus might interest Peter. She took a breath and was about to tell him when she bumped into the switch and accidentally turned on the light.

It took Peter a few seconds to compose himself and understand what had happened. Then he looked at the photo paper, now useless, and launched into Soledad. He rudely threw her out of the room and locked himself in there all morning.

She stayed the whole time waiting on the other side of the door. If Peter didn't finish on time they'd have to change the appointment with Lola. Sol felt so guilty that when Peter came out and showed her the prints he had chosen, she couldn't believe he wasn't still mad. And so, when he asked her to stay in the studio to print another series he had promised to take to the dealer the next day, Soledad thought he was punishing her. Peter well knew that Lola had also insisted on seeing her work.

"Your photos. Ah...sure," said Peter distractedly while he changed clothes. "But you can see her some other day."

Soledad felt Peter didn't care at all about her things. He had just put on his white linen suit he wore to openings and was tying his shoelaces. Finally he cast a glance at himself in the mirror in Montero's room. Soledad watched him the whole time. She watched him smooth his eyebrows and beard, completely lost in self-contemplation. She discovered then that this man (without whom she couldn't imagine surviving) didn't need anyone to exist in the world. Moreover, his very presence that filled the mirror became intolerable.

Peter didn't know at what moment she fell upon him. She knocked him to the ground without him able to avoid falling. They were trapped in a fight of biting and scratching (Soledad biting and scratching and Peter hitting back in self-defense). Montero arrived just then and managed to separate them. Peter finally recovered from his surprise and then indeed wanted to hit her, but his friend convinced him to have a shot of *pálinka* and leave with him. As they were heading out Soledad remarked that Peter's jacket was ripped in back. He didn't dignify her with a glance, not even one of anger.

As soon as they left, the girl got up and hurried to look through Peter's photos. They were on a little table in the room with the installation of shadows. She ran out the studio and down the stairs: she had to make him forgive her no matter what.

Lola (for Dolores; Sol had already passed all the tests and so the woman insisted the girl call her by her first name) opened the door at her apartment in Tabacalera. It didn't seem strange to see the girl arrive without Peter. Soledad forced herself to be pleasant and as soon as she could handed her Peter's work. Lola immersed herself in the images because for her the only pleasure in the world comparable to taking photographs was looking at good photographs. When she'd gone through them all she asked to see Soledad's own work. The girl found herself on the other side of the table, by a vase filled with long-petaled gladiolas, unable to respond. Lola sat there a long while looking at her and suddenly made a gesture with her forehead that preceded getting up for her camera or disarming an interviewer with a question. She did neither one nor the other. Instead she said, "You can't go on like this. Make a decision. Do something."

At that moment someone knocked on the door. They remained silent while the cook Jacinta returned to tell Lola that the Hungarian photographer and the crazy painter—that's what Jacinta called Montero—wished to see her. Lola looked inquisitively at Soledad but the girl lowered her head. She told the servant to send them in.

As soon as they saw Lola they covered her with kisses and she threatened them with her cane for being "rude vagrants." Peter and Montero looked at her in surprise and apologized for being so late, but Lola told them they well knew what she meant. Peter and Montero were unsure and when Lola winked at Soledad, they looked at each other and smiled in complicity. Peter's gaze stopped on the photos in the middle of the table and then he said to Lola, "Ah, now I see what you're talking about. Has she been here long?"

Lola looked at him with that tender gaze with which at times she looked at her son Manuel and answered, "Peter, you just don't do that…You just can't ignore people."

"Lola, dear," Montero plowed in, finally understanding they were discussing Soledad, "don't go defending her. Just look at what she did to Peter…" And casting a glance at where the girl sat, he added maliciously, "She even tore his jacket. That's why he decided to punish her. No, Peter?"

Peter made a vague gesture, preferring to keep silent.

"But what a pair of devils," laughed Lola as she sat down beside the girl. "You should be actors. What a way you have of tricking people. Get out of here. Out of my house. Treating others so roughly," she added, resting her hand on Soledad's leg. "And don't come back until you want to make peace. Jacinta, the Hungarian and the painter are leaving."

The whole scene turned out humorously. Soledad would have also enjoyed it if Peter hadn't marched off without asking another question. Something in his attitude made her suspicious. When he and Montero left, she couldn't keep her gaze from following after them, or better said, after Peter who headed down the hallway towards the door. Until the last moment she hoped and waited for him to shout out that the joke was over. But then all she heard was the door shutting and Jacinta dragging her feet down the hallway. She lowered her gaze to find her own hands grasping her legs: only thus could she understand she hadn't run after Peter.

"He carries off your body and you stay in the shadows, isn't that so?" Lola said, caressing her hair. "I know very well what that is. I was like Manuel's arm, an extension of his will. I had to get away. And you know what, my girl? It hurt more than an amputation. Well, I've never had anything amputated, no? But my soul ached in my body with a physical pain. You know what I'm talking about."

Darkness Lesson 2
Notes on designing a shadow

Take any body and submit it to different climates, temperatures, intensities, emotions (all gradation is proportional to a strict level of survival)…The result will be an illuminated shadow, perfect in obedience and condition.

I will speak later of transparency and shadows. The visible and the invisible, that which makes sense and that which doesn't.

….

To think with light you have to consider shadow and penumbra: the contour of a body is distinguished from its background in the measure to which an intimate and secret will beats in the object, negating to die at all, to be seen—touched—at all. But only submerging it in fog, in blindness, provoking those states of being that result from disorder and loss...When unease shuts its aperture to lower the respiratory intensity and is concentrated in desperation (the same for an excess of high love specular sources rather than cold key absence) contiguous with darkness. Thus you will attain the eyelid of the night. The instantaneous, mortal knife's edge like Medusa's loving gaze that impregnates you with an immortality finally found.

From this you will discover that every gaze is loving and contains death. Only shadows cast light over the soul.

....

Written with light and shadows, the origin of photography is memory: to perpetuate the beloved image, to invoke the cessation of time and forgetfulness. On the path toward the visible world, Orpheus discovered that Eurydice was nothing more than the incarnation of his desire. For that reason he looked at her too soon, in order to recuperate her in his memory and permanent invention of her.

....

The knowledge of shadows must therefore persevere in the processes of casting into shadow the desired objects. Submitting to the most secret will. Capturing the lines of force that establish the organization of the ensemble. Determining the distance vision has traveled and thus attain, on the paper's silvery surface, clipped off but still beating, the dark dawn of things. (Only thus can she attenuate the tyranny that her desire—a dark and profound hunger—imposes upon her.)

....

Techniques for the physical manipulation of the model exist: deformation from large angles, solarizations, infrared film, decomposition of continuous movement, the *flou* effect, destruction of the visible quality, all these augment the creative experimental possibilities. But beginning with the submission of the object, the perfect subversion is achieved: the crystallization of the conscience and the will to convert itself into an imaginary and not real body, to be shadow, aura, cloud, trace, dream…

….

(Photography is the mirror where our dreams are reflected: eternity. There are resplendent photos that signal to us like the finger of god. And experimental and abstract photography. The same thing. The end result of our future memories. The dreams and again the desires that although we don't long for still choose us as their own.)

XXXIII

It was as if Peter's hand had shut off the light and the darkness made her lose all point of reference: where the sky was, what floor she walked upon, what her life used to be. Uncertainty surrounded her. She closed her eyes and it made no difference. She stumbled and no one prevented her from falling. She waited to hear the gunshot that Peter had once pretended to point at her temple, but only the echo of memory dulled her soul. At one moment someone came up and touched her shoulder. She thought it was Lucía with the letter from Peter she had been waiting for, but it was just the hotel cleaning woman. As Soledad was unable to respond—she had gone days without eating—the maid reported her to the front desk. They made her drink a cup of hot tea. As soon as she revived, the manager told them to throw her out in the street with her luggage. The cleaning woman looked at her with guilty eyes, and when the manager walked off, she gave Soledad a slip of paper.

"Forgive me, I didn't know. If you need a room, here's an address. My cousin Mode is a concierge at a building over on Cuauhtémoc. She might…"

She helped her catch a taxi. Soledad handed the driver the address the woman had given her. She still had some of her savings for Hungary. Anyways, she had to look for work. The world had become too vast and heavy for her to know where to begin. Suddenly through the open window of the taxi flew in a pale yellow butterfly that fluttered confusedly about her. Soledad took that as a good sign.

Part Three

Subterrarean Dreams
and
Other Choices

XXXIV

It was still day when she decided to come down from the Castle. Pressed against the walls, fleeing from the passing people, she descended the little marble steps and then the ramp extending to the foot of the hill. Near the old sentry box she came across a unique little structure, right between the fort's merlons and a church with ojival arches. The doors were open and from inside came peals of laughter. Out of curiosity she went in. There was no furniture in the house. Groups of students stood alone by the walls, walked about, made funny faces, laughed nervously or teased each other. From the walls surged the visitors' deformed reflections: subtlety stretched-out legs or giant bony hands, giraffe-like necks, midget-like torsos, completely hydrocephalitic heads. It was the House of Mirrors with its measure of anguished magic.

Soledad wanted to know what would happen if she stood before one of the mirrors. There appeared a body with a little head and trunk and elongated limbs: her own body in a momentary and spider-like deformity. She tried other mirrors and in each one the answer of her monstrous reflection illuminated a smile on her face: perhaps the spell was broken; perhaps all those distorting mirrors had ended up newly reforming her shape.

A loud group of teenagers in school uniforms shook her from her ruminations. One of them, a fat prattling boy whom she'd heard called Lard, tried to stand in front of Soledad's mirror. But he couldn't. It was as if the air made him bounce off, or as if in mid-movement he changed his mind. Looking at him on the floor, his classmates made jokes about him that he brushed off like flies, accustomed as he was to being an object of ridicule.

"Look at Lard. He saw himself in one of those mirrors and now he thinks he's a gazelle."

"You received your greatest wish, eh, lard butt? You're finally skinny?"

"Now all you have to do is not have such a dark face, make your hair spiky, straighten out your legs and you'll be like new..."

Three slender girls with their school sweaters tied around the waist came in the room, their tennis shoes adding to their light, bouncing steps.

"Come on, Lard, the princesses are looking for their knight in shining armor."

Lard got down on his knees whiles the girls walked by him at a distance. The boy started to follow them on all fours, wagging his tongue. The teens seized on his new performance, shouting, "Go, go, go..."

Watching it all and feeling bad for him, Soledad huddled against the wall of mirrors. She looked at Lard and his little companions and their tyrannical game and remembered the Ángeles sisters with whom she and Rosa once played. She recalled how one word of approval, one gesture of criticism, was enough to make them rise or fall from the clouds.

The boys finally left. For a moment the House of Mirrors remained in solitude. Soledad saw her eyes as if they were two fish bowls and tried to widen them. Then she remembered Lucía and her oriental features and how she hadn't seen her since they had gone into the vase together, after the fairy tale they'd experienced at the Palace of Fine Arts. That had already happened several times, but why did it seem that on this occasion the coin tossed into the fountain of desire took so long to fall? Or would this enchantment never end? She thought it might have been better never to have left the Morgue, where she'd gone to work after Peter departed. And she would have been even better off never leaving the Chinese vase.

But always that stubborn call to wander with desire still not fulfilled, like the sleepwalker who doesn't realize he's walking through life.

XXXV

The archives at the Palace of Fine Arts were called the Morgue. There in the bowels of the palace, next to the electrical and ironwork and mechanical workshops, near the mobile platforms of the auditorium and its huge mechanism for raising curtains and rotating stages, it shared the heavy steel structure that held up the Palace of Fine Arts, a white water lily ever on the verge of opening its marble petals.

But below in the subbasement were the soccer games and drunken revelries of the workers in the tunnel that served as a parking ramp for the bureaucrats, the altars of San Jude Tadeo and the Virgin of Guadalupe surrounded by little Christmas lights and posters of beautiful naked women, the concentrated odor of humidity and piss…As well, the deeper one dared go down those unending corridors, the scarcer the fluorescent lights that three levels below served as a guide so one wouldn't get lost on the subterranean banks of that hidden river which, according to legend, went all the way to Chapultepec and the Hill of the Star.

The archives were a world apart, a kind of grotto where stalactites of documents and boxes seemed to create a balance of irregular columns that held up both the floor and ceiling. There were sinuous corridors, passages that suddenly emerged and then dead-ended by the impetuous will of paper. The first time Soledad passed over its threshold she tripped several times because the sleepy light blurred the edges of boxes and packages. After several tries she finally reached a corridor a bit wider than the others, where an older man sitting at a metal desk was making notations in an accounting book. He had distinct indigenous features and for a moment Soledad recalled those *tlacuilos* from the codices with a roll of bark paper upon their legs. While she approached she also discovered a young man sitting on an improvised bench of papers reading names and numbers from a thick folder. The two men wore blue smocks with the Fine Arts emblem on them. Then Soledad remembered why she had come to this place.

"Señor Agapito?" she asked the older man.

He glanced at her before returning to his notebook. Soledad thought he hadn't heard. She was about to repeat the question when the young man came forward and asked, "Are you here on behalf of Señor Rueda?"

She nodded yes.

"Then come in."

Soledad didn't know whether she should ask to take leave of the older man. Anyways she mumbled "with your permission" and followed the boy, who had a noticeable limp. He led her down the same corridor by which she'd entered, but before reaching the exit he turned down a passage hidden by three hanging archives. He pushed them aside to dive into a small cubicle of diffuse light piled high with boxes spilling with papers and photos.

"You can begin here," he told her and went off with that involuntary sideways tilt that almost made him graze against the paper walls.

Soledad was astonished to find herself suddenly in the guts of that place so many tourists visited throughout the year and she remembered the gleaming white wall of its exterior that dazzled the eyes in the midday sun. What a contrast to the rarified air of the subbasements and the permanent penumbra one could touch by hand. She leaned over a box where a black and white photo, which looked recently taken, showed the director of Fine Arts presenting a famous ballerina a bouquet of flowers. They were on the stage of the Palace, surrounded by other important people and dance personalities who were applauding. Suddenly the absence of light in a far corner of the photo caught her attention: there, in that area of penumbra created on the margins, she discovered a shadow from which barely emerged gleaming eyes and hands reflecting light. She hesitated a moment, discerned the sharp nose and predatory air of a hunter lurking in the shadow and no longer had any doubts. It was Martín Rueda.

XXXVI

She had come to the Morgue recommended by Rafa, Señor Rueda's driver and the husband of the caretaker at the building where for the last few weeks she had rented a room on the rooftop.

Usually on the weekends Rafa helped his wife clean the building on Villalongín Street, a couple blocks from the Garden of Art. One day he was cleaning the entranceway when he observed a girl take a suitcase from a taxi and drag it stumbling to the door. For a moment Rafa put the mop to one side, ready to help, but he stopped; although the girl looked rather skinny, her hands were welded onto the trunk. He thought how funny it would be if one of those February winds dragged her through the air, she and the suitcase floating off like a kite, because Rafa was sure she would never let go of her luggage even if every February wind came at once or she had to piss in her pants. He couldn't help but smile when Soledad held out the little piece of paper the hotel chambermaid had given her.

The caretaker Mode was the cousin of the woman at the hotel, and as soon as Rafa introduced Soledad, Mode told her she could have the room. The girl put down the suitcase for a moment and began rummaging through her pants pockets.

"Here's the money," she said quickly.

"But, girl…you haven't even seen the room yet," Rafa responded, looking at his wife.

"Nor have we even told you how much the landlord wants for rent," intervened Mode smiling. "You have to see it first, though I think you're going to like it."

"A painter used to live there," said Rafael as if revealing a secret. Then he bent down to pick up the suitcase and head to the roof, but Soledad moved to take it. They were about to head down the hallway when Modesta's voice stopped them both.

"Wait, Rafa. First I'm going to give this girl a cup of *atole*. Just look at her face."

"But that's not necessary," said Soledad. "Don't worry, señora…"

"Modesta at your service. But people call me Mode and don't tell me you're going to refuse a little *atole,* because that I won't accept."

When the three finally went up to the rooftop, Soledad was surprised by the room: a diamond of light situated in a corner, with natural curtains created by the leaves of a willow and a *pirul*. The space was broad and among the old things the previous renter had left behind was a dilapidated sofa that would serve for a time as Soledad's bed. She went up to one of the windows, dizzy from the asymmetry and clarity of the space. She thought she wouldn't be able to install a dark room here, but in exchange she'd be able to photograph the light. She took from her suitcase the Leica camera Peter had given her shortly before he left for Hungary, when she still thought they'd travel together. Rafael saw her place a hand on the window glass, against the clarity filling the room, and then take a photo of that suddenly ghost-like hand. But as soon as the shutter clicked, Soledad let out a moan and the camera almost fell to the floor, startling Modesta and Rafa. Soledad looked at the palms of her hands and found them red and inflamed. What the hell was wrong with them?

"It must be from carrying that suitcase. It gave you blisters," said Rafa, looking over Soledad's shoulder.

"Blisters my ass," objected Mode while she inspected the young woman's hands. "You'll have to forgive me, girl, but this is what happens when you play with fire…"

"But these aren't from burns," replied Rafa, already convinced Soledad must have been carrying that suitcase her whole life.

"Men," said Mode, winking at Soledad, "they never understand anything…"

But Soledad didn't understand either, and she smiled at the care-taker with a gesture that more than showing agreement revealed doubt.

XXXVII

The appointment was set for Friday afternoon. She was asked to wait: Señor Rueda wouldn't be long. All Soledad really needed to get the job was an interview with the head of the department of warehousing and inventory, but Rafael requested his boss meet her. Martín Rueda had frowned and asked, "Why? Is she really hot, or why do you want me to see her?"

Rafa smiled and looked at him in the rearview mirror. "No, well, she's not up to your standards…but you told me yourself it was urgent to contract someone for all the lost photos. And she's really a great photographer."

"And who told you I was looking for a photographer of weddings and birthday parties…What I need is someone who can help me with very particular information. Not some dumb bitch who surely waived her ass at you and now you're getting ready to dump Modesta for. And how's her bladder?"

"Mode's? Good. The pills your wife sent her worked great. Now she insists on making you rabbit in *adobo* sauce. Tell your wife and just let me know when."

104

"And the other?

"The other? Her name is Soledad. She needs the work. Mode herself told me to tell you. Maybe you can help her out."

There was a moment of silence while the car stopped at a light. When they finally started moving, Martín Rueda frowned again.

"So not my type at all, eh?"

"Well, she's not bad. She even looks a bit like that woman who used to be your advisor and now is…"

"Patricia Ledesma?"

"But not nearly so old, I mean, ten years younger and not so clever. She's a bit shy, but you'll see what pretty pictures she takes. Sometimes there's nothing more than light and a few shadows, but when I start to look at them memories and strange things occur to me…So, boss, do I tell her to come see you at the Palace?"

"Strange things, like what?" Martín Rueda's interest suddenly perked up.

"I don't know…Dreams, caves, grottoes…"

"OK, Rafa, now I see you're getting senile, you bastard. What do you mean dreams and grottoes?" He picked up his newspaper and began to page through it.

"Why don't you just look at them so you don't think I'm kidding around? That girl's photos have something. You start out seeing clouds and a little later they look like the guts of the earth. And that's not all. It happened to Mode, too, that she's looking at a photo and suddenly everything disappears. Like your eyes have turned within."

"What did I say, you bastard? Now you're turning poet on me."

"So, boss, Friday afternoon?"

XXXVIII

First they made her wait in a reception area that offered a panorama of empty desks, the coming and going of a couple secretaries already tired from the week's hustle and bustle, the diminishing ringing of the phones, and beyond that, near the elevator, a few employees standing in line at the Palace's cashier.

"You have to demand they teach you the basics. How many years have you been on the payroll?" Soledad's attention was caught by a dark young woman, her ample bust ready to stop anybody about to butt in front of her. She showed up just after getting paid and was lecturing a cleaning girl while going over to a desk piled with documents waiting to be filed. "That Leonardo Ramírez is a magician. I used to clean the box seats in the theater and now look at me. I'm a secretary."

"It's really possible?" asked the cleaning girl, leaning on the other woman's desk.

From an office in back paneled all in wood emerged a thin woman who approached the girls with a hurried air. Her movements were anxious, as if she were afraid of something. Although a bit on in years, the woman had retained her beauty.

"Girls, the boss is arriving any minute," she told them in an educated voice.

"And so what, Florecita? He's going to eat us alive or what?" said the young woman at the desk spilling with papers, rolling her smiling little eyes.

"That's what you'd like, Maru," responded from behind her a secretary with green eyes that had kept out of things but now laughed suspiciously.

"Me?" she answered. "I pass. I'm still not as desperate as others."

"Girls," again said the woman who'd emerged from the paneled office. "Please, quiet. The good thing is the accountants have already left."

"No," responded the young woman, Maru. "The damn collectors went to the Opera. Because today is payday. Unfortunately they didn't invite us."

"To the opera? Isn't the performance later?"

"Yes, the Opera Restaurant is where María Conesa danced a can-can showing her tail up to here," Maru said, shaking her butt in response to the question.

Señorita Flor let out an amused laugh. Returning to her office she noticed Soledad. "Have you already been helped? Can I get you something?" she asked the girl.

Soledad mumbled a few words that forced Señorita Flor to request she repeat her reply. Maru saved her the effort.

"She's here to see Señor Rueda."

"Did he know you were coming? You see...I don't have it noted in his appointment book," she softly clarified.

"It should be. Well, that's what Don Rafa told me."

"Ah, you're the person coming about the Morgue? But he didn't confirm it with Rafita. Didn't he tell you that Señor Rueda was going to be a little... busy?"

Soledad nodded.

"Well, just wait. He won't be long. Would you like a cup of coffee or tea in the meanwhile?"

She said yes. Flor approached the young woman who had stuck out her chest to make way between hordes of invisible enemies, but before she could say anything the other replied, "Yes, Florecita, you only need ask because your wish is my command. Can I get you something, too?"

Maru began to march off, and Soledad discovered then something curious in her way of walking. Perhaps it was the rubber-soled shoes she wore, but some kind of flexible movement in her robust body made her rise and fall, rhythmically and confidently, with each step.

"Olé," Soledad heard a group of workers in line at the cashier shout at Maru, to which she raised her hand in acknowledgement like a bullfighter. Then she headed to a small room with a nicely stocked kitchenette, Soledad following behind. Maru flipped the light switch back and forth several times. Sol stood right behind the woman who, irritated because the light didn't work, began mumbling under her breath.

"Damned Pedro," exclaimed Maru. "I've told him a thousand times to fix this," she said before turning around and bumping into Soledad.

"Ah, look how dumb you are, sister, to stand behind an animal my size," replied Maru, seeing Soledad hadn't been hurt. Then she noticed the girl was wearing white gloves and immediately asked, "What are the gloves for? You have scabies or something?"

"I..." said Soledad catching her breath, "came to get a cup of coffee."

"Ah, yes. Now I remember. Rafa told us you burned yourself with the solutions for developing photos. Are they really that strong?"

Soledad didn't have time to answer. They heard the elevator bell and then firm steps coming down the hallway. The workers in line at the cashier turned quiet, expectant. Señorita Flor, busy arranging some magazines on a table in the middle of the reception area, ran

to her desk and adjusted her dress before sitting down. The recep-
tionist began taking down a union announcement fixed to a window
pane. Maru herself came out of the kitchenette and went back to
her work next to the archives. Someone in a nearby office cleared
her throat. What had prompted all that uproar? Soledad vaguely
recalled the first time she followed Lucía into the vase and that
unease when she got lost in the labyrinth's passages and the fear,
after each turn, of tripping over the beast asleep at its center. She
preferred hiding in the penumbra of the kitchenette. The closer the
steps got, the deeper into a funnel of silence fell the office. Instead
of him walking down the corridors, it was the corridors that came
toward the owner of those steps. The man continued on his way,
but passing before the entrance to the shadowy kitchenette he
stopped a moment. Soledad managed to see his predatory gaze
before she hid inside the vase.

XXXIX

Martín Rueda pointed to a chair in front of his desk while he took a
phone call. Soledad would have rather remained outside, but now
she found herself waiting, legs together and gloved hands one atop
the other. On the desk were the photos Soledad had given Rafa, a
necessary condition before his boss would grant her an appointment. It seemed strange to the girl to see only portraits and not one
of those works she had, for the time being, entitled "Writing With
Light." She thought Rafa had carelessly forgotten to put them into
the portfolio.

Meanwhile Martín Rueda's long fingers and manicured nails
rapidly passed from one photo to another, barely pausing at a couple
of portraits. Soledad tried to avoid looking at his face but when he
picked up the portrait of Genet sprawled upon a divan like some
odalisque and put it next to the photo of Lola Álvarez where she
tried to guard herself with a hand over her face, her intimacy
suddenly violated, Soledad glimpsed the man's nose, triangular and
fine, pointing at her and she started.

"No, I'm not busy." Martín Rueda's jaw had tensed and Soledad
could tell there existed an instinctive movement between that
clenched jaw and his flaring nostrils.

"Guess who I have here in front of me…No less than your dear Lola. I don't think you've seen this photo. Not even with all your experience curating exhibits. In it the woman places a hand between her face and the camera. Well, you'll just have to see it. When would you like to have dinner?...A Hungarian photographer has one just like it? Peter Nagy…?"

Soledad must have been somewhere else, for how could she explain the lack of emotion with which she reacted to hearing Peter's name? Instead, she took off her gloves and looked at her naked hands. She tried to touch them with her fingertips and verify the feeling. In fact, the pain was lessening. A feeling of relief—she thought the bottle must have finally reached an island—comforted her.

"So anyways, you want the photo…" Martín Rueda watched Soledad above the photographs while she took off her gloves. He parted them a bit to observe her. "Anyways, you'll want it for the homage you told me about. Let's have lunch or dinner sometime this week. OK, bye."

A few moments passed before Soledad noticed he was no longer talking on the phone. The man watched her look at her naked hands, touch them, test the definition of their contours…And Martín Rueda observed all that with the same care he'd used to hang up the phone and gauge the reaction of the girl now that she'd lifted her gaze from her hands and was watching him watching her. Soledad had the urge to cover herself but the gentleman stopped her, "Don't put them on. You don't need them anymore."

Soledad obeyed and left the gloves on her lap. The man had an intense, penetrating gaze. How far could he follow her into the labyrinth? She lowered her eyes and bit her lip before a wish could escape them.

"If you want to work with me," he began saying without taking his gaze from her, "no faking it. No gloves, no disguises, no masks…Do you understand?"

Perplexed, Soledad nodded in agreement. How was it possible for this man to penetrate her like that? She looked into his dark, dark eyes and for a moment thought Martín Rueda indeed had the power to pass through objects and bodies.

"Do you know a photographer named Peter Nagy?"

Soledad pronounced the name to herself. She heard it run through her guts like a hollow sound bouncing from one wall to another.

"Peter Nagy," she repeated as if some unknown person had been mentioned. Martín Rueda frowned, exasperated. Suddenly a distant echo reached Soledad: the memory of a man walking toward an intense source of light, of whom she could discern nothing but blurry contours. Soledad felt unharmed. Then she added, "Yes, I was his assistant while he was in Mexico. Both of us took photos of Doña Lola, but they're separate work."

"Well, I'm going to need all the photos you have of this woman. A good photographer, don't you think?" asked Martín Rueda while he took several photos between his hands. "A friend of mine is organizing an exhibit of portraits of photographers. An homage…" He passed his long index finger over the edge of the images and looked at Soledad before going on. "My friend also knows that photographer…Peter?…It seems he was robbed of his portfolio at the airport…"

Soledad couldn't help smiling and inquired, "At the airport in Mexico?"

"No, in Bucharest, or wherever he's from. So you can understand, my friend and I are in your hands."

Soledad instinctively looked at her hands. She thought she held before herself a notebook of blank pages. Thinking how the new sketches would once again depend on her, she trembled.

But Martín Rueda had other plans. She'd have to bury herself everyday in the Morgue until she came up with the photos which reconstructed that pictorial history of the Fine Arts subbasement, especially those 1905 photographs of the excavations mounted after the discovery of a tile fountain depicting human figures and musical instruments.

"My investigations lead me to surmise this is Quetzalcóatl, that marvelous civilizing deity, giving music to mankind as Prometheus earlier gave them fire," said Martín Rueda. Soledad was surprised to hear the comparison between pre-Hispanic and classical myths, but above all it seemed strange that he'd mentioned a pre-Hispanic fountain made with tiles. The Aztecs knew how to make tiles?

Martín Rueda didn't pay attention to the girl's doubting face. He was now telling her about a more important task: she would have to photograph the Palace's unknown winding passages, descend to those levels where one loses all stellar orientation and begins to follow the layered, veiled routes of the underworld...Soledad discovered that Martín Rueda's face had become illuminated. An exaltation that grew as he listened to himself speak lit his gaze and honed his marauder features. The girl thought the man burned like a flame and could transform himself because a hidden desire fed that fire.

"Of course that area can be dangerous: rabbit-sized rats, spores that prodigiously flourish in the human lung, bat dung..."

She would be well paid. But first she had to locate the photos in the archives. As to the other affair, better to use discretion. He would give her instructions later.

It was after nine when Martín Rueda offered her a ride home. "That way," he said, "we can continue talking." But getting into the car he picked up a little tape recorder from the back seat and murmured into it a kind of detailed summary of everything he had discussed with Soledad. With no self-consciousness he described the girl as if she weren't even there. "Opaque, but translucent, I foresee in her an ideal servant," he said and Soledad thought he was talking about somebody else.

XL

The good thing about that job was one could get completely lost. As soon as she arrived she took refuge in the sort of nook that Filemón, the limping boy, had formed out of the boxes and files of documents to be gone through. Silence surrounded her, an invisible protective net that allowed her to enter her heart and hear its palpitations as if she were a visitor to her own self. She went around inside, went back to visit the vase and pass through the labyrinth of red walls, to encounter the sleeping dragon and contemplate it, as if her true mission was to guard its sleep. In the meantime, Lucía rummaged through the mountains of paper. But she soon got impatient and then Soledad returned to the archives. Lucía, on the other hand, preferred to visit the halls of the Palace and prowl through the area.

"You should go up to the top of that building," she said, referring to the Latin American Tower. "Besides the view, you meet all kinds of foreigners, one better than the next. In fact I just became friends with a group. And where do you think we went? Aha, to that cantina that makes the snails you like so much! And you'll never guess, there were two Finns and another guy from you know where."

Soledad listened with a smile. She closed her eyes and then remembered: yes, the viewers at the top of the Latin American Tower, and three boys who had smiled at her before asking she take their picture. They ran into each other again later in the elevator and while they descended the forty-two floors Lazslo asked if she knew any good bars and...

"And that's why you didn't come home last night?"

"Don't think so hard," Lucía answered, raising her hands to her temples. "My neurons rumble just to hear you."

"You're hung over raw."

"No, cooked rather, deliciously cooked..."

"Is that better?"

"Hey, thanks for taking care of the dragon alone," said Lucía, planting a kiss on her cheek.

"Forget it, I didn't do it for you. I just thought I'd tell him stories I knew as a child. I think he liked it."

"Ay, Soledad, you truly were born a simpleton. Who do you think told you those stories? Your papa?"

Soledad couldn't help but throw a punch at her. Lucía avoided it but fell into the vase.

"Anyways, I wanted to go back in," she said joking.

Soledad preferred returning to the archives, but although she tried not to think about it, she asked herself time and again why she and Lucía couldn't get along like they did when they were children.

XLI

Soledad had been submerged in those papers for a week, not sharing any more words than necessary with Filemón, since Don Agapito had continued to be intractable and as soon as seeing her cast that look of a pre-Hispanic deity with which he warned off anyone approaching him, when she heard steps and then voices and laughter that fell in that desert of sounds like an unseasonable rain. She got up and went to investigate but no matter how many corridors she passed down, she only came across Filemón asleep atop an improvised bed of piled documents.

112

She was returning to her desk when she again heard laughter in the next passage. She looked around but didn't see anybody. And then that muffled silence fell. It was past mid-morning and she remembered Mode had packed her a sandwich for lunch. She was getting ready to eat when she discovered where the voices came from: a door locked shut.

"I don't like it when they watch over me," said a broken voice.

"No, Don Agapito, that's not why they sent her. But you remember what Leonardo says: the collective worker. A thousand eyes, a thousand mouths…don't be stubborn with me, because if you get mad you'll lose."

"OK, Marita. Just because you say so."

Maru, was it Maru? Soledad hastened out. When she got to where the voices came from nobody was there. She decided to walk a bit and went around the high-tension fence, the gray lockers standing in a row like upright caskets. Mr. Rueda's car was still in the tunnel and Rafa was joking around with the parking lot security. Seeing her, he raised his arm and began walking over to say hi, but Soledad hurried to the bathroom. She heard the sing-song voice of Maru near the sinks. She approached from behind, fearing she'd interrupt her, while the dark-skinned girl recounted to a ring of her laughing co-workers how she had scored the last point during a softball game in which she was the only woman. She had barely paused when a member of the group said, "There's someone here looking for you, Marufa."

The woman turned with a gracious movement that feigned surprise. "Behind me again?" she laughed and added, "Hi, Shadow! You're precisely the person I was looking for. You all know her? Let me introduce a new colleague, Soledad García, alias the Shadow." She laughed again. "That's not true. Just Soledad García. She's going to work for Mr. Rueda, or rather she's already working."

"Nice to meet you," a couple women said. And another added, "Hmmm, off to a bad start."

"Don't be like that with our colleague. What's she going to think? If you could only choose the boss you had to work with. So what's going on, Miss Shadow, are you coming to eat with us?"

"I can't," said Soledad.

"Why not? Don't you know your forty-five hour work week includes a half-hour for lunch?"

"But I don't…"

"It doesn't matter…We're not going to let you turn down our invitation. Right, girls?"

They went to a Chinese restaurant. At first the women looked suspiciously at Soledad, but whether due to her harmless air or gaining trust because Maru herself had issued the invitation, what's certain is that soon they were talking about their men, their children, their worries, their pastimes. When they stopped to pay at the register, Sole was once again right behind Maru.

"Didn't I tell you she was my shadow?" she joked to the others. "Come here, little sister," she said, putting her arm around her shoulders and softly pushing her foreword. "Stand here in front. What are you so afraid of? No, woman, be brave—if they don't see you they squish you."

Soledad was confused but liked that the woman patted her on the back. She took the spot in line in front of Maru.

The boy at the cash register was taking a long time to ring up the bill, and so Maru raised her voice. "Damn Chinaman. Once again you can't figure out the bill. Doesn't everyone in communist China have a right to an education? They must have held you back…"

The young man dressed in denim, with a fragile air and beautiful girlish features, bowed his head slightly.

"Patience is a spiritual quality, Miss Maru," the boy responded while his face flashed a tenuous smile.

"Ay, Chinito, not even you think that. But OK, I'll forgive you for your rising sun smile…"

"Miss Maru, you offend me. I'm Chinese, not Japanese."

"Well, all right already. You want them not to pay us for the day, eh? Charge us and we'll settle the other point later."

Soledad looked back and forth from the girl to the cashier. She perceived in the boy's diligence and measured words a sign of respect for the young woman with the clear, firm voice. It was a joy listening to her.

XLII

The first few times Martín Rueda wanted to see Soledad he made an appointment with her in his office. Later, when he noticed the solicitude with which she answered him on the phone or recounted to him her latest findings, he began asking to meet in a café on Reforma Avenue, near the entertainment district known as the Pink Zone.

Soledad was used to arriving early, for she found it inconceivable that such a busy man should have to wait for her. And so on several occasions she had time to wander about the area before sitting down to wait. One of her favorite places were the stone benches around the monument of the angel on Reforma. From a sole observation point, she focused with her camera on the stationary flight of that winged victory through the clouds and shadows that made the splendor of its metallic body shine.

One time when she'd already taken two rolls of film and was about to begin another (Mode used to tell her that she only lived in order to feed those at the camera store), a car with darkened windows and diplomatic plates stopped beside her. Through the backlight could be seen the silhouette of a man and woman in the rear seat.

At first the couple seemed to be observing her. After a few moments of stillness, the woman's silhouette moved with strenuous laughter. Perhaps the man was laughing, too, but his sharp-featured form stayed still. Lucía immediately reacted, taking the camera and heading towards the car. Soledad stopped her.

"What are you doing? That's Martín Rueda…"

"Exactly. Let's make fun of his grandmother," replied Lucía, trying to slip free.

They struggled until Soledad managed to grab the camera. Meanwhile, the car had taken off. Lucía dropped her arms and let out a disgusted sigh. Soledad looked toward the car, already turning onto the traffic circle. Coming the other way, a boy on a brilliant red motorcycle approached at full speed. Sol discovered her friend signaling to him and the kid waved back and stopped a few feet away. Then, according to what she could make out, Lucía grabbed back the camera, ran to the motorcycle and climbed on, shouting at Soledad, "See you later!"

She met Mr. Rueda in the usual café.

"You're late. I wanted to introduce you to a friend, but…she got impatient and left."

"I'm sorry."

He looked at her disdainfully. The girl felt the man's gaze, but strangely she didn't feel guilty: it was the first time Martín Rueda had so distinctly devoted such a feeling to her.

"Anyways, she looked at your photos," he continued before taking a sip of coffee.

"Excuse me. What photos?" she responded.

Rueda exhaled with impatience. "Those of Lola Álvarez," he added without looking at her. He was following with his gaze a young woman who'd just entered, accompanied by a boy. The kid was holding a helmet. The woman sat down on the other side of the place, exactly facing Rueda. He looked at her closely, his feelings of a hunter on alert. The woman must have possessed something extraordinarily enchanting—a smell, an unusual luminosity—because otherwise he wouldn't have kept looking at her so insistently. Soledad turned slightly to see. As she suspected, the woman resembled Lucía.

"And what did your friend think of the photos?" she ventured.

Martín Rueda fixed his gaze on the eyes of Soledad. The girl didn't even try to move.

"She says they're not bad," he said, passing his eyes over the shoulders of Soledad, over her breasts, her hips. "Hmm," he said to her and turned his gaze again toward the woman on the other side of the room. She was posing and laughed each time her companion focused the camera on her as if it were some kind of photo session. Without moving his gaze, Rueda commented to Soledad, "She might include them in the exhibit."

Soledad almost started with pleasure. It occurred to her she might see Lola at the opening.

"But don't get ahead of yourself, Soledad. The openings Nadja organizes are very select. Her husband is a member of the diplomatic service. First you have to wait for the invitation…"

Soledad was perplexed. Had she thought out loud or did Martín Rueda have the power to divine her thoughts?

"You know, you're very predictable, but also trustworthy." He smiled before getting up and taking the latest portfolio of materials compiled by Soledad.

Martín Rueda was walking toward the exit when someone shouted at him, "You, stop." He turned instinctively to meet the flash of a camera. By the time he gathered himself, the woman and young man had gotten on the motorcycle and taken off into traffic. He caught her blowing him a kiss before she waved goodbye.

XLIII

One might say that during those days Soledad was happy. She worked in the archives, saw Lucía from time to time, and Mode and Rafa worried about her like the good aunt and uncle she didn't have. She saw Martín Rueda and although the meetings were fairly infrequent, it was enough to believe that someone like him, with such an irreducible presence, trusted her with important secret tasks for her to feel like she finally had a place in the world.

"Shadow, you're in love with that son of a bitch," Maru scolded one day when she saw her getting all ready for a meeting with him.

("No, that's not love," Lucía responded from inside the labyrinth, but of course Maru couldn't hear her. "Devotion, adoration, destiny. A complete desire that goes beyond Rueda himself, beyond me, beyond the dragon, because although I fight all the time with her, I can't help but recognize that Soledad is more and more fulfilling herself.")

Soledad was confused to hear both their voices.

"I'm not in love, nor do I even admire him," she stammered between astonishment and anger.

"No, my friend, I didn't say you were so in love with him, but fish get trapped by their own mouths."

Maru adjusted her bra from atop her clothing, not paying much attention to what her companion was saying. On the other hand, Soledad wanted to complain to Lucía: in the end it was her, as always, who'd thrown everything into confusion. But Lucía, more agile in those shadowy rounds, cut her off, saying curtly, "I wasn't even talking to you. I was thinking of Maru but she doesn't even hear me. Just pretend I was talking to myself."

Soledad became furious. "For once in your life, could you leave me alone?"

"Sure. I've never seen you angry. That's it, sis, get mad, even though I'm the one you're fighting with. But be careful," added Maru, grabbing Soledad by the shoulders. "And for Mr. Rueda, don't even mention it. To each her own. Me, I don't trust him. In fact, I know a few girls who are afraid of him. He was the one who brought that gangster Rodolfo Mata to Fine Arts. But him, he's quite a looker…Look at Flor, she's the president of the fan club of his silent admirers. Because despite seeming so modest, she has the hots for Mr. Rueda."

Maru took out her make-up bag and retouched her eyebrows and lips before continuing, "And along that line, how's your research going?"

"It's advancing," Soledad replied quickly before starting to brush her teeth.

"You know, it's very strange…" said Maru.

"What's strange?"

"That they hired you. Look, we have a photo workshop and darkroom here. Besides, Rueda must know about maestro Gallegos. We call him 'the living archive.' He's about to finish fifty years here at Fine Arts. You still haven't met him? I'll introduce you. He might be able to help you with the information you need. Not today because you're going to see your boss, but tomorrow there's a staff assembly for everyone. Why don't you come for a bit? Gallegos will definitely be there. He knows everything about the Palace, about the convent that used to be here and the ghosts of nuns that frightened people at the first performances, about the canoe they found on the subterranean river and sent over to the Museum of Anthropology, the tunnels that connect it to the Hill of the Star and Los Pinos. In fact, I think he has photos of that fountain you've been looking for."

Soledad spit toothpaste into the sink. "How do you know what I'm looking for?"

Maru took a long look at Soledad. "Look, Shadow. Let me get straight to the point. I don't know you very well, but I know you. I like you. So I'm going to tell you something: we're very careful around here. These are difficult times for democratic unions. They've already knocked the shit out of the teachers' movement and the delegation from the Polytechnic School. Now they're going after Fine Arts. We don't know how, but they're going to try. But we're not crippled either. We have a thousand eyes and a thousand hands. We follow the steps of the authorities, especially Rodolfo Mata. That son of a bitch was the one who broke the subway workers' movement. That's why they 'rewarded' him by bringing him here. And it seems like that was your boss Rueda's idea. At first we thought they'd sent you here to spy on us, but then Leonardo saw you and said that only a real bitch would be able to fake it so damn well and appear so…innocent."

"Well, I don't know any Leonardo."

"He's heading the meeting tomorrow."

Soledad said goodbye. On her way to the café where she was going to meet Mr. Rueda she tried to imagine the Leonardo whom Maru so admired. At what moment had he seen her if she never left the Morgue? She smiled to think that someone had been observing her without her knowing it. How many more things was she unaware of? She began to worry. If it was true that they'd suspected her, maybe it was better not to go to the meeting. What if other people thought she was going to spy on them, as surely Don Agapito thought, whose somberness that first day had kept up throughout the weeks she'd worked there? But on the other hand, if maestro Gallegos had information about the tile fountain…Without mentioning Maru or Leonardo or the meeting, after going around it a thousand times, she mentioned something to Rueda. She was surprised when he replied, "Go see him, Soledad, and see what Gallegos has. Tomorrow there's a meeting of the workers. Look for him there. Make yourself at home." And while he spoke, Martín Rueda's predatory features softened with a smile.

XLIV

She left late from her meeting with Mr. Rueda. She didn't have any reason to go back to work and decided to walk to the building where she lived. Before going home, she felt like wandering around for awhile. After a few minutes going here and there she came to the Garden of Art. She remembered how as a little girl she had roller-skated in that park. She was barely seven blocks away from the house of the portals and despite such a short distance, her mother and brother seldom used to come there. Carmen preferred the Alameda de Santa María with its Moorish kiosk where she nestled in her dreams like the little cocoons that each summer hung from its trellises. Perhaps they reminded her of the kiosk in the plaza in the village where she was born. For that reason, as the lethargy of Sunday afternoon fell, she would take her children to the Alameda to weave in the air lace and stories like those that as a girl she had surely thread in the fading light of sleepy afternoons when she awaited the arrival of some prince or film star.

However, they seldom went to the Garden of Art, located in the other direction, even though it was much closer. They barely went the occasional Sunday when the painters took out their easels to create their decorative *naïve* paintings and tourists gathered there to hunt for some new native or nationalist spoils. In those moments of crowds haggling over prices it was difficult to skate freely and the girl Sol preferred to contemplate the drab birds in a pair of giant cages found within the garden.

She directed her steps there and found the cages empty, with no trace of recent occupation. After thinking a few moments—the light had begun to fade among the bowers of the *colorines* and poplars—she sat down on a concrete bench. Her hair covered part of her face and she tried to see the park through that filter. Only then did she notice how long her hair had grown and how much time had passed since Peter's departure. She heard her own even breath and with a calm feeling tossed her hair to the side with a slight movement of her head. Then she discovered she wasn't alone on the bench. An older woman looked at her through laughing little eyes. She was about to run away, when she saw it was her mother.

"Sorry about frightening you," said Carmen's sweet and friendly voice. "But it's …you know, you look a lot like my daughter."

Soledad didn't know what to say. She smiled and let her hair fall again over her face.

"You know, she's about your age. Maybe a bit taller and lankier. Here, try this ring on. She always wanted me to give it to her, but it was my mother's and I was afraid she'd lose it." Carmen took off her mother Marina's thick wedding band that her sister Refugio had given her and held it out to the girl.

Soledad didn't dare refuse, but she took the ring and put it on. It had been weeks since she'd worn the gloves. She remembered that she had still been wearing them when she decided to send Carmen a post card from the Soviet Union she came across at a stall on Juárez Avenue. Drawing a circular figure that looked like

120

cancellation marks on a piece of beet had been easy, just like the Cyrillic letters she copied from a dictionary. The complicated thing was making up a message to send her mother to explain the change in plans that instead of Hungary had taken her to Russia.

"Look, it fits you perfectly," said Carmen. "It probably would have been a bit big for my daughter. The truth is Sole has always been different from what I hoped for her. I would've loved her to be a model or a stewardess, but children today do whatever they damn want. She's studying photography in Russia now. In my day," continued Carmen, talking more to herself, "if my mother Marina had said the sun rises in the west, well, it rose in the west. You didn't dare contradict her. And to travel so far away, and by yourself...out of the question. The worst thing is my dumb Soledad didn't write down her address. And now I have no way of writing back. Her brother, my other child, is getting married next month and I wanted her to come back for the wedding."

The woman remained silent for a few moments and then added, "I'd also like to write her that I miss her. If you knew how many nights I've stayed up crying because she went away. Of course I never told her. I'm telling you because you look like her and in some way I feel it's like saying it to her."

Carmen got up and went off. Soledad let her depart among the shadows falling over the park. Then she cried with the feeling that perhaps much time would pass before she saw her mother again and she hadn't even been able to say goodbye, much less tell her that she also loved her. Suddenly she remembered her grandmother's ring that still shone on her finger. She had forgotten to give it back and her mother didn't remember to ask for it. And while she twirled it around her finger, she couldn't stop thinking about the strange ways wishes have of being granted.

XLV

The next day right after she arrived to the archives, Don Agapito confronted her in one of those passages walled with paper.

"Out! Out!" he said. Filemón finally showed his face when his limping made him stop to lean upon Don Agapito's shoulder. "To the meeting," he gestured, seeing Soledad's surprised face.

Soledad clasped the camera strap over her shoulder and let herself be led along. She smiled when the older man said to her seriously, but now without a trace of brusqueness, "And be careful of coming to work without my permission, eh? Those who do such piggish things we call corkscrews and you're not one of them, right?"

"They're not called corkscrews, Don Agapo," Filemón clarified condescendingly. "They're called strike-breakers."

But the man was already leaving the tunnel to take the stairs to the ground floor. It was the first time Soledad had seen him move with such energy and enthusiasm.

"Now, yes...now let those clowns try to drive me out of here," they heard, as if instead of the Palace they were entering a rodeo resounding with laughter, applause and whistling.

"And who are you going to vote for? Laura Gómez or Jorge Flores Miranda?" Filemón asked, inviting her to go up with him.

Soledad didn't know whom the boy was talking about.

"They're not going to re-elect Leonardo?" she asked when they'd almost reached the grand lobby of the Palace.

"No, and that's really too bad. He can't run again, but they say he's supporting Laura Gómez. Although who knows. He also gets along well with Jorge—I've seen them having a beer in the tunnel parking ramp and they even play on the same team."

They'd stopped at the foot of the stairs of the left wing, right near the bookstore on whose glass door hung a little sign that said, "We're done working for today, and tomorrow...not either." Soledad observed Filemón. Although he'd never acted hostile, frankly his present tone was friendly. Then she saw him wave at the guard standing by the entrance to the Palace through whose main door, just barely open, gathered in line the workers coming for the assembly. Soledad had never attended such a meeting before but she supposed that from the number of people arriving and heading to the theater this was an important one.

"And the plain truth is that Jorge would give you the shirt off his back. He could just as well get drunk with you as find you twenty tickets for 'Swan Lake' at the theater on the little island in Chapultepec. On the other hand Laura is a fraud, talking about historical materialism, Rosa Luxemburg and who knows how many other famous thinkers. Look, here she comes, like a black widow spider sticking out her antennas."

Soledad encountered a girl a couple years older than herself, with disheveled hair and short arms and legs. Her timid walk—because she was walking cautiously, as if she feared the Palace would fall down atop her—contrasted with a permanent smile and sweet eyes that seemed to want to absorb everything. She went up to a group of workers waiting beside a counter. A man wearing glasses and a buck-toothed smile welcomed her with a hug.

"That's Leonardo Ramírez," came a woman's voice from behind Soledad.

She turned to find Maru.

"Hi, Body," joked Soledad, alluding to the name Shadow which Maru usually called her. "I felt very lost without you."

"A shadow without an owner, how could even a dog bark at you?"

Soledad laughed.

"OK, am I just a piece of furniture or what?" interrupted Filemón

"No, little brother," said Maru, covering him with kisses. "You know you're my little golden gimp, but ..." And she suddenly stopped as if remembering something. "You already have an owner and she's looking for you. So you better limp off or later they'll accuse me of trying to butt in line."

Filemón bid farewell effusively to Maru and Soledad. As soon as she saw him disappear the secretary turned to the girl, "Come along, Shadow, we've got at least an hour before this little number starts. Did you bring a camera? Let's go, I have a surprise for you."

Soledad thought she was going to introduce her to Leonardo and his people, but that wasn't the case. Instead of heading towards the vestibule, they walked around the Palace to the balconies and climbed up to the gallery. Soledad barely noticed the people settling into their seats, the long table at the edge of the stage, the growing hubbub like some kind of inevitable human detritus. On the other hand, she was enraptured by the filtered atmosphere of the lights off to the side, the warm surroundings, the artful roundness of the arch, the velvet seats, the stylized design of the brass fixtures. She took her camera out of the bag and absorbed the details while adjusting the lens.

"What do you think?" Maru interrupted her. "Wonderful, no? And you don't know the half of it. All those figures," she pointed at the vaulted soffits of the architrave as well as the proscenium arch, "were made by a Hungarian artist. And along that line, did that fucking photographer you used to go out with ever answer?"

Soledad wrinkled her brow: that Lucía again. Could she still trust her? Would it come to the point where she'd end up regretting having ever known her? She suddenly stood up: a movement of the dragon, barely a tremor, forced her to hold her breath. Perceiving that the beast was pursuing her dream, the air softly stirring, she was thankful she hadn't ended up forming any desire.

"But that's not all. Here's the real surprise. Come, Shadow," Maru said and they went back to the stairs, but instead of going down they went through a metal door leading to the roof. They came out onto a terrace overlooking the Alameda and from there walked above the low arches on the main façade. Above the marble, between the railings of the staircases that passed among the arches, were huge moths. A few of them were dead, others were beating their wings with difficulty. She took a few photos as she discovered that the contrast between the moth and the marble created an instantaneous play of light and shadow.

They finally came to the balcony leading to the main façade. Looking behind her, Soledad was thankful she had brought the wide-angle lens so that she could take a few panoramas. Minutes passed before either woman spoke again. The transit of people and cars, the shouts of vendors on Juárez Avenue and the horns of the desperate drivers confronted by the inefficient police trying to get traffic to flow, the hurry, the ever new hurry and agitation, because life is always on the point of departing, all were distant situations, incomprehensible from the Palace roof where one could look at the sky up close—a sky that ever more permitted a new reference in the gamut of colors: a gray sky—and with a little effort on that polluted morning separate the mountain of Tepeyac and the triangular tower of Tlatelolco.

"I often come up here," said Maru after filling her lungs with a deep breath. "Here I contemplate the madness of the world and feel sure of seeing my own madness. Because that's the truth, we're all crazy, although it's more obvious in some than others. Here I think about my children, about the dope who left me a widow, about how I came to work at Fine Arts (the director asked me what job I wanted and I replied, 'I want to start at the bottom'). From up here I see swarms of people coming and going and I discover myself alone in the world. Then I imagine the Palace in the middle of a forest and me the only one living there. I can scream in pain and nobody will answer. I feel the air on my cheeks and don't know why but I smile. Did you know there are ants on the Palace roof? Those moths you were taking pictures of, they carry around a fucking ton of them. Then I think, yes, we are alone but there are a lot of things we can do with the help of others. There are many unjust things. If you start to think about it, who wouldn't like to come up here and look around and feel themselves the owner of all this? Everybody has the right to be well, to feel complete."

"Yes," replied Soledad looking at the waves of transients crossing the busy avenue, "everybody has the right to feel alone."

"That's not what I said. I said 'to feel complete.' On the other hand, you fulfill that right of feeling alone very well, no?" confirmed Maru.

Soledad barely moved; hunched over the battlement she seemed smaller than she really was. Maru discerned that she was peering closely at the panorama part by part, as if she didn't dare take it in all at once, grasp it in one complete gaze. She must have remembered something the girl had recounted because suddenly she asked, "And your mother really sent you off to live with an aunt after your twin sister died? So how guilty could you have been if she drowned when you were both so little?"

"It must have been an accident," answered Soledad testily. "But I must not have been without desire: Lucía used to invent all kinds of stories and get me in all sorts of trouble…"

"I never had sisters, only brothers, but I always wanted to have one. Really, you didn't love her?"

"Yeah, a lot…but I prefer not talking about her."

Maru turned to look behind her and sighed deeply. She smiled, as if she'd just thought of something.

"Listen, Shadow, now that we're almost in the clouds, tell me that story you made up with that friend of yours, the one whose brother got killed in '68. What did you say you used to call that game? Lessons for flying among the clouds?"

Soledad wrinkled her brow and looked toward Tlatelolco. Triangular, a spear tip, its tower hung there in the distance.

"She also told you about Rosa? That is, she told you all about Rosa?"

"Yes, since you told me, I've been thinking about what would have happened here if we had reacted like they did in Hungary in '56. To call bread 'bread' and killers by their names. Maybe they would have squashed us, but not completely."

After a while she looked at Soledad out of the corner of her eye and ventured to say, "Perhaps she would have helped you stop being scared."

"But not completely," joked Soledad, repeating the very words of her friend. "Besides, you were telling me how you imagine the Palace, about the ants and I don't know how many other things."

But Maru was no longer listening. She stood on the balcony, extended her arm and pointed toward Juárez Avenue. "Shadow, let's leave that for later. Look, that little old man carrying the newspaper is maestro Gallegos. Let's go see him before the assembly starts."

Soledad peered that direction. An old man with thick glasses stopped at a light waiting to cross the street. He contemplated the Palace as if looking at it for the first time.

XLVI

She accompanied maestro Gallegos to his office. Impassioned by the history of the Palace, Gallegos unhesitatingly let her see his personal archive: two thick portfolios with negatives, photos, plans and articles from yellowing newspapers, all of which he had gathered in his free time.

The maestro adjusted his glasses and proudly pointed to a bent-cornered photo. "Look here, young woman, here's the photo of the fountain. It belonged to the convent of Santa Isabel. The Palace is constructed over part of what used to be the convent."

Soledad took the photo and the lupe the man held out to her. It showed an excavation that uncovered the remains of a rather large font; on the picture appeared the date November 1905.

"And this other one is of the *cuauhxicalli* they found precisely in the excavations, when Boari directed the project during the era of Don Porfirio. They sent it the National Museum and now it's on exhibit in the Museum of Anthropology's Mexican Gallery, where you can take photos of it."

126

The young woman encountered a piece in carved stone—not the canoe Maru had told her about—with two serpents uncoiling to both the left and right. Soledad recalled her elementary school classes and that pyramid of Teotihuacán decorated with plumed serpents: stories of long dragons that also related gods and goddesses, princes and princesses, desires and punishments.

"Are they plumed serpents? The *cuauhxicalli* was consecrated to Quetzalcóatl?"

"They do look alike. But no, these are fire serpents. Quetzalcóatl wasn't a bloody god. And the *cuauhxicallis* had to do with sacrifice...They served to gather the hearts of the chosen."

Maestro Gallegos smiled at the opportunity to display something of his personal research. Although he had only studied in technical school, at sixteen he began at the Palace as a maintenance helper. But from the very outset, the young Gallegos had experienced the Palace as the family home he never had. He wanted to know all about its past and so took on the task of accumulating data, clippings, photos, as if he were tracing his own genealogical tree, the digits of a personal identity number. Perhaps nobody had so caressed an onyx vein on the whitest marble of the entrance, or had cried seeing a metal sculpture rusting away without the authorities, alerted by him, moving a sole finger. So if Soledad wanted to do some investigating, she had found the right person.

"For the Mexica, the heart of man was the food of the gods. Now concentrate on this detail: when the Mexica found the emblem of their founding, the eagle wasn't devouring the serpent; that was a contamination of the Spanish empire: what happens simply is that the eagle, a solar divinity, is resting upon a nopal cactus brimming with *tuna* fruit. The *tuna* symbolized the human heart that was in turn the food of the gods. And *cuauhxicalli*, which signifies 'the house of the eagle,' is the receptacle for the hearts obtained during sacrifices. What better house for a heart than the abode of the eagle, which would take charge of bringing it to the sun and the repose of the gods. Fascinating, no?"

The man's eyes sparkled. They clouded over, nonetheless, when Soledad asked, "And the subterranean river, does it really go all the way to Chapultepec?"

Maestro Gallegos softly closed the photo album. He smiled, answering, "Those are pure fantasies invented by people...That there are tunnels to the National Palace, to the escarpment of Nochistango, to the Hill of the Star...We would be talking about a subterranean city and that's not possible. A city built beneath the lake. And the Mexicas had theirs but to perforate beneath the marshy city...impossible. The only underground city would be the actual deep sewage system. Or if you wish to see it in an urbanist sense, that mythic, unconscious, subterranean world would be the pre-Hispanic city over which was constructed the colonial, and over the colonial, the modern...so that at this late date, believe me, such a world of tunnels is more in our heads than in the subbasement."

The words of Maestro Gallegos still resonated in her head. The assembly had ended and just a few people remained at the Palace. She walked to the Morgue, and in the deserted tunnel she found the figure of Filemón limping toward her.

"Is it true you want to know about the subterranean rivers and the tunnels?" he tossed out as soon as he met her.

Instinctively Soledad took a step back.

"Don't be frightened. Señor Rueda spoke with Jorge and they put me in charge of it. I'll be your guide. Put on your tennis shoes and I'll lend you a smock. You're going to need a big flashlight because it's really dark. Friday...yeah, Friday, because there's an assembly to ratify Jorge."

"Jorge? Then Laura Gómez lost?" asked Soledad, who hadn't yet heard the final result of hte vote.

"No..." A derisive grimace flashed across Filemón's face. "But Friday's assembly will be it. But who knows, maybe Jorge wins. People are going to be very preoccupied and there won't be anybody worrying about the basements. So, we'll leave it until Friday, no? Let's meet at the archives before Don Agapito arrives. And not a word to Maru or anyone else."

XLVII

Did the subterranean world below Fine Arts really exist? What the hell did Filemón have to do with it? Had Martín Rueda indeed given him instructions to be her guide? And if that wasn't the case, how had he learned about it?

It was almost evening, like the first day when Martín Rueda interviewed her. As if she had been working at the Palace for years, she ran through the tunnel; from the maintenance workshops she passed into the foyer, took a narrow set of stairs up to the dressing rooms, then circled behind the stage and finally took the elevator to the fourth floor. Maybe she'd run across her boss and could ask him if he had really given that order. But as soon as she found the waiting room empty, she stopped before the big window: she might doubt the intentions of Filemón but the information he had given her squared perfectly with Rueda's interests. Then why did she feel such uneasiness, as if suddenly she were a pawn in a vast game of chess where she came and went according to secret designs? Because although she didn't know much about union issues, what Filemón had said about the new assembly was very strange. Did that have to do with the authorities playing both sides, as Maru said, in order to aim a low blow at the Fine Arts workers? And was that what was really bothering her, or was it that for an issue she'd believed so personal as the Palace's subterranean world there now came intermediaries with orders that Martín Rueda used to give her directly?

Suddenly she noticed voices coming from Señor Rueda's office, a hushed murmur from which all at once arose abrupt, sharp sounds. His voice—because suddenly it sounded to Soledad so distinct—changed. The other, barely audible from being so fragile, was a woman's voice that suddenly broke into sobs. That situation, the woman's voice weaker and weaker and her uncontrollable sobbing, exasperated the man even more and he began throwing and breaking things. A dry blow, a slap stamping against a soft surface, ended that sudden burst of noise. Martín Rueda stormed out of his office without Soledad able to take refuge in the kitchenette as she had the first day. She was instantly struck with terror. Then without thinking twice, she wished the man couldn't see her. She shut her eyes. Opening them she found Martín Rueda standing there looking at her furiously. Like at other times, she felt like his gaze went right through her and no labyrinth's wall or dragon could hide her. The man looked at her a long time until he was certain no one was there, nor had anyone heard anything, nor would anybody have anything to accuse him with.

XLVIII

Maru went to look for her at the Morgue. They went up to the roof but this time ascended to the cupola crowned by an Aztec eagle sitting not atop a cactus but the world. It was a cold morning and climbing up the spiral staircase that curved around the dome, the winds cut like knives against their faces and hands. Once up top they leaned upon the stair railing, for there was no other way to keep standing. Maru was higher than Soledad and had to bend over to be heard.

"Up here you can allow yourself the luxury of dreaming." Maru smiled broadly and her cheeks settled into a childish look. "OK, Shadow, if being here you were granted your greatest wish, what would you ask for?"

Soledad looked for Maru's face: she wanted to make sure it wasn't Lucía who'd just spoken to her. But no, it was that fat girl who with every movement carried the impulse of her entire body, that vigorous woman who instead of walking jumped along and who made one feel secure instead of distrustful.

"Why does everyone talk about desires?" Soledad finally said and then ran her gaze over those buildings that from down below impeded a complete view of the valley.

"Well, that's because man is an animal of desires, dreams, aspirations…We wouldn't have reached the moon, we wouldn't have constructed pyramids, or this city…We wouldn't have invented stories or union struggles…But you, Shadow, what would you ask for?"

Soledad looked up. That opaque morning her friend's face seemed an enthusiastic sun. She wondered how that woman could live so vigorously. It was as if a fire, a wind-proof flame, was lit inside her. Maru's feet were at about the height of Soledad's head. She thought that if one of those earthquakes the inhabitants of Mexico have become accustomed to should shake her, she'd still be able to grab onto those feet without any fear.

"Well, if you don't want, don't tell me," replied Maru, not getting any response from Soledad. "Me, I'll tell you my wish. You probably think I'd like for us workers at Fine Arts to create a great union. You probably think I'd ask for my kids to grow up well and have a good career…Or the Palace be the only thing here in the valley, with the lake and the herons from long ago, and the little adobe houses and the floating gardens and the canoes here and there in the canals...But no, Shadow...What I'd ask for, and for just one day, because I don't need anything else, is to be invisible."

Soledad had a sudden moment of blindness. A white splendor hid the city, the valley, the sky, Maru's legs. About to faint, she pressed her body against the staircase and grabbed on hard to the metal.

"Can you imagine, Shadow, the hell I could raise? Man, even the president would remember me..."

When they finally came down, Maru was no longer speaking about desires. Instead she recounted the incident of Señorita Flor and Señor Rueda. They had stopped on the balcony facing the main façade, near those sort of box seats that Fine Arts reserved on very rare occasions for its visitors. Soledad noticed that to both left and right a monumental angel protected with its body and immense wings a nude woman and man.

"Go figure, the bastard slapped her in the face...And all because Florecita sent a bouquet of flowers to the wrong person, to his wife but with a note for someone else...A big deal...No doubt Flor screwed up but to hit her after so many years of adoration...We want to file a complaint against him. Imagine, such a delicate river flower wanting to go after him...But there aren't any witnesses. She said there was someone in the waiting room, and with you able to appear without anyone noticing, I thought maybe you..."

"I don't know anything about it," Soledad cut her off.

Her reaction was so abrupt that Maru, contrary to normal, waited a moment to respond. "I didn't know you before, Shadow. But you know what? I don't believe you don't know what happened. Just look at your attitude..." she said, fixing her gaze on her. "I believe, and it hurts me to say it, we were wrong about you."

XLIX

They arrived to the floor where stood the gigantic hydraulic jacks that held up the auditorium's stage. They had barely passed through the metal door separating that room with machines from the flooded basement when a couple of men greeted Filemón. They didn't exchange a word, just a slight signal that the men understood as to hurry up and grease those moving columns. Soledad thought that after the assembly convoked that day the Palace would have a grand performance, for she recalled the stage pit was ten feet deep so all the musicians in the orchestra could fit. But now that it was covered with numerous security guards, Soledad began to have suspicions. Perhaps that pit was to be used for other ends, because right now it created an inexpugnable barrier between the audience and the table of those presiding over the assembly. Moreover on the mezzanines holding up the auditorium, they came across some people from the mechanical workshop, the dominion of Jorge Flores Miranda, stretched out on little striped mattresses and plaid blankets. They were beneath the stage, among the beams and metal structures that forced them to walk hunched over. Filemón, whose limping made him move sideways, seemed like the clapper inside a bell, about to bump into one beam or another. They continued going down. A few security guards asked them where they were heading. Filemón said they'd been sent on a special task by Señor Mata, and the guards let them go on. But after that Soledad no longer had any doubts: she didn't know how, but those men were orchestrating a fraud at the assembly of Fine Arts workers. It occurred to her she could invent some excuse, argue she had to use the bathroom and then escape to look for a telephone and call Maru. But maybe Maru wouldn't believe her after that affair with Señorita Flor. And, instead, Martín Rueda—because undoubtedly he was part of the authorities organizing the fraud—wouldn't forgive her. She imagined his predatory gaze running over her guts and through the depths of her soul without her able to take refuge behind some excuse. That feeling so conquered her she didn't think she could take it. She would die or lose complete control. Then she began having difficulty breathing and realized that perhaps she wasn't so lost. If she faced it head on perhaps she could live her life without fear. Make a pact with Lucía instead of wandering and hiding in the corners of herself. Joke about Martín Rueda, Peter Nagy, the dragon itself from which she had extracted all that annulling force of submission. She would be able to regain possession of herself and never again have to ask anybody permission to do so. "And desire?" asked Lucía with a softness that sought to not wake her friend. Sol frowned and answered fearfully, "Well, I'll live without it." Such was the fearlessness of that moment that Soledad perceived herself atop a tower, dividing to the left and right territories to conquer: forests, citadels, houses spread out like a model that a sole glance would take in. At that moment anything seemed possible: to stretch out her hand and cover herself with the sky or disappear from Martín Rueda. Was this lightness of standing on the edge of the void while still sure of falling intact on her feet freedom?

Everything was near, clear, of an oppressive clarity that lost all limit and proportion. Vertigo forced down her gaze. Two feet next to her own made her step upon the land.

Filemón said to her, "So, you've gone to the bathroom? OK, can we go now?"

L

They descended into the subterranean world. Vestiges of other cities, dark tunnels, ruined patios, a tiled fountain where the nuns from the Santa Isabel convent used to feed carp brought from China by ship. As well the canal, although holding little water, that used to lead to Tlatelolco and right before reaching there sloped down to an abandoned pier. Off to the side they could discern the shore of the islet of the ancient city with its mortared dikes and terraces used to regain land from the water. By flashlight they discovered the statue of an old man incrusted in the cypress palisades, as well as casks made from opened stomachs where skeletons gestated in the fetal position.

They walked aimlessly, letting themselves be carried along by the rotund feeling of each new appearance, going back and discovering other narrow passages. When one of their flashlights died, they arrived in the dark to the next intersection and there, at a convenient height, were a lantern and a can of kerosene to wet the hemp wick. They descended several more levels but that darkness wasn't frightening: neither animals nor odors, only an agreeable warmth, unforeseen, blanketing, seasoned by filters in the ceiling that cooled their face and clothes. Soledad took photos knowing that no fragment would be capable of revealing that subterranean world.

Time passed. The artificial suns of the flashlights dissolved in the perplexing shadows. Soledad thought she had already passed through such penetrating darkness, those nebulous grottos like memory, in her dreams.

"Look," said Filemón. "Do you see the cages placed in the walls? They say those are the remains of Moctezuma's zoo."

Soledad glimmered those compartments down a perspective that became lost in the tunnel itself. Suddenly she thought she discerned the crystalline gleam of a gaze shining in the darkness: she looked closely and it seemed it wasn't just a sole pair of eyes that gazed at her with a hunger of centuries. Without thinking she hurried her step. Farther on she discovered a kind of altar: chrysanthemums and lilies surrounded a Christ with a sweet and sorrowful look: his wounded hand revealed a heart in flames. On one edge the image was partially covered by a piece of brilliant white linen hemmed with two red ribbons. Soledad stopped, and Filemón came back to look for her.

"Hurry up," he said. "This is the Evening Adoration."

Soledad looked at him, not knowing what he was talking about.

"I'm not joking. They're like evening angels: they used to praise God so that this world and this city weren't lost in darkness and would survive until dawn. They're also very jealous: they fear being joked about or misinterpreted. They pray the whole night through, but that doesn't mean they should come early and find us. Their temple is right above. One of their basements reaches all the way here, so you better hurry up."

Soledad felt her head spinning. Was it possible that in all their coming and going the residents of the city didn't know what was here? They went on in silence, Filemón holding out his hand to help her up or pointing out some find with his index finger. Encountering enormous roots of the ash trees in the Alameda that reminded Soledad of some nocturnal or inverted forest, she realized they were returning to the Palace. As they climbed up to the exterior world, she began to feel like the ground was moving. The clarity distorted that world which had just emerged out of the nothingness and presented it, suddenly, as something distant. She shut her eyes and began again her nocturnal wandering. And in the blindness that memory unfailingly led by chance, she thought that perhaps she hadn't gone down into any basement or subterranean gallery, that perhaps she hadn't left the archives nor even Lucía's vase and that this subterranean city was just a dream, glimpsed by others who also dreamt of her.

LI

She finally opened her eyes, went up the staircase, wanting to leave the Palace, and the world came out atop her in the figure of several workers from Fine Arts struggling in the vestibule with some guards. During one foray, a worker managed to steal in and the impulse led another to step all over Soledad, who couldn't find a place. The rest happened in a tumult: crowds chanted sayings, attacked, organized themselves in face of the guards who refused to let them enter the assembly. Soledad didn't understand what was going on. Whether out of inertia or in some attempt to order the world, she began to take photos inside the Palace. Providential screwdrivers appeared in the hands of a few workers so they could take out the glass in the entrance door. A first pane passed above the heads of the crowd and was lost in the distance. The response was bruising. One of the guards shouted to the others, "We'll beat the shit out of you if you try to get by," and he picked up a fire extinguisher as a warning. Through the newly formed void in the door sprayed the tank's contents. The people in front looked like ghosts and backed up coughing. One man was in complete disbelief, saying. "I'm the orchestra's piano player. I'm a cultural worker…You can't do that to me…"

Soledad finally came across Maru bathed in white dust, shaking herself and the ghost that had been erected over the indignant pianist. Maru laughed while telling her, "These bastards don't know the favor they did us, now we're dressed for the union ball." Behind her everyone remained stunned and then an emboldened force ran through the crowd: "Strike! Strike! Strike!"

A sudden immobility took hold of Soledad, as if she'd been bewitched and her body formed part of that same marble extending through the floors and walls of the Palace. Outside a girl with the legs of a dancer climbed up a column of the portico and fixed a banner atop it. People applauded that gesture of rebellion with the childish fascination of discovering that someone has thrown a ball at us a moment before we realize we wanted to play. Soledad, on the other hand, closed her eyes: she was afraid to confirm that the girl with the fearless legs was Lucía.

LII

When she could finally move, she headed to Rueda's office. As soon as he saw her enter he hurried to hang up the phone and invited her to sit down. Soledad hadn't even settled into the chair and was placing the camera upon her lap when the man began to pepper her with questions.

"And so? Did you go down into the subterranean world? What did you see? Did you take many photos?"

"I went there, Filemón took me."

"Is it as..."—the man paused a moment—"...extraordinary as they say? Did you find any information that lets one find the route of Quetzalcóatl from Tula? Or is it another entrance to the underworld like that in Chapultepec?"

The girl could tell Martin Rueda was overcome with anxiety. She asked herself why, if he was so interested, he hadn't gone down there himself.

"Extraordinary? I don't know if that's the word. Perhaps..." Soledad stopped to observe his jaw was trembling slightly. His thin lips opened a bit to stutter words the girl couldn't believe hearing.

"Please, Soledad," begged Martin Rueda while his face softened into a childish gesture. "Tell me everything."

The girl then perceived that for some unknown reason the man was in her hands. She hurried to tell him what she'd seen, the photos she'd taken...The man's gesture of approval before each of her words, the fascination shining in his eyes, disarmed Soledad: she felt an inner warmth flooding her and remembered that forgotten flame of desire her father had spoken to her about. It was an almost physical sensation, as if hands—soft and warm—were passing over her insides and she could, finally, feel complete.

For his part, Rueda listened with all his feelings placed upon the girl. He almost smiled to confirm he hadn't been wrong: this opaque, silent girl was the ideal witness for reconstructing that subterranean voyage he hadn't dared take. This idea made him comment in a tenuous voice, "You talk about it as if you knew that world your entire life."

Soledad couldn't resist the temptation to tell him about Lucía and the dragon, about the labyrinth and darkness where she used to take refuge when she was a little girl. The man looked at her in marvel and almost vehemently urged her to go on. There came out Rosa and the slippers, the story of the Ángeles and Commander Pucheros, there came out the Hungarian rhapsody that had bewitched her.

While all this was going on, Lucía and the dragon remained silent, making no movement, no objection. It was as if when the words resounded a sortilege had come undone and the words vanished in the air.

"Go on, Soledad. Trust me. I won't hurt you…"

Soledad kept talking. She felt like she could trust him, speak of the anguish and the emptiness that dragged her through dark tunnels like the city she had just seen. Finally she spoke about desire: how when she was a girl she discovered they were fulfilled in the opposite way.

Martín Rueda looked at her a long while. "And now what is the desire you don't dare desire?"

Soledad didn't hesitate a moment. If she had thought about it perhaps she would have said it another way. (Lucía would tell her later, "Clearly, Sole, you didn't act prudently.") But at that moment, as if she had lost all idea and proportion, instead of jumping into the emptiness of reason, she followed the impulse that led her by the tail toward desire made fact, made rattlesnake. Then she told him.

All night long she worked in the bathroom of her little rooftop home, converted into a darkroom. The images of the Fine Arts underworld surged forth in luminous shadows, lighting memories and future dreams. She was so excited that she almost didn't notice the envelope Modesta brought up to her. It didn't have a return address so she put it in her pants pocket, gave the concierge a kiss and closed herself up again with the negatives. Contrary to what she thought, the photographs were much more suggestive due to the penumbra and the marked chiaroscuro. One might say she had cut strips of memory and, still fresh, with the edges sharp and stripped clean, she offered them to the innocence of the eye. And in every case they were demented photos, for although not knowing their origin, the gaze discovered in them grimaces of a primordial chaos.

Soledad was in a hurry to wrap up, as she was as well in a hurry to see Martín Rueda again and show him those photos and what she was capable of doing. When she finished the last roll, precisely the one in which the Fine Arts workers appeared forcing their way into the Palace, an unknown fatigue overwhelmed her, even more so when she considered she'd done nothing to feel that way. She lay down on the sofa the painter Ismael had left behind and Mode had covered with cushions and pillows to make more comfortable. She still had a few hours before her appointment with Martín Rueda that afternoon at five. Her body weighed her down with a joyful gravity, but she still couldn't sleep. She contemplated the diamond of light that was this rooftop room, with white-washed walls that Rafa had helped her paint; over by the window was the photography equipment resting upon a design table and, standing up, the suitcase she brought when she arrived. With her eyes half shut, it was easy to dilute the contours and dream of a white sea. The transparency sunk everything, including the ship in which she was now slipping along that carried her farther and farther away within herself. The horizon disappeared when she discerned an isle with figures: she recognized a few people like Mode, her mother, Peter. As well there were other unknown people: a girl with agile legs who climbed the palm trees in order to see her crystal ship, a man dressed in white who said to a fat woman, "How nice you're wearing your dress from the union ball." Suddenly they all began to tell her goodbye. A little girl dressed in a kimono with a fishing rod in her lap flung the orange fish she had caught into the sea and then joined her hands together in that Asian gesture one can interpret as either a plea or a farewell. Soledad raised her hand and the girl also bid her farewell.

LIII

That seemed like a story with a happy ending to Soledad. The Fine Arts workers had triumphed and now were celebrating their victory with a party in the Palace foyer. Accompanying them were musicians from the orchestra that played classical works as well as

138

mambos and cha-cha-chas, and the people dusted off their dance steps on conquered territory, the marble esplanade in front of the Palace of Fine Arts. Perhaps it was the amber light of the arches spilling over that June afternoon, or perhaps it was the happiness of the participants who saw an unknown dream fulfilled: to dance in the street, in front of the Palace, with the symphony orchestra. Each time the music waned, the gathering also turned into a political act, with slogans, exclamations and calls for democratic unions and resistance to the committee forced upon them by the churls…Then Soledad noticed what the banners and signs said: an enormous NO to fraud and imposed conditions. And so Rodolfo Mata and Jorge Flores had come out with their own sign…

A man asked Soledad to dance. The orchestra played a well-known waltz. She declined because she was carrying the photos from the subterranean world, but she couldn't fail to recognize the man with a beaver smile issuing the invitation: Leonardo Ramírez. The portfolio had a strap she could wear across her chest to free her hands.

They took a few steps over the dance floor that had just cleared. Leonardo was an expert at twirls and knew how to lead his partner's movements with just a slight pressure of the hand. On the other hand, Soledad felt ever more clumsy, but the leader's infallible buck-toothed smile relaxed her. The music had a nice tempo and although loud still let her hear her dance partner's voice. A few couples kept up conversations splashed with laughter; others were left lethargic from the rhythm of the waltz that more than upon the waves kept them among the clouds. Soledad recognized the man directing the orchestra: he was the same person dusted with white powder by the fire extinguisher the day before. Although a pianist, the man had picked up the baton and was beginning his career as an understudy. Suddenly Leonardo's voice shook her from her caviling. "How does it feel," he said without losing a shred of his smile, "to always be between two waters, between day and night, and never decide?"

Soledad didn't understand what he meant. Were his words directed at her? Farther away, among the crowd that served as a barrier, she saw Filemón with his arm around a girl from general services. The boy waved to her and began dancing on the improvised dance floor. It was curious to see how his limping was accentuated by the beat of the music: he really did look like a ship listing upon the waves.

"Don't think I know much about books by what I'm going to say," said Leonardo after a spin. "My father used to read to us *The Divine Comedy* when we were children. We didn't have anything to eat but we distracted ourselves from hunger by consuming the cantos about Hell and Purgatory. Not Heaven because papa hadn't quite managed to save the whole book from the boiler in the public restroom where he worked. But Hell and Purgatory I know by heart. For that reason, you won't think I'm very well read, but I can tell you that the worst of sins are committed by indecision."

And as if the orchestra knew that song had to end, the music stopped and applause and whistles broke out again. Leonardo bid Soledad farewell and she knew she had to go.

She entered the Palace on Hidalgo Avenue. At first the guards wouldn't let her by but then apologized after consulting Mr. Rueda by phone. Knowing she was on her way to see him dissipated the questions that kept resonating in her head from Leonardo's words. When she reached the fourth floor the bell announcing the arrival of the elevator sounded ever more clearly amidst the silence reigning through the offices. Feverish, almost running, she crossed the waiting room and stopped a few steps from the half-open door. Martín Rueda was talking to a woman who had a strange accent.

"She won't be long. But remember, don't say anything about publishing her photos in the homage book. Don't worry about her."

"But how did that ever occur to you? What if she finds it in a bookstore and asks us about it?" The woman's serious voice enunciated every syllable.

"Her, no way. I'm telling you she's crazy, she believes in a ghost that grants the wishes she asks for."

"Really?"

"Seriously. So don't even worry about the rights, I'll take care of everything."

"But tell me more about her 'ghost'…"

"Later…at dinner. We're having dinner tonight, no?"

Soledad couldn't believe it. What kind of joke was this? She felt like the skin on her face and hands was burning and she had an instantaneous reaction: to go away, to flee. It was just that the bundle of photos encumbered her. She put them down on Señorita

Flor's desk. She crossed back through the reception area but this time she didn't wait for the elevator and ran down the stairs.

Leaving the parking garage, she ran into Maru, who asked, "Shadow, what's wrong?"

Soledad barely nodded. "I have to go," she finally replied.

"Listen," Maru said, looking at her with concern, "if you'd like I can come with you."

"No…no…They need you more here. They're on strike, right?" Soledad acted agitated, as if she wanted to excuse herself. "You know…I found out they put people in the auditorium. I wanted to advise you. If I had told you perhaps none of this would have happened and…and…"

"And nothing." Maru went back to being the friendly girl from before. "Those bastards have wanted to beat us up for a long time. And you really think little old you could have stopped it? No, Shadow, don't put that death upon your shoulders. The day before they told us they were recruiting people to vote for Jorge Flores. They called Leonardo and other people and warned them. And now you see. They gave us a bunch of bullshit…but we're stopping it: almost all of Fine Arts—museums, schools, warehouses—is on strike. People aren't going to sit with their arms folded. We were hundreds, now we're thousands. And you, ma'am, *compañera* Shadow, don't blame yourself for something beyond your control. Instead come dance to the orchestra. Sergio Cárdenas, the director, is coming to support his guys. We've even received banners of support from workers in Spain and Poland…"

Maru's face was radiant. They were walking near the main entrance of the Palace and had barely reached the portico when a boy from administration invited the secretary to dance.

Soledad remained alone in the middle of the crowd. Night had fallen and a light rain refreshed the dancers. Soledad, on the contrary, felt cold. She contemplated Maru, the other workers, applauding and hugging each other when a man wearing glasses and holding a baton mounted the podium. They shouted slogans. They sang and danced even without music. It was, in a certain way, a story with a happy ending…They held onto each other. But Soledad knew she wasn't part of that. More than ever she wanted to disappear, to no longer exist, and she felt life no longer burdened her with that weight which made her drag along her feet and soul.

If she could only carry it like a little girl with her hat hanging down the back, perhaps she could then jump over puddles and disillusion now and then.

Then Lucía stopped her heart to say, "Come on, Sole, we're going into the vase together." They walked along in silence. And when they'd almost reached their destination, Lucía insisted again, "Let's go…It's a matter of your most secret desire." Soledad felt exhausted, with no other desire before her. She looked at the supple legs of her friend and then at her own. How hard could it be to jump into the vase?

Part Four

Shadows that Dance Alone

LIV

Invocation

Sing, Eco, of that damsel of unraveling understanding and
fragile will, who after destroying the ramparts of her body
wandered in pilgrimage at night from clearing to clearing
and during the day from tumult to tumult, who admired from
the Cathedral's bell tower the city she saw born, sharing the
happiness and grief of other such people with those whose
difference she had discovered, and whose spirit lacked a
great number of labors during her navigation through the
shadows. Unfeeling damsel who thought she was air and
who drunk on renewed illusion wished to gulp down the
sunrays in the middle of the city square, insolent and trust-
ing because no one could see her. But the gods that had
granted so many gifts also stopped stopping her and so in
the end abandoned her to her fate. Oh, nymph of extinct
lakes, of this once crystalline valley where the sky-gazers
contemplated the migrations of birds, the path of the wind
and the suns to come. You, nymph who goes out endlessly
through the streets unpopulated by voices into the half-
built structures, the blind subterranean worlds where lost
children are lulled in their sleep, tell us even just a part of
such things.

(But the echoes don't drone on. The city remains silent,
deaf to the obstinate throb of the damsel, to her transparent
blood and her exhausted desires. Thus must I lend my voice
to the shadowless damsel, who is only shadow.)

LV

After leaving the House of Mirrors, Soledad tried to sneak through the grates and the less frequented areas. Where to? Her steps led her to the main entrance of the forest, where a flowery baroque gate opened to visitors. To the left and right were the statues of the famous lions adorning the entrance to Chapultepec Park. Soledad observed they weren't the same, for while one was roaring the other lifted its paw slightly in a sign of alertness. She remembered how Peter once told her about the palace of the Esterházy princes and the lions found at the foot of the steps: one lowered its head to the arrival of the nobles; the other roared and protested when they left…But, on the other hand, she who felt a little less than nonexistent wouldn't have provoked even the slightest yawn in those copies made of…bronze? She had her doubts. She remembered as a little girl her friend Rosa used to repeat the riddle, "What are the lions at the entrance to Chapultepec made of?" And Sol could respond with every metal imagined and invented, and all the known materials of the world as well as any other kind, but her answer was always wrong. Did she ever admit she was wrong so that, finally, Rosa would give her the answer, or was she once right? Whatever the case, she couldn't recall. And while she went out to wander around, suddenly reinvigorated, she asked herself again, what are the lions at the entrance to Chapultepec made of?

LVI

She walked down Paseo de la Reforma. If she had to walk during the day, it was better to do so on the leafy boulevard full of flower beds where she could avoid passers-by. It was just that after walking a few seconds new questions and doubts began to emerge. Where to? What to do in a similar circumstance? Whom to ask for help and advice? It would have been so simple to throw herself off one of the precipices on Chapultepec Hill or at this very moment climb up the column of the Angel of Independence and rain herself down from above. What could have stopped her now that she knew herself to be absolute owner of her life and her death?

"I see myself in mirrors. I look there and I am the same—those are my hands and my legs and my lips. I touch myself and I am real and true to myself, but...to others? Do I cease to be because they can't see me? And if that's the case, is what I see not real? Which is the truth? Theirs? Mine? So does this city exist or do I just imagine it? If I'm myself and what I see doesn't exist, then is it true that it's all reflection or illusion?...Lucía, where has Lucía gone? And the dragons at the entrance to Chapultepec, I mean the lions, what are they made of? I'm sure Lucía would remember."

And she went back to walking from tree to tree, statue to statue. The stiffness of a bronze figure that, from atop a pedestal, stopped time and prevented movement on the avenue reminded her she was entering the boulevard of heroes, champions of the movements of Independence and Reform in her country, elevated along the length of the roadway like a three-dimensional history lesson that few people—or no one—read any longer. Driven lives, sacrifices, honor for the Fatherland...But in the end the cars and pedestrians passed before the statues as if they didn't exist. The column of the Angel, the Castle, the statue of Columbus were situated in strategic locations that forced the view to stop upon them. But these effigies to the side, erected on the planters at the edge of the traffic, looking at the passing of cars and time, with their back to the wanderer who to see them had to cross to the other side of the avenue or step right into the middle of traffic and play bullfighter with the vehicles...These statues were condemned to pass unnoticed. Soledad felt pity: in the end they were just as invisible as she was. She looked from one statue to the other, observing their gestures, their clothing, their attitudes. Most of them had been soldiers and their military uniforms were imposing despite the grime and the stiffness of the metal; others were dressed in frock coats, or at least in a tabard or civilian garb. Among the combatants was a particular standard: most carried a kind of stirrup in their hands. Soledad asked herself what that might be or signify. She observed the statue now before her, whose plaque at the base of the pedestal revealed its source:

GUADALUPE VICTORIA
INSURGENT
BORN IN TAMAZULA, DURANGO

IN THE YEAR 1786
HE DEFENDED INDEPENDENCE WITH VALOR
THE FIRST PRESIDENT OF THE REPUBLIC
AN EXEMPLARY CITIZEN
DIED IN PEROTE IN 1842

The metal simulated the folds of his skin and clothing; the man stood immobile for eternity. Forever with his left hand—large with long, slender fingers—upon his chest, for all time in a dignified pose that seemed to proclaim, "For my honor and my Fatherland." Soledad asked herself, beyond that glory that paralyzed him what were his deepest desires? Had one of them been fulfilled precisely with this statue that immortalized him? But the metallic skin, on the verge of sweating, remained silent. Only the adroit hand holding up that sort of stirrup seemed to assail the tempestuous winds of forgetfulness. Then the girl discovered that it was no stirrup, but the hilt of what had once been a sword. She murmured with more pain than irony, "Guadalupe Victoria, unarmed…what a failure."

LVII

Go straight ahead or turn? Before her spread an intersection of streets but she couldn't decide. Why go on? Might she by some chance find an answer? Why if she possessed such a marvelous gift did she feel so vulnerable, unprotected, alone? No, she couldn't believe that such a deep desire had to end in that disastrously wrong way. She looked at her feet and legs: they still held her up and carried her along. And her heart? Was it the flame from a light-house that threw off sparks to guide her among the blinding transparency or had it gone out and now she walked along carried by wind and chance?

A group of women crossing the avenue pushed her from her thoughts and Soledad fell headlong. A paperboy ran by, kicking her. A vendor of lottery tickets stumbled while stepping on her hand. A crowd of workers got off a bus and the girl had to jump out of the way, in danger of being squashed.

"Miss…miss," Soledad heard coming from above her in a firm and friendly voice. "Take refuge up here on the pedestal."

She did so, putting her back right up against the stone base, staying still until the traffic and the flow of people subsided. Then she lifted her gaze. She was surprised by the disproportionate angle of a face that seen from below had a full goatee, fleshy cheeks like those of a child, and a westward-looking gaze. Soledad moved back a bit and discovered the complete figure of a flesh-and-blood man mounted atop the pedestal.

"What are you doing there...standing?" stammered the girl, still incredulous he had spoken to her.

Then she noticed his attire: a blue frock coat that allowed a glimpse of a white shirt and a thick belt and a buckle with the eagle of the national shield. The man's left hand rested upon a curving saber that, descending behind him, touched the heel of his military boots.

Sole had a feeling. It was crazy, but what could she do. She went up to the plaque and read the name on the statue.

"Sir...are you Leandro Valle?"

The man seemed not to change. After a few seconds, Soledad discovered he was trying to see her out of the corner of one of his green eyes, immobilized as he was in that pose of a statue.

"I beg you," the man began to say, "to step in front of me. I get a stiff neck each time I try to turn my eyes...and not even an elixir of *garuz* can help me in these trances..."

Soledad stood before the man at the edge of the stream of traffic. The ideal place to see and speak with him was found in the middle of the roadway, although the incessant flow of cars, buses and trucks made each attempt impossible.

"Thanks. Now we can continue. Tell me your business, affiliation, caste, family, religion..."

Soledad smiled to hear him speak: she who had felt like she was going crazy was finally seen and heard.

"Tell me about the state of things. Can I finally rest? And my aged mother, have her sorrows at last come to an end? Are the hundred pesos the government of the capital pays her enough? And did Miguel Miramón die facing straight ahead or like a traitor? You know, they shot me in the back like cowards and it vexes me not to know if his 'Highness' will be able to bet on the cockfights again with me. They last time we did so was before fighting in Calpulapan, him with the conservatives, me with the liberals. As his soldiers fell from the sword thrusts of mine, Miguel embraced me before bidding farewell. 'My general,' he said to me. 'Your Highness,' I answered, because that's the way we had joked around since the military college we attended together in our youth. Miguel went on then with a rigorous officiousness: 'If I don't get out of this battle alive, I'll wait to parry with you in the beyond.' But my childhood friend didn't die until years later. I died first on the Mount of the Crosses before he fell on the Mountain of the Bells, with that poor little emperor Ferdinand Maximilian those spurious conservatives brought from Europe, according to what I've heard recounted. Do you understand why it is so vitally important that just like me, Miguel died by the sword?"

"Did you say his surname was Miramón?" asked Soledad, perplexed by that allusion to memory and history. "I remember Maximiliano, but your friend…to be honest, I don't know much about history."

"The same old noise." The man's voice sounded irritated. "When I want to speak, they don't listen to me, and when they listen to me, they don't understand or don't know what I'm talking about. Such a sinister destiny to die and wake up a statue…"

Suddenly feeling cold, Soledad couldn't help involuntarily grabbing her own arms.

"Yes, a statue. It took me a while to understand. Imagine my mother crying at my feet and me not able to offer her a word of solace…And the same for my fiancée, who learning of my order by the supreme government to apprehend Tigre Márquez gave me a relic with the Virgin de los Remedios which, certainly, wasn't very miraculous…"

A tumult of horns made Soledad seek refuge once again at the foot of the statue. From there she heard the man, deaf to the city's movement, continue talking. And she thought if that wasn't madness—to walk about with others not seeing her, to listen to a dead man erected as a hero— then it still sure seemed extraordinary.

"Madness? You call it madness, dementia, alienation? You don't know the adage about the cactus?"

Soledad barely dared shake her head no.

"Well, it squares perfectly with me: *Unfortunate justice astonishes me because I am like the nopal cactus, which does no one harm, but casts a wicked shadow.* When I regained consciousness I was standing on a pedestal. At the Tacubaya Foundry they lifted me onto a carriage and brought me here. I thought Tigre Márquez had lied about my death and now they were taking me prisoner to Toluca. After hours on the road, I recognized the turret of Belén but not the roadway nine or ten rods wide through the routes of the Teja hacienda. They left me there, alone, with my tight suit, unable to move and not understanding at all what was happening. Conscious, I recalled a story that my sister Augustina used to tell me about a Philippine rifleman who came through the air and left by the sea, who posted on the ramparts of Manila found his mind had completely vanished and upon regaining his spirit discovered himself in the main plaza of New Spain. Thus I remembered having died—but now everything seems like a dream—in the year 1861 on the Mount of Crosses, that same hill where Father Hidalgo held mass for the last time, and then I awoke decades later, in '89, as years later I came to understand...

"I would have gone completely mad if one night, when the watch had already lit the street lamps, a man elevated on a little pillar hadn't alleviated my pain. It was Don Ignacio Ramírez, the statue on the sidewalk facing us. How my misfortunes dissipated with this new confidant and friend of whom I'd heard spoken so much thunder. Don Ignacio was my second father, brother and desire. As he had perished in '79, he told me about Juárez and the Empire and the death of my brother Miguel Miramón beside Maximiliano and the Indian Mejía. He couldn't tell me with certitude—perhaps he didn't wish to do so—whether Miramón faced the bullets head on or like a traitor...Don Ignacio and I listened to the passers-by, we saw them parade before our eyes, and at night, amidst the quietude in which the Paseo de la Reforma slept, we told each other the things we'd just heard: real gossip about society recounted by the servants walking down Reforma who stopped to talk about life with their peers. That's how we learned the Café Colón had replaced the Café Gran Sociedad; how Mr. Joseph Bush contrived the idea of resuming the failed project of the '50s steamship that navigated Lake Texcoco, to use it on Lake Xochimilco's marshy passage; about the funeral rites of the last daughter of Soledad Lafragua, the virgin betrothed at twelve who laughed at her husband so she could hide and play with her rag dolls...And among the parade of vanities, moments of dishonor and betrayal: Tigre Márquez, forgiven by the intercession of the spurious Romero Rubio, returning from exile. He had the courage to come back and see me. His wrinkles and big belly consoled me when he said, not without envy, "The good thing is I made you a hero at a young age…Just look who had to come tell me. Me with a case of gout that doesn't let up for a moment and you a kid for all eternity…"

Traffic on the avenue had eased. Soledad listened point by point as the man lamented, got all riled, or cried out. The long silence that followed his last spoken words forced the girl to search out his gaze. The man suddenly composed himself and asked her, "And so? Let's continue with the introductions. José María Leandro Francisco Paula Valle Martínez, brigadier general of the Reform Army. *Conde del Nopalito*, at your orders and those of the free fatherland. And you?"

Soledad bowed her head. Why continue that dialogue if everything seemed absurd and useless? Nevertheless, as the man hoarsly sought out a reply, she murmured, "Well, I suppose that now my complete name is Lucía Soledad García Maldonado…Marquess of shadows and crepuscular armies."

"Into the mist we go, eh? But, my child, you must have some affiliation, caste or family. Or are you one of these modern day women who work and even support their husbands?"

"Work, yes I work, that is, I used to work…But I'm not married."

"Well, you're almost too old to merit it…" The man observed Soledad smiling. "Although as I understand, you don't care at all about such things anymore. But tell me, how can you hear me? Only crazy people, the blind and little children pay any attention and take me for real."

Suddenly Soledad didn't know how to explain herself. Tell him she had turned invisible thanks to a desire that, like others, had been fulfilled in a failed manner? Without stopping more to think about it, she added, "I lost my body, sir, and people can't see me."

"As they say, you're one of those pained souls who prowl the world."

"I don't know…I only wanted to disappear, for someone to take the reins of my life…and look where I've come to stand."

"According to what I see, on the boulevard of ghosts and heroes. Do you want me to make a place for you?" joked the man. Soledad smiled in reply, but suddenly she couldn't contain herself, there were already too many jokes and ironies in life, and a cry broke from her. The man on the pedestal kept silent and waited until the girl composed herself again.

"Pardon, bald old Valle never has been the pristine carnation of diplomacy. In my defense I will tell you of an illness (in this place one hears so much about people's business and pains) that has your symptoms. They call it 'loss of shadow.'"

"And what's that?" inquired Soledad in better spirits.

"From what I've heard it's when the soul, which they also call shadow, has a great fright. Then it departs from the body like a person who leaves a house on fire at midnight and runs about in a daze and when he wants to go back home can no longer find the way."

Soledad listened attentively. For the first time it occurred to her she might be ill and if that were the case there might be some cure. She was absorbed in this new possibility and didn't care that people getting off the buses on that busy corner began pushing her. The pressure was moving her like a surge of waves and she took refuge near the pedestal at the most intense moments.

"Did you have a big scare before the loss you mentioned?" asked the man with that clear-eyed gaze that reminded Soledad of the unease of a child who can't find his parents, but now that look had a star-like quality: it shone distantly, its solitary brilliance a kind of balm.

"A scare in particular? I don't think so," the girl finally responded. "That is, I've always been scared. My whole life."

"That is to say it forms part of your natural condition. Then you must have lost your body on other occasions…"

"Yes," said Soledad, bowing her head. "Many."

Two women trying to cross the avenue stopped close to the statue. It seemed one of them heard Soledad because she asked the other, "Many what? I didn't quite hear."

"Huh? I haven't opened my mouth. Come on, let's cross now with the light."

Soledad watched them go off. One was fat and the other tall. They were carrying shopping bags and wore white smocks like the cooks and janitors from the hotels that abound around Bucareli.

"OK, all is not lost. I still have my voice," added Soledad, letting out a sigh. "And sense of touch as well. I can touch them, although they can't see me nor even explain what's happening…"

"Listen, haven't you disappeared yet? I mean, died...That's another possibility. There are a lot of souls wandering around here by the Cathedral that don't know at just what moment they died. They're sudden deaths, from assault or mishap...For example, I had a rapid death but saved myself from a pilgrimage on the Mount of Crosses, because when I was captured, before shooting me they gave me time to write my parents. I also bid farewell to Señorita Laura Jáueregui, she who didn't manage to become Señora de Valle."

Soledad thought that must be a joke. She thought about the occasions prior to her disappearance and remembered that, recently, in the subterranean world of Fine Arts she had slipped and bumped her head but that Filemón helped her stand and waited a few moments for her to gather herself before going on. She also remembered when one night, returning to her room on the rooftop, a man seemed to follow her as she crossed the Garden of Art near the building where she lived. Only she had a very clear image of having hurried and entered the building just when Modesta was coming back from buying bread. Ever polite, Mode had invited her for a hot chocolate and pastry but Soledad, anxious to develop the pictures from the subterranean world, declined the invitation. Finally she remembered jumping into the vase with Lucía and falling inside, but who could die from jumping into a Chinese vase?

"No, Don Leandro." Soledad wondered if she should call him by his military rank. "I don't believe I'm dead. Rather, I believe I've fulfilled a very strong desire I've always had."

The man's gaze still shone; his chest seemed to be holding in his breath.

"I, too, know about desire," he finally said and his gaze became frustrated again. "I was born in '33, the same year the steam locomotive was seen for the first time in Europe. Like its passing, which devoured time, my life was brief. A breath of wind, barely a fleeting comet. But always the same dream of immortality: to leave behind a page written in history....Now how long is my eternity."

Soledad felt compassion for the man. Detained forever in that gesture of looking towards the horizon, he was once again a sad, unsheltered little boy. And then, as if suddenly he had found in Soledad something he knew he'd lost, he added, "You, at least, can move. Me, on the other hand..." The man paused and then, resuming his serene gaze of a statue, continued, "Well, fine, let's return to your business. If you're not sure whether or not you're dead, go to the home of Don Francisco Ortega at 6 Escalerillas Street, behind the Cathedral. He is a most eminent physician. But if he can't help you, go see the caretaker of his house, Nana Eulalia, a famous herbalist. She'll know how to understand your afflictions and cure them. You better go, because you've been talking too much and your throat must be dry by now."

"Yes, general, I'm going now, but first I must tell you something," said Soledad, touching the edge of the saber that fell from the man's left hand. "Down the *paseo*, as you call it, there are other statues, very stiff and made of solid bronze. Many of these monuments, like that of Guadalupe Victoria, don't have..."

"That wasn't his real name," interrupted the man. "The homeland was still being forged and Don Miguel Fernández Félix, a marvelous, intelligent man, understood that to command people of bronze...You must know the devotion of the people to their patron saint, the Virgin of Guadalupe, so here was the first part of the plan. The second, the name Victoria, was to make his opponents despondent, like that black warrior of black fate...He was also a man of character. My esteemed father knew him and used to speak of the goodness of his soul and his serious but humble nature."

The man suddenly became quiet, as if a cauldron of memories were taking shape before him. The girl directed her gaze towards the end of the avenue and made out the castle amidst the clouds of smog. Lost among the poplars of the boulevard must have been those other statues he was talking about.

"Well, those statues," she insisted again, "in contrast to you don't have any more life....nor do they have a sword. Someone stole it from them, as they say profaned them, and now they only have a sort of stirrup in their hand."

"The hilt," mused the man on the pedestal, as if Soledad were only confirming what he already knew.

"Yes, that, the hilt."

"And it's not a sword but a saber. There is a notable difference, with one you touch your enemy and the other you dismember him...well, the art of war is full of subtleties. Don Ignacio fought with the pen and is so immortalized, and a squad of soldiers emboldened by alcohol managed to take from him with a pistol shot the duck feather he carried with his bundle of papers. Since then he has remained silent. That was during the uprising of one Victoriano Huerte. They tried to strip me of my saber, but the sculptor who conceived my monument fastened it to my back."

"But then…perhaps if you let go of the saber," Soledad dared suggest.

"You better believe not…Almost a century asking for a response and now you tell me to do something so clumsy. No, impossible. I will continue unscathed in face of the strong winds of a city, of a politics, of a world no longer mine. Turned into a pillar of salt, if you wish, paralyzed in face of destruction and chaos, I will await an answer. Surrender first? Never…"

Soledad thought the man's voice was breaking, surely out of indignation. His chest seemed to fill with anger, his eyes flashed with daring. The girl took off towards the Cathedral.

"Come back soon with news," she heard the man beseech her. She turned to look at him. He appeared small atop his pedestal and as helpless as Soledad herself.

LVIII

To reach the Palace of Fine Arts had been a triumph. The city in its daily traffic and commerce had become a forced and difficult undertaking. Perhaps it was just her imagination, but since she had discovered that people couldn't see her she walked along with an unusual lightness, her feet were quicker and the mass of her body weighed less. Despite everything, reaching that point had taken her a long time. Precisely because of her new lightness, she encountered the heavy corporeal presence of the passers-by who moved through and occupied space with an undeniable animalism.

For a moment she thought of going into the Palace to look for Martín Rueda and play a joke on him. She'd fake being a shadow from the subterranean levels, sent by the god Quetzalcóatl or one of those Aztec deities that seemed to fascinate him. An intempestive happiness took hold of Soledad. Yes, she would have to go down into the subworld of Fine Arts and wander through its dark, surprising passages. Something told her that Martín Rueda didn't like the darkness or dripping humidity of the tunnels, so that abandoning him without a flashlight in that inverted labyrinth would be like losing a little child…Then she would remind him of the rabbit-rats, the spores that flourished in the human lung, she would invent a flinty wind, the subterranean river on which were shipwrecked the souls of the disappeared…Soledad stopped all of a sudden: how could she be sure she wouldn't be shipwrecked on that river or lost among the tunnels, being she didn't know that unusual world? That time she went with Filemón they didn't run across a sole person, but who could swear it wasn't inhabited by beings used to the darkness? How difficult would it be for them to recognize her? And what if they said, as Lucía once did, "Why go back to the outer world if you're already dead?" But no, she was alive. At least she thought so. She looked around: a guy selling balloons passed by whistling, a few office workers joked among themselves, a group of tourists got off a bus and began taking pictures…As well a girl in a nurse's uniform crossed the street; her mien was cautious, like a nun's, she walked in short rapid steps and soon was lost among the lanes of ash and poplar. How long ago now since she had worn a nurse's uniform…She had felt herself part of a game and being used by other people had granted her the fleeting illusion of identity. Now, on the other hand, she knew neither who she was or what was happening. That girl others had known as Soledad García— was that really her? She looked at her hands, she recognized her grandmother Marina's ring on her own finger, and nevertheless she had the sensation that the past she now recalled more and more distantly someone else had actually lived. A man selling cotton candy stood with his tree of pink clouds near Soledad. She stretched out her hand and took a few of those rosy clouds, sweet and ethereal on her palate. And while she was eating she felt tears burning her face. Was this what they called madness?

She preferred not to move until the sun and the city settled down, which was still hours away. She clambered up one of the big Palace windows, pulled her legs in and put her arms around them. She shut her eyes. At first the exterior sounds kept coming through, but little by little she could hear the silent sounds of her own body: her heart as persistent as desire, her guts spilling out in sudden cascades, the air in the labyrinth of her hearing. Within, in that distance traveled inside herself, now that the boundaries of her body seemed to have been erased, Soledad discovered herself obstinately alive. It would have been worthless to let life spill out like a wound, to remain motionless, to shut off all desire, to make no noise, to ask Lucía to change places with her. Each rebellious throb, each stubborn breath, spoke to her now of a secret force like that of seeds: that germ, that paltry little plant, made of still inexistent stalk and leaves, refused to disappear. Perhaps it was hearing that awakening of cells that accompanies germination, or perhaps it was because she hadn't eaten and the sun was sapping her brains and strength…She felt hungry. The man with the cotton candy had left a while ago. She stuck her hand in her pants pocket hoping to find a piece of gum. Then she found the letter Modesta had given her. She looked at it carefully and discovered that although it had no return address, the stamps revealed its origin: Magyar Posta. Budapest. It must be a letter from Peter. How many times had she written him before getting an answer? Three? Five? Ten? What would he think now if he knew that she had become a shadow of herself, submitted to the will of a desire she had once thought her own? For a moment she thought maybe Peter was informing her of his return. How would she approach him now? Would she be able to confront him and attempt a new relation? No, she recognized that Peter, like Martín Rueda, incarnated for her a permanent threat, the unpredictable danger of what lies outside us. She held onto the envelope a few more seconds. Perhaps it would be better to leave it closed and bet that life would continue complying with her desires.

> Dear Soledad,
> This isn't a letter. I am a ghost, and so are you. No, that's too much. But there is something real: memories and photographs. Stop. I hope you're well. I send you these lines. They're not important. I might have a show in Madrid in October…(Title: The Poetics of Shadows [??]). This is only a form of silence. Forgive me.
> Yours, Peter

Soledad breathed with relief: she was alone, she didn't have to respond to anyone or anything for her actions. The city and its streets could turn themselves into a labyrinth and who knows, perhaps she'd find coming around some corner, more than the dragon or Lucía, her own face.

LIX

There was no Escalerillas Street behind the cathedral. It was night but the metallic signs said only República and Guatemala. Soledad remembered how once as a little girl she had been fascinated by the Street of the Lost Child. In her imagination surged scenes of a child stolen by gypsies from a fair who transformed him into an unrecognizable lizard child. Soledad had squeezed her mother's hand to exorcise those images not so much because her desire to disappear might convert her into the first turtle girl of the area. No. She squeezed her mother's hand, she measured her short steps while her head filled with the memory of other streets with suggestive names she hadn't recognized but formed part of her city's map of legends which her father occasionally told her about at night: Get Out If You Can Alley, Street of the Scares, Monster Street, Good Death Street...But just like the Lost Child, those streets no longer existed: by the work and grace of a bureaucratic toponomy that throughout the cathedral's neighborhood thanked the republics of the world and the recognition of the revolutionary government, the city was forgetting its names and past. And 6 Escalerillas, Soledad asked herself while going down Guatemala Street looking for some sign that would tell her where to stop. Not a trace of the office of Dr. Ortega, much less his caretaker there. She suddenly stopped. What was she looking for? General Valle had died a century earlier and surely, like those old people who speak of their past as if it were a perpetual present, he had sent her to look for a doctor dead and buried long before. How hadn't she thought of that? She looked at the street empty except for a couple dogs sniffing around a pile of garbage near the Templo Mayor. To the left and right a drizzly light spread through the scant foliage, leaving in the darkness zones of a deceitful reality. Was that bundle hiding in a door really a child sleeping on its haunches or was it just a trick created by the shadows? And the Cathedral lit askew by a waxing moon that covered it in clouds of a ghostly halo, was it really there or was it a lithograph from the past century? And wasn't that silence by chance like that of dreams—a dark blow to the chest when the street and one's own steps are lost? In a wall of the Cathedral she discovered a figure carved in stone: the body half in flames begging from mercy made her recognize in that sculpted image a soul in Purgatory. A sign hanging from a nearby screen confirmed:

Chapel of the Souls
Hours of service
Monday-Friday 9 a.m.-5 p.m.
Saturdays and Sundays 10 a.m.-noon

Soledad felt cold. If the souls atoned for their sins with fire, crackling like pieces of human wood, could they also like her feel cold, hunger, fear? She walked a few steps closer to see if she could discern the features of that image delineated in the stone stocks. She tripped over a can of beer and the yelps of dogs passed through the air. The girl turned to look at them: after a few seconds, one of them turned to root through the garbage with its pointed snout, still looking at her. Soledad remained still; perhaps if she pretended to be a shadow on the street it would leave her alone. She thought of the petrified image resting behind her and she remained immobile a few minutes. When she decided to look, the dogs had disappeared. Where to now? She arrived to the corner of Brasil Street and looked closely at the cupolas of Santo Domingo. Her steps—not her will—led her in that direction.

LX

It was small and vast, open and pressing, illuminated but its portals hidden by shadow. The Plaza Santo Domingo presided with its fountain of the Corregidora Domínguez over the traffic of the days—wandering passers-by, cars, pigeons. Only now, at this hour of the night, among those buildings that sleep a sleep of stone, the Corregidora—sitting on her bronze horse—was also sleeping. In the light of the somnolent streetlights, Soledad contemplated the empty plaza with its perennial church and buildings that belonged to the Inquisition and Customs House and sat in awe before that image which emerged in the neighborhood's amber night.

She approached the fountain, its waters silenced so not to wake the present. The Corregidora seemed to thank it with a gesture of majestic calm. Barely a moment's rest, a catnap before dawn and already the folder of papers she held in her right hand threatened to slip free. Soledad glimpsed a feathered ornament crowning the head of the statue and wondered whether that woman, a heroine of the Independence movement, would have liked to pass into posterity dressed like that. But there was no way of asking her: compared to Leandro Valle, whom at first she had confused for a flesh-and-blood man atop the pedestal, that bronze woman remained unchanged and silent. It was too bad she didn't speak, especially now that the night was so dark and the plaza's streetlights only accentuated and adorned other shadows, but not Soledad's. She erupted with a gesture of desperation and rage: not only did the statue refuse to help her, but as well her shadow remained silent.

"Speak!" she suddenly shouted at the Corregidora.

In reply, the ornament atop the statue lifted into flight. Astonished, Soledad began running toward the portals. But the ornament alit upon the ground flapping its wings and strutting about looked sidewise at the girl. Soledad broke into a laugh that was also a cry.

"Things aren't so painful and difficult in themselves," said a voice. "But our cowardice and lack of substance make them so."

Soledad looked for the place from where the dark portals had spoken. Like a bolt of lightening she made out the presence of some ghost, one of those tormented in the name of religion or the sorrowful soul of that poet famous for "Nocturne for Rosario" who committed suicide at twenty-four precisely in a building on the plaza. And while the girl feared the appearance of Manuel Acuña, the suicidal poet, there emerged from the darkness a little cane and behind it a man. He was elderly, plump, dressed in an old dark suit, like something taken out of a chest from the nineteenth-century, and he wore his riotous hair in a volatile mane that lent him a certain gallantry. He took a few more steps and stood there before the girl with a fixed gaze and a face filled with emotion. For her part, Soledad remained astonished. The man must have understood the situation because he broke into a broad smile and added, "Michel de Montaigne…"

"What? Are you…?" asked Soledad surprised.

"Am I? You flatter me, child…No, I'm not Michel de Montaigne.

He's a good friend of mine. But the phrase I just told you about sorrow comes precisely from him, the first among French essayists. Well, you know that famous saying about the essayist, because long ago one only 'assayed' the meal before the great lords because they didn't want to be poisoned. And as they say where I come from, 'Fear doesn't ride a donkey.' So better that others assailed or assayed the meal, and attempted or assayed to die poisoned…"

Soledad didn't understand what was happening. Was this man really talking or had he emerged from some absurd novel? As the silence extended, the man excused himself: "Pardon, I'm all done talking. Allow me to introduce myself: Matías Torres at your service, in past times librarian at San Agustín and now an evangelist of the portals on Santo Domingo. Do you need a letter to dissuade your lover? A missive to beg the pardon of a prideful father? Or is there a bureaucratic situation that needs remedy? Tell me, girl, so I might make myself useful."

"You said evangelist? One of those who goes knocking door to door announcing the New Testament?" asked Soledad wiping her eyes.

"Of course they also call themselves evangelists, although as a Catholic I have only the faith of baptism, for I share more opinions with agnostics…But they call us evangelists, too, the scriveners of these now calm portals."

Soledad recalled the daily life of that part of the city, the long corridor flanked by the portals where little hand presses printed invitations for weddings, baptisms, or funeral announcements; the haranguing printers on the corners of the plaza looking for potential clients; and, as well, in the portals a few desks with typewriters worked by men quite proud of their knowledge before the ignorant maid wanting to send a few lines to her village or the applicant for a chauffeur's job needing a letter of recommendation.

"Thanks, but that kind of help, no," responded Soledad with a thin voice. "What I need is to speak and for someone to listen to me."

"Understood, my child, because speaking and being listened to is a divine privilege. But look, Lucretius said that the cause of all evil resides in our hearts…I don't know what yours are, but understanding how relative our passions are ends up being satisfying. I

162

can tell you that nobody is evil much longer than they want to be..."

The man suddenly became quiet, directed his face towards the atrium of Santo Domingo and waited a few moments. Soledad discerned the figure of a dog. It looked like one of those that had been barking on Escalerillas Street.

"Listen, here comes Marbles."

The excited animal ran towards the man wagging its tail insistently. It came up and stood on its legs, greeting him with licks of its tongue. Almost getting knocked over, the old man responded with pets and hugs. After a few moments he told the dog to settle down.

"OK, OK, Marbles, can't you see we have a visitor?"

Marbles turned toward Soledad and let out a howl.

"No, Marbles, the young lady is our friend. Come..." and he bent over, calling to the dog until it came to him. Then he held a hand in the air, asking Soledad for hers. The girl hesitated a moment but then let Matías guide her along the animal's flank. "Pet him, and that way he'll trust you."

Soledad obeyed and the dog began wagging its tail again excitedly. She discovered that Marbles had different colored eyes: a blue marble on the right and a green one on the left.

"That's it," nodded the man, looking at the emptiness.

Soledad was in front of him and she turned from looking at the dog's eyes to those of the man.

"Señor Matías," she asked, "how long have you been sightless?"

"My child, that's a story I share with Don Quixote. Although I only have half his adventures and knowledge, we both lost something from reading so much."

LXI

Matías lived in a hotel on Brasil Street, and although he was blind he wasn't deaf and could tell by the conversations and moans that more than a cheap hotel, the Río de Janeiro was a place for quickies: his dingy room was the only one not used for a little afternoon delight. But then why did the blind man prefer to live in such a total dump? Well, certainly in part it was the proximity to the portals where every day he sat at a desk with an Olympia typewriter and waited for the young maids, people from the provinces, old men and women, or those who didn't know how to write or so seldom did that they preferred to hire the services of a professional scrivener like Don Matías (whom his own competitors always recommended for difficult cases of failed love or injustice). It was also an advantage to live in that dump on Brasil because the owner gave him a good discount for the dark, dank back room that even the prostitutes preferred to avoid. But the real reason why the blind man had chosen the Río de Janeiro was simply its name. "Hotel Río de Janeiro, 27 Brasil Street, Downtown," was for Matías an echo of the stories that he liked to invent about himself: that life on Central Avenue in Río de Janeiro, when his wife and daughter would go out shopping and he would wait for them with *The Mines of King Salomon* on his lap, recalling the words Sir Henry had once told him: "There is no journey on earth that a man can't accomplish if he puts his effort into it, if love guides him and he defends his life without importance, ready to save it or lose it according to the will of Providence." Then, ready to continue his travels, that old man who lived in the Río neighborhood was granted a stop on his itinerary: the parallel life of a blind man living near the portals on a populous plaza in Mexico, the alchemical city that had bewitched him and that he loved like those things which are our perdition.

In these passions and penumbra navigated Matías Torres, who owed to books his blindness and the pleasure of finding in disgrace his servitude, for as the same blind man said to Soledad a few days after their first encounter, to navigate through shadows was cruel and inhuman, but it also gave him the opportunity of inventing alone a world for himself, a world where just the pronunciation of a word was enough to create its meaning. Then he remembered his insightful Montaigne, who bragged about his bad memory, for when rereading a book he thought he was reading it for the first time. And so Matías Torres, ready to travel to a country uncreated and unformed, once again completely reinvented his image and desire.

The girl wasn't surprised to learn from their growing closeness and increasing conversations that the dictionary was his favorite book. With his hand resting on the *Abridged Larousse* and its worn-out red glue, Don Matías said, "Here, in one sole hand, I possess the Universe."

Another time at dawn, the two of them sitting on the pedestal of the flagpole in the Zócalo, the Cathedral asleep to one side and before them the silent Palace of Government, Soledad thought of asking the blind man what he would do if the president asked his advice about governing. In that plaza, with its legacy of *tlatoanis*, viceroys, strongmen and presidents, Don Matías wouldn't resist proffering a few of his opinions; moreover, the lamentable events of San Juan Ixhuatepec had recently occurred, and although the deaths were rumored in the thousands, the authorities insisted they had everything under control. Matías answered that he couldn't respond because pride wasn't one of his favorite sins; he preferred to remain silent rather than pretend to put the world in order. Soledad said nothing. The breeze in the plaza blew papers about and high above them the waxing moon illuminated a part of the blind man's face. The girl observed that despite his messy hair and overgrown eyebrows, he always maintained an air of dignity.

"Excuse me," added the man pensively. "Not to answer you is also a form of vanity. The poet Octavio Paz relates how Tzu-Lu asks Confucius, 'If the duke of Wei called you to administer his country, what would be your first measure?' Confucius answered without joking, 'The reform of language.' The poet adds, not knowing where evil begins, in words or in things, that when words are corrupted and meanings become uncertain, the meaning of our acts and works also stumbles. I believe that as well: things are sustained by their names and vice-versa.

"And returning to your question, I would speak to the president about my taste for heroes and fairy tales. As to the first, like Homer said a man who holds his life for nothing, who's capable of risking it for anything, isn't just any man. When Alexander the Great was a boy—although in truth he never was—they asked him what destiny he would prefer, that of Achilles (brief but magnificent) or that of Homer, who sang of the hero's feats throughout his long life. Alexander answered that he would prefer the destiny of the hero and his life fulfilled that command. (But, the poet added, we wouldn't know of Achilles' feats if Homer hadn't sung of them.)"

Soledad felt the urge to touch the blind man, to caress his venerable face and embrace him with the warmth of that flame that revived inside her with the incantation of the stories he recounted. She remembered her father and the legends he narrated to help her fall asleep, promising they'd pick up the game of life the next day. She didn't know at what moment she leaned her head upon the shoulder of Matías. She began to fall asleep covered with that mantle of words with which the blind man conjured up the world and other unknown realms.

"Returning to my story, I return again to my taste for fairy tales, not for their happy, cohesive endings, but their prophetic symbolism. Recall the story of the emperor's clothes. Perhaps it's missing someone shouting, 'The emperor is wearing no clothes, the president is gray-haired, the Pope is a man.' So that things are called by their name, that they call *tragedy* tragedy. I think the fate of man didn't begin so much with the expulsion from paradise but with the birth of language: the tiger ceased being that bag of muscle and bone with prodigious reflexes and became a word with which we grasped its fleetness and threatening reality. Well, when we don't pay attention to words, the last redoubt where we may seize reality, when the dead of San Juan or those from '68 can be counted on two hands in the official version, then we're lost, as if filter upon filter were placed between us and the named reality. Divided, more and more separated from ourselves. And look what remains of the modern adventure. Every life is a departure and the patience to reach port. Ulysses, not so much the adventurer but the patient one, leaves Ithaca in order to return to Ithaca, he says *no* to the call of the sirens, to Circe, he disguises himself as Nobody in order to cruelly fool the cyclops Polyphemus...And his return justifies twenty years of hazards, pleasures, and punishments. The man of today has to say no to the world just to go shut himself up inside his house and watch some boxing match or soccer game or soap opera on TV. And all for what? So the beast named anguish devours him like the entrails of Prometheus. And those in command believe that anguish is exorcized with veils, falsehood, lies. Can you imagine, Soledad, if we got up one day and the Pope was talking about his own little concerns, if he just said, 'I want a little wine, my corns hurt, what time are they putting the miter on me, doesn't that nun have a nice ass?' It's scary, no? If one day the president said, 'Yeah, I'm not interested in those miserable people, but what do they want, I have to act like it's important because if not the pressure cooker will explode...give them instead a little spit so they can clean off their grime.' If he said that, the world would get nervous. Then those young office workers would be able to confront their boss and tell him, 'You think you're doing me a favor giving me a job but I'm the one who gives you the power to command, I solve this and that for you, what you pay me doesn't justify me handing over my life, my soul, my hours here.' Or you, girl, you could go say to your mother, 'Look how much you've denied me, your daughter, look what you've done to me, an enemy wouldn't do me so wrong.' And then what? Man's existence is encoded in lies, in conventions, but conventions choke us and ground us even less. In any case people should have the option of choosing the lies that most suit them. Like me, who chose the paradise of words."

The blind man paused. Then, turning his gaze towards 20 de Noviembre Avenue, quiet and almost empty of cars at that hour, he began again, "Or like Jorge, who chose to be a hunter in this asphalt jungle, with his tribal shields converted into wings…"

"Jorge? A hunter? In this city? Wings?" replied the girl about to turn around.

"What? Haven't I told you about Jorge Estrella, who silences the city when he raises his angel wings?"

"No…"

"How is that possible? And I haven't told you about the lost children who wake from their dreams when the city sleeps…of the members of the Nocturnal Adoration who free the country from the sins of the nation…nor even of Mr. Polo and his bellmen from the Cathedral who with each peal call to the beings of light so that this world doesn't become lost? Well, what have we been talking about, child, all these dawns?"

LXII

I close my eyes and everything becomes a threat. I walk slowly, softly, as if they'd turned me inside out and now my skin was the deepest part of me. I discover in this upheaval where feelings turn inward, where feet are transformed into another pair of hands in order to touch the earth, in this foggy upheaval the body is converted, curved upon itself into a big question mark that requests an answer with each step.

Here, with useless eyes I am the most vulnerable being in the universe. All the fear of which I used to be capable is a

167

child's game compared to this absolute anguish. Still, I keep my eyes closed; I walk through the Plaza de Santo Domingo at an hour of the dawn where it becomes solitary and passable. The paving stones on the ground are so uneven that I stagger and my pace slows even more. But I must not open my eyes. The air becomes a presence, a shapeless and unknown body that my hands and the skin of my face discover in astonishment.

After a while I have tripped and fallen, crashed into a column, and when I thought I was going north I got lost on the east side of the plaza, just about run over by a car that fleetingly and suddenly appeared. But my senses are alert and now I recognize other vibrations in the air, the presence of massive stones that surround the plaza because the light they reflect turns dense, and as well the column of the Corregidora Domínguez surges like a lighthouse from the shadow...

Little by little, recognizing that something within me awakes with this limitation of my eyes, the fear diminishes and I discover that darkness can also be protective. As if unaware, or some shapeless knowledge filled an unnamable anxiety. Before, with Lucía, I experienced something similar, when we entered the vase's labyrinth and walking between those reddish walls the pain and sorrow eased and we didn't even think about them when we saw the sleeping dragon and so became drowsy, not worrying about leaving or waking. Just that tranquilizing feeling of losing oneself, of no longer existing apart. Of melting.

Soledad had been sitting on the edge of the fountain, her eyes still shut in a sort of somnambulistic sleep when she perceived movement around her. In contrast to the auto that almost ran her over which she recognized by the movement of the air and the squeal of the brakes, now she didn't quite recognize what was happening. At first she thought it must be a flock of doves alighting on the plaza to begin their courting rituals. Then when a dog came up and rested its snout upon her legs, she recognized Marbles and thought it was the blind man Matías approaching. But no matter how hard she tried to find the metallic noise of the old man's cane, she couldn't hear it. Perplexed, she tilted her head to funnel the noise and find among the buzz of the electric streetlights illuminating the plaza the latent rumor of the sleeping city and the murmur of water from the fountain where insects and garbage lay strewn, and recognize the little swirls of battering air as if the wind itself had begun to play around in amusement.

Suddenly she heard chirps of laughter, like feathers must feel when they're tickled. Marbles left Soledad and a little later the girl heard him whining as if asking for something. Then she heard clapping and imagined the dog leaping up while wagging its tail and turning round and round. Soledad didn't know at what moment she began to smile. It was if her skin recognized before she did that jumping and exuberant happiness that ran and rolled about in mischief where bodies—because no doubt they were bodies—were in joyful control of themselves: a hand was the movement of that hand and the desire to touch turned into a caress or blow…And legs stretched out or were tucked under in a flash that was the act of fleeing or finding…The mouth slurped or left hanging out a thick bumpy tongue. A few little nips. Soledad could perceive the almost painful struggle to keep teeth from tearing into her. And in that holding back was a resplendent trembling, cascades and rivers that don't flow out but ebb, the open fall toward within.

Marbles was jumping up to lick her face. Soledad, who still had her eyes shut, fell into the fountain. The freezing water woke her, making her sit right up. Before her a group of children were frozen by the uproar and surprise: they were watching Marbles come up to the fountain and play with its front paws suspended in the air and couldn't understand why it tensed its muscles ready to attack—or flee. Soledad observed how as the moments passed their bodies squatted to take up less space, they sunk their chests and pulled their shoulders in as if protecting something. It was enough then that Marbles continued wagging its tail for the children to once again unfold their bodies. One of them, with a defiant chin, came up to the dog and petted its head while it sniffed the air. Soledad felt the closeness of the child, that vehement reality of his skin and its heat, and she waited. The child neared her face, stuck out his tongue, and tasted her wet arm. The others looked at him expectantly and even Marbles calmed down beside him. Soledad felt the area where she had been touched radiating a fire to the rest of her body that made her forget having just fallen into the water. Then the boy rested his head upon Soledad's lap and she felt an overwhelming happiness light up that dark room that was her body. She hadn't disappeared; she was there, they recognized her.

The enchantment disappeared as if by magic. Marbles barked and pulled the boy to wake him from his airy dream. The others ran off and Soledad saw them disappear through the portals, appearing later on a distant corner of the plaza with the boy who had touched her and finally they were gone completely. They escaped in a surprising way: despite not lifting her gaze from them, Soledad could have sworn that while running or rapidly moving they vanished in the air; only when they stopped could one discern them, as if in transit from one place to another they managed to escape from sight and stopping they exposed themselves to view. But they were no longer there. Marbles must have first heard a distance rumor growing in the air and rebounding in an incomprehensible word.

"Sope-Sope-Sope," repeated a chorus of voices that seemed to come from a street alongside Santo Domingo. Soledad crossed the plaza and found a crowd of boys and girls watching a blond-haired boy about twelve walking on the edge of one of the church's cornices. The voices became hushed as the boy challenged more and more the empty air. Just about to fall, he jumped and grabbed onto one of the columns holding up the balustrade and from there leapt to an ash tree and in a truly acrobatic act landed and continued rolling until he finally could stop.

The group of kids began to shout in chorus again, "Sope-Sope-Sope." Among the crowd emerged a girl with big eyes and a lost gaze. She was wearing an embroidered blouse and a short skirt that displayed her legs, thin and innocent despite revealing an endless desire that began with her skin. Instead of walking toward the blond boy she headed to an abandoned truck, once painted but now all rusty. The boy followed her inside. When the truck began to move with growing fury, a chorus rose again with that word that had alerted Marbles but seemed unintelligible to Soledad. Little by little the voices and movements stopped. Only the hand of the blond boy appeared in a window and flung out a plastic bag the others hurried to grab. Then began an unusual race and soon they disappeared behind the ruined portal which Soledad saw was a kind of dwelling. She threw a glance at the still truck and the suddenly quiet street. On the corner, attached to a stone wall, she came across a blue plaque with white letters saying Leandro Valle Street.

LXIII

One night she decided to follow the children, but it didn't prove easy. She'd barely turn her eyes and when she looked back they were no longer there. Finally she found them thanks to Marbles, wagging his tail near a lamp post. Bewildered by the bulk of its body, they stayed still as larvae, five little sacks that squatted next to the post while a police car prowled through the area. As soon as they saw it go by they got up from the ground and continued on their way through the shadows. When they reached the Plaza de Santo Domingo they preferred the dark passage where men sat with their typewriters and then carefully approached a building entrance. Anybody who didn't know the place might have passed by without noticing the silhouette of a man leaning against a wall. Instead, the penetrating smell of marihuana mixed with the aroma of freshly made tortillas would have caught their attention. Stopping by the entrance leading to a shadowy interior patio, perhaps that person would have felt tempted to enter without being seen, without running the risk of being hurt, and explore that pregnant world of the city's downtown, full of latent violence.

The children, on the contrary, stopped as soon as they discerned the man's figure. The kid in the lead jumped to hide behind one of the columns; the others did the same, each behind a different one. Marbles, on guard as soon as they reached the portals, turned the corner and disappeared down Cuba Street.

"I know you're here," said the man and from the wall emerged a hand holding a beer can that headed to a another spot in the wall where his mouth must have been. He took a drink: a snake slurping from a puddle. "You think you're very clever because you're as small as rats and can scurry away to escape. But you'll grow up or…" —the snake took another sip— "or perhaps not. Maybe none of you will grow old, maybe not even reach thirty like me. If I'm alive, I'll tell those who ask: they were lost children, with neither father nor mother, well, perhaps with parents, or perhaps it was the fathers and mothers who were lost...Enough stories. Or perhaps not. To see children with rags on their feet, rat children, mischievous urchins. 'And so the story goes,' no?"

But instead of an answer, the child furthest down the corridor took a wad of bills that made a bulge over the skinny belly beneath his shirt and waved it in the air.

"Ah...you've come for your medicine. I could also say I was their shaman, their doctor, even their pharmacy. I, too, could say that I always helped ease their death."

The wad of cash waved around again. Then the man murmured, "Let's be clear I didn't look for you. You were the ones looking for me. And for sure I don't want any problems with Sope. Come here...Well, come in," said the man and with his other hand brushed the bulge from a gun he carried in the waistband of his pants.

But the kids didn't move. They remained with one leg in the air, ready to run off at any moment.

"All right," agreed the man. He moved his large figure away from the wall and entered the building. A few minutes passed in which the children's eyes didn't stop moving, watching the shadows, the plaza, the street. The man returned; besides the can of beer he carried a little box of medicine that, just crossing the threshold, he decided to guard in his back pocket. He took a few steps toward the first child in line, the one used to lifting his chin in timid defiance.

"First things first," said the man and held out his hand.

The money passed forward from one kid to another but before reaching the last one, the boy with the defiant chin made a gesture with his head and the wave of hands stopped.

"I got it here," the man signaled to his back pocket. "So now you don't trust me?"

There was no response. The man smiled scathingly and took a few steps toward the first child in line.

"Well, you're distrustful because you choose to be. But the truth is I'm very trustworthy...And if you don't believe me," the man drank from his beer with that animal hiss, "you can ask Ruth...Just looking at those legs you touch the heavens, imagine what it's like having them here open for your ready. I'm not very demanding, I take whatever I can get, needs are needs, but you and your sister are different. What do you say, Clarín? Do you accept? Or should

I say Clara? Come on, Clara-Clarín, the medicine shouldn't have to cost you…so much."

Soledad witnessed that scene: she looked at the man—his eyes shining despite the darkness—she contemplated the children—that threatening fragility growing in their messy hair, the big pants held up by suspenders, the naked feet in shoes without laces—and she witnessed in the plaza's silence and the solitude the violence of a bubble about to burst. She observed that the face of the boy who had earlier touched her radiated a pure rage now that he'd heard his name. Soledad didn't know how things quite developed, just that suddenly she discovered the line of children had broken up and two kids were now on the man's back shaking their thin arms in the air and Marbles, running out from who knows where, was growling. Hearing the animal, the man ceased advancing towards the first child and instead brought his hand to his waistband. His back and head turned in an explosive movement but Soledad, who had stayed back and could already see the hand of the armed man perfectly framed, knew she had to do something. And that certainty stripped her of all fear: she fell upon the man, the impact knocking him down. Not knowing what was happening, looking from side to side as if he feared he wasn't so drunk as to fall all by himself, the man tried to retreat and take out his gun, but then discovered a void where the revolver had caused a bulge and immediately brought his hand to his back pocket, only to realize the box wasn't there either.

Soledad, who'd also fallen to the ground from the impact, jumped up when she saw Marbles' tail wagging at the end of the corridor as it headed toward Leandro Valle Street. Although she ran to catch up with the children she found only an empty street. In front of a dwelling she came across Marbles licking a paw. She went up to the dog, which wet her cheek with its tongue, and although she asked him where the kids had gone, Marbles only looked at her with the double confusion of his different colored eyes.

Soledad cast a glance to the dark interior of the dwelling. The stench of drains and long rotting garbage made her step back, but then she took a breath of air and got up the courage to enter. The building was silent, dark except for the rectangles of light coming from some upper window. She poked through the shadows without finding them. About to leave, she discovered a staircase leading to a kind of basement and understood the children must have escaped that way, and she left the building accompanied by Marbles.

"That's how you take care of lost children and blind people like Matías, and accompany ghosts that don't know if they're ghosts?" she asked petting the dog. "What other secrets do your transparent eyes hide?"

LXIV

Little by little she discovered it wasn't so difficult to speak and be heard by the blind like Matías, religious women, the indigents who attracted by some preacher downtown wandered through the streets, entered churches and slept under the portals and in public plazas. All she had to do was find the right person to converse with: that guy in a dirty torn trench coat and a red and white scarf around his neck, jabbering unintelligible prayers on a kneeler in the church, turned to look at her like he knew her.

"Francisca," the man began saying, "you leave me neither sun nor shadow, but now I ask for you at the hour of my prayer. You must know and for this very reason you should loosen the straps around me. I'm a dog, I've been your guardian. I was your twig, now I'm your dog. But above all I'm the dog of our Lord Jesus Christ." The man let out a deep sigh and added in litany, "Divine Savior of souls, my face covered with confusion, I bow before your sovereign presence, rent my painful heart in pieces to see the forgetfulness in which redemption holds you, to see your blood sterile and your sacrifices barren and your love incarnated…"

Soledad thought she had seen the man before. She observed that he carried a book with a red mottled cover between his fingers with long dirty fingernails and she vaguely remembered the theft from the Librería Francesa, that book of photos of clouds she had so wanted to have, the episode of the police on Reforma, and then that man who'd snatched the book. Months had passed since then. Now the man's clothing was even more worn out, his head completely shaved and with a new wound in his ear, but it was the same person.

"What are you doing here?" Soledad whispered in his ear, adding, "It's been a while since we saw each other on Reforma."

"What do you mean what am I doing here?" the man asked in a loud voice, the few parishioners turning to look at him. "I pray for your soul and my soul and that of others who commit sins and don't beg forgiveness. Have you forgotten already that today is my evening vigil? Ah, now I see that no…You remember and you want to exasperate me so I'll commit a sin with my rage and then go before the Most Holy Virgin dirtier than some blasphemous journalist, one of those who aggravate our holy mother the Church and our Lord God."

"No," the girl answered. "I didn't want to bother you. Excuse me, I have to go."

The man got up behind Soledad. His head sunken between his shoulders, he begged in a murmur, "Forgive me."

Soledad remained silent. After a few seconds of waiting while the man moved his head from side to side as if searching for someone or waiting to hear a call from the heavens, he sat down on a nearby bench. The girl watched him all the way there.

"It's just I'm not Francisca," she confessed to him.

"I know," answered the man. "And what's your real name?"

"Soledad."

"'Solitude.' The same name we all carry on our shoulders."

"The very same."

"And what have you been doing? You said we once saw each other on Reforma."

"Yeah, a few weeks ago, or maybe it was a few months. I don't remember now."

"But are you a spirit, a soul in sorrow like my dead Francisca?"

"Not that I know. Although it seems incredible, I simply disappeared…That is, I'm here but people can't see me."

"Holy mother of God, aren't you an angel who's lost her memory?"

Soledad smiled before adding, "I don't think so. I still have my memory and it's not quite the life of an angel that I remember. Although in truth, I remember less and less. But no. I was once a girl who lost her father and since then several of my desires have been fulfilled." The girl paused. "And, well, I always wanted to disappear, for someone else to take the reins of my life because, you know, life scares me."

"Be careful what you ask for because you just might get it, my mother used to say," said the man, who knelt and joined his hands together in prayer. A priest wearing a white robe paused beside him, listening to him speak.

"Take comfort, my son," said the priest, patting him on the shoulder. "In the infinite wisdom of God, there is no loss that doesn't also have its profit. One need only see and accept it."

The other man seemed not to listen, for he went on, "One asks without knowing. And then it ends up that desires have a tail and the tail coils around and chokes you…"

But the priest didn't give up. Moving his head in an obvious gesture of disapproval, he said, "Pascual, my son, I know you're very busy now, but when your prayers allow you, the Lord and I will thank you to help us…I know you're a good shot. In turn, I've got my hands full with so many pigeons profaning the house of the Lord."

His smile floated in the air without the man noting it. Then the priest opted for the most practical path: he took the man's ear between his snow white hands and lightly pulled on it.

The man instantly grumbled, "Yes, father, I'll get right on the pigeons." The priest let go of his ear and laughing good-naturedly headed off to the sacristy.

"Easier to kill doves than stop making wishes. But if one asks on behalf of others, then things change and Francisca falls asleep and I rest as well. When I speak with God and tell him about my things, He understands and forgives me. I speak to him and He answers me like you who doesn't have a body but I hear your voice and I know you're there. In my greatest solitude, when not even Francisca accompanies me, I have searched for the face of the Lord and then like water that washes my heart, in my eyes brim tears tasting of forgiveness."

Soledad listened to the man whom the priest had called Pascual and she seemed to understand him despite his confusing words. She squatted down on the kneeler right beside him. She hadn't joined her hands in prayer since she was a girl. She closed her eyes and tried to think of the god she'd just heard the man talking about. She didn't feel Him but his absence, that hollow in the flesh of the soul capable of devouring illusions. Instead she remembered her father. It had been centuries since she thought of him and still she felt like his image had never abandoned her, that in some way he was always there, stopping the train of life so she could choose her whim. Tenuous but luminous surged forth the memory: "Quickly!" Javier García urged her again. "Make a wish." Soledad buried her face in her hands. From some unknown source now flowed calming tears. Then she said, "I don't want to fall lost and alone."

A hand reached through the air and caressed her head.

"Now, girl, everything will pass," Pascual said to her. "If you allow, I'll pray for you tonight, Solitude that has no body but exists in every heart."

LXV

The children were not used to entering the church of Santo Domingo. Immense, with its central nave like the long aisle that separated its parishioners from heaven and that altar of brilliant golds and marble columns proclaiming the reign of an inaccessible god, it was anything but welcoming. Nor did the side entrance help, which let in the winds off Colombia and Brasil Streets, for inside formed a freezing draft of air that cut to the soul of the few penitents who went there to pray. For others who entered the church to snooze, the silence was enough to let them take refuge in a tenacious sleep in which they drooled all over themselves with copious threads of salvia running from their mouths. Feeling the draft, they hugged themselves, if only with their soul and torpor.

For Soledad it was a privileged site: she could remain there for hours resting without much chance of being bothered. Now that it seemed she'd dropped all her questions and limited herself to experiencing in an immediate way whatever she confronted, she discovered that she and that other with whom she was always fighting seemed finally to walk together, as if she and her shadow were heading the same direction. It was enough for one to want to sleep for the other to lay down upon a bench, for one to know about the lives of the saints that filled the altars for them to enter the sacristy and take possession of *The Golden Legend* by Santiago de la Vorágine and discover the portents of St. Martin of Pores and the punishments of Isabel of Hungary; or for one of them to make a joke about the priest who, rifle in hand, went to shoot pigeons on the front of the church for the two of them to say in his ear without even thinking about it, "My son, remember: for me your life is no more important than that of the ugly bird you just finished pluck-ing…" And laugh their heads off when the priest, in a daze, sought out the prior and the altar boy and the office secretary to tell them, "The Lord has spoken to me! He told me, 'Don't let those pigeons continue harming my house!'" And she breathed easy because to contemplate the madness of others, Soledad—she who was herself and the other—discerned, finally, her place in the world.

Now that the distance between desire and action had lessened, Soledad could abandon herself to the present moment and enjoy that plenitude of childhood which fills or mends every hollow and every emptiness. As nobody could see her, she also discovered that first innocence, that state of grace preceding the judgment coming from every gaze. And so, unconcerned, protected from the tyranny that had subjugated her before, she finally dared to savor life like ice cream on a sunny afternoon.

Nor was it that great things happened to her: no longer having to take into account what she did or undid, what she was or had stopped being, still with her voice and touch (for she could touch or make herself be heard or touched), Soledad finally felt complete: she stretched out her hand for a piece of bread, she jumped over puddles or bathed in the Corregidora fountain, and her hands and feet and entire body were all one with her, and she felt neither guilt nor fear. Never like then had she slept as they say do children and crazy people, as if she were blessed.

LXVI

I'm not moved, my God, to love you
by the heaven that you promised me
Nor am I moved by the fear of hell
to stop offending you…

read Soledad in a painting, the words written in Gothic letters, hanging at the feet of a Christ on the Cross in whose stigmatized body seemed concentrated all the world's misery. Perhaps for that reason—because of the sorrow incarnated in the plaster figure, or perhaps from the glass eyes that some master artisan had provided with such infinite compassion, or perhaps because of the contradiction that rolled around the brain but made greater to the soul this mystery of lavish love after having received such ridicule—the so-called Christ of the Good Death received daily visits, prayers and requests from the crowd of parishioners.

One time Soledad seemed to discover a face she recognized: the challenging jaw, the brilliant eyes and the lips both fine and fleshy made her think of the boy (or was it a girl? Soledad hesitated a moment) who always went at the front of the lost children, the one they called Clarín. But that was surely a girl with her pants hiked up to show a pair of legs unquestioningly beautiful, legs that would "make you touch the heavens," at least that's what the man in the portals had said, the guy the kids had made fun of the other night. Was he referring to that same girl? Soledad followed her to the kneeler by the altar, she watched her cross herself and caress with a hand the wounded feet of Christ. Then she raised the same hand to her lips and said with her gaze fixed on the face that also gazed back at her, "I'm not moved, my God, to love you." It seemed to Soledad that upon her lips those words weren't a prayer but a true declaration of love, that her long and anxious gaze said everything the words couldn't stammer. Suddenly she heard a whistle. The girl jumped up all at once and without thinking bumped into the table full of candles in front of her. Her lips rested intensely on that plaster skin that could only thus withstand a caress without shattering. And she took off running to a second whistle that insistently echoed off the church walls. Soledad thought of following the girl but the overturned candles made her stop. She hastily arranged them and then ran after the girl, but by the time she reached the church door the other had already disappeared.

Something told her that the amorous date with the Christ of the Good Death was a kind of farewell. She snooped around the plaza crowded at that hour of the day and after giving it some thought decided to walk around the church, sticking close to the walls. She was going to try to get close to the dwelling that gave access to the basements where the children seemed to seek protection, when on the rooftop appeared the girl she was looking for, scanning the horizon of buildings and then resting her gaze upon the cupolas of the church facing her. Someone must have called to her because the girl suddenly turned her face and stepped back from the cornice.

Soledad took a breath and crossed like a gust of air Leandro Valle Street until she reached the dwelling's entrance. She climbed the three steps of the staircase and then the flight up to the rooftop. The access door was ajar so all she had to do was push it open a bit more. But there was no one on the rooftop. Her heart pounding, she let out a long sigh. Deceived, she walked from one side to the other while she caught her breath. Despite the brownish cloud marring her view, she discovered that the northern part of the valley was visible, like that from the Palace of Fine Arts when she climbed up there with her forceful, assertive friend Maru. She missed her but then recalled the curt words the last time she'd looked for her, that "Who are you?" when she tapped her on the shoulder and Maru turned around, irritated not to find anyone. Soledad had at that moment feared her rejection and hesitated to answer. The voice turned her into a knot and she could only touch her again on the shoulder. Maru jumped, infuriated. "Aren't you going to tell me who you are?" she mumbled. "Go fuck yourself, because I can't do anything for you." Soledad had to swallow her cry watching leave that friend whom she so needed now that she was more alone than ever, but alone above all due to the devilish, paralyzing fear that sealed her lips like her own tomb.

Now that time had passed and she found herself before another panorama, she tried to say it, although it was useless: "Soledad, I'm Soledad." She heard her voice and recognized it as her own: it was neither sweet nor serious, but resonated in the air as if it had passed through labyrinths and dark groves before seeing the light. A voice from the shadows but firmly clear. She was thinking about this, recognizing her voice, when from the distance came the sound of pealing bells, not from Santo Domingo but the Plaza Mayor. They must have been coming then from the Cathedral. And while the echo still floated a few moments, she thought how she herself was like those bells that without being seen could still be recognized by their voice. She thought that if there was something true, deep, certain about herself, it was her voice. Then she felt the need to hear it until she became lost within herself. She took a breath and let it circulate inside before letting it out. But she couldn't. A burst of laughter broke out on the other side of a row of cisterns that formed a separate space. She walked over and skirted around the obstacle. Before her eyes the girl from the Christ of the Good

Death was sobbing and two boys laughed and made fun of her.

"You're really scared?" said the blond kid Soledad had seen the other night upon the cornices of Santo Domingo whom everyone called in chorus Sope. But instead of answering, the girl began sobbing again.

"Well, if you can't decide, I'll help you," said Sope while he winked at his friend. "You'll see, you'll be filled with a desire that neither he nor I together could fulfill. What do you say?" he asked, trying to grab the girl's arm, but she wrenched it free with a brusque movement. Soledad saw then the sharp flash of a syringe.

"If I'm going to do it, I can do it by myself," she answered.

"Well, get going, idiot. What are you waiting for?" said the other boy, who had until then remained silent.

"Don't call me an idiot," the girl cut him off. "Even if you're my older brother, at least call me by my name."

"OK then, you little whore, make a decision, or besides being a slut are you a wimp, too?"

The girl took the syringe and turned in the direction of Soledad. She took a few steps while testing the needle, squirting a couple drops of liquid into the air. Then she rubbed her empty hand with the cloth of her pants until the veins beneath her skin turned blue. She brought the needle close but two tears that had yet decided to fall blurred her sight. Soledad ran through her memories and didn't stop until she came across the name with which the guy in the portals had referred to the girl. He had mentioned Clarín, that boy or girl with a defiant jaw, but he had also mentioned the name of the girl. Still, the memory didn't surface. Suddenly, a syllable came back to her that vibrated on the smoke from a locomotive: Ruth, that was the name. Then she went up to the girl and murmured it in her ear. To hear her name as if it were being said for the first time, her entire name, her own name, which belonged to her and nobody else, the girl felt like the tears were forming a watery mirror and in it was reflected her own image, a true image and not that dream she had been living until then. To see it for the first time and feel she could lose it forever...The syringe fell from her hands. The boys shrugged their shoulders as they watched her run off.

"But when you want it, we won't give it to you," exclaimed one of the boys while the girl fled down the steps. Her heart was beating so loudly she didn't hear him.

LXVII

The power of language was incredible. According to Matías it was enough for a madman like Flores Magón to toss into the air a few words like "liberty" and "dignity" for others no less feverish to dream of converting them into action. Matías used to say give me a man who dreams and I'll populate a thousand worlds. They were just words, volatile, pregnant with air, but with neither the burden nor flesh of reality; it was enough then for a man to take one by the tail and mount it in a dream for that Lazarus we all carry within ourselves to awake to real life…from another dream. At least that's what Matías thought had happened to words like "revolution," "brotherhood," "love," "democracy."

They talked about the events of '68 in Mexico. Soledad told him about Rosa and Miguel Blanco, and about the game they invented when the death of Miguel was a truth sharper than the bayonets stuck in him. Matías kept silent. They had just about come to the Ciudadela and the old man leaned upon his cane and the arm of Soledad. The Ciudadela had been an arms depot and military barracks on numerous occasions, but now it housed the Mexico City Library and the Design School. The girl recalled that it had been precisely there where Peter Nagy had exhibited his photography for the first time in Mexico. Just a few steps away, the Hungarian sorcerer—as Lucía used to call him—had taken Soledad by the hand and initiated her into that ritual of shadows which for others was known as love. It was only that now, turned into a shadow of herself, she could vaguely recognize a secret thread that stitched together this and that circumstance. She took a deep breath: whatever the case, the girl she had been and the girl she was now were no longer the same person.

A watchman noticed Matías leaning against one of the cannons in the little plaza and was about to go toss him out, but his partner stopped him.

"Let the old man be. He's blind and crazy. Don't you see how he wanders around talking to himself?" he said, and the other suspiciously walked up to Matías to see if he really was as mad as they said.

Soledad noticed the man hovering behind them, but Matías was talking and it was impossible to get him to start walking again.

"But if words can ignite the soul, man has also created the way to turn them into water. Do you know how, Soledad? With the game of equivocation…a game we play marvelously in this country. If the chief of police says 'white' in reality it's 'black,' if the newspapers announce the price of gas won't rise, the next day there will be new taxes on it…But tell me, Soledad, what can you expect of a city that calls one of its most important avenues 'Thiers'? You'll wonder why I mention a foreigner when in the nation's history there are plenty of examples, like right here in the Ciudadela. Well, because Thiers has to do with one of the most glorious moments in the vanguard of human history: the Paris Commune, when man looked himself in the face and recognized himself, when he discovered the glory of his misery and decided to launch an attack on the heavens, according to the words of Marx spoken by that admirable young writer Agustín Ramos. With all your studies you must know him."

Soledad, noticing the watchman was right near by looking at them, preferred not to answer. And she wondered why instead of the Paris Commune, Matías, with the great hearing he had, being blind, didn't perceive the other man's presence.

"You prefer not to answer. You know I enjoy talking, but it's far from me to teach you any lessons. You don't respond to that either. Ah, Soledad, at times so silent. If at some moment you get fed up with me or I make you uncomfortable, all you have to do is ask me to shut up. Well, I'll return then to my story and the city that calls one of its avenues 'Thiers,' which comes out onto Reforma, in homage to that general who in 1871 put down the Paris Commune by commanding the army to kill in cold blood more than twenty thousand men, women and children in scenes of unnamable suffering and cruelty. Many of the people passing down that street, whether walking or hurrying, those who have their luxurious houses on one side of the street or another, perhaps they don't know but Thiers, the general for whom that paved street in the Anzures neighborhood is named, was proud to have 'paved' the streets of Paris with the cadavers of *les misérables*. Isn't that a cruel irony?"

Soledad, who had been on guard while the watchman was keeping his eye on Matías, relaxed when she finally saw the guy head toward the main door of the old building. He walked up to his partner and said, "He might be old and blind, but he knows what he's talking about."

"That's Matías, one of the evangelists from Santo Domingo. He's really good at writing love letters and even helping sue for inheritances. They say he lost his sight from reading so much, especially at the San Agustín Library where he was a librarian for many years. People thought he was some kind of wise man when he came to take a place in the Portals of Santo Domingo with his typewriter and later when he went to live in a nearby hotel. They used to say his wife had abandoned him when he went blind, that his children turned their back on him…all kinds of stories, but what's certain is that after a few months now the old man is getting senile. He talks and talks with a ghost of a woman—some say it's his daughter who was killed accidentally by the police. You'll see."

Soledad looked at Matías with curiosity. Was it true what they said about the blind, that when some eyes close then others open? What did Matías know about her? Did he imagine her with flesh and bones or did he know her real state?

"Matías," she asked with a thin voice. "Do you know what I am, or rather what I'm not?"

"The only thing I know, my child, is that nobody exists until death comes. Then we recognize ourselves. All the moving about comes to an end and we rest," he said, taking her hand and gently patting it. "Don't get discouraged that every state of being is transitory. And what remains is the trace, that grace we touch and for which we're remembered or that touches us and through memory brings us back to life…As Don Quixote might have said, 'What do you think about that, Sancho? Are there enchantments that work against true bravery? The enchanters can well take away my happiness, but my strength and spirit, impossible.'"

The blind man shut up. A cold draft ruffled the part in his hair around his face and Soledad noticed for the first time the man was always impeccably shaved.

"The celestial troops always come to one's succor," he hurried to say as if reading Soledad's thoughts. "But let's get going. It must be past 3 a.m. On our way, if I haven't already bored you, I'll tell you the story of a hero who is in reality all heroes, the same way that the sea is in each grain of sand."

Gifts and countergifts
(or a brief parable of desires that bite their own tails)

Once upon a time there was a man whom the complacent gods let fulfill all his desires. As soon as he felt the fever of gold boiling in his veins, his fingers received the gift of turning to gold everything they touched. And so the man obtained a palace as shiny as a golden cage, a court of metallic servants who could no longer complete the tasks of the kingdom, a woman as golden as the sun but as cold as the moon, children turned into statues of youth as perfect as death, a meal as resplendent as only the immortals certainly used to have, their teeth harder than diamonds able to chew the golden apples of their dreams, an amber water curdled in an eternal anxiety of thirst…And the man was about to die the richest being on this earth, sad and alone due to his wish fulfilled, unable to eat or drink. Finally he formulated a new desire: he wanted to be immortal. Amused, the gods told him that he had to drink from the waters of a marvelous river. The man began his search. He passed through deserts, he leapt over abysses, he got lost on rough seas and discovered the most varied waters existing: waters to prevent baldness, waters to make one beautiful, waters to clear eyes that won't see, waters to quit the thirst of desire, waters to unplug a constipated bladder, waters so one never stops wishing, waters to scale the skin and fill it with *xiote* sauce…And of course the water of immortality.

It happened then that the man met a young woman of solar beauty: her face shone or sunk according to the movement of the sun. In order to contain her in those dark moments and conquer his numerous rivals, the man asked for a new desire: to play the silent music of the stars. What most moved the young woman when she heard the new suitor wasn't the solar happiness that blossomed in her soul despite the darkness of the night, but the effects it caused in other people: his rivals made way for him, the waters ceased to flow and the birds stopped in full flight to hear his music. Victorious, the man gave his beloved the most perfect wedding present: he asked the gods to choose for his future wife the most marvelous gift. A serpent finished the givers' generous act. The man then tried to take his life but his life no longer belonged to him: he was immortal, as long as he undertook the road in search of the fruits of mortality. He preferred to descend to the reign of the dead and move the watchmen with his music: he wanted his beloved to come back to life. Once again he was granted his desire: the shadow of his beloved would follow him toward the path of light as long as he didn't turn to look at her. In absolute darkness, unable to hear the footsteps of the young woman, there finally arrived the moment when the man could no longer resist and he cast a furtive gaze: the shadow of his beloved vanished, absolutely, like a shadow.

Burdened by this nightmare, the man still had the strength to ask for a new desire. The gods stopped smiling when they heard him ask for the gift of forgetfulness. Thus, with the successes of neither life nor death leaving a trace in him, he managed to make the gods forget about him, too.

("Matías," the young woman said while they waited at a stop light, "that subterranean world the man in your story descends reminds me of some tunnels beneath the Palace of Fine Arts. I saw them when I worked there but even today they seem a dream. Then the other day I followed the lost children and saw a door leading to a subterranean passage. Suddenly I thought maybe that tunnel connected with those others I'd walked through. Is it true there's a subterranean world below the city?"

"A straight oar looks curved beneath the water," replied the blind man as he started walking again. "As the old man of the mountain would say, it's not what the object is but how it's looked at. What would you say if I told you that what we're walking through now is a subterranean city, the hidden face of another city in the air that we can't see but only fleetingly discern? You could say I'm blind and talk so because I navigate through the darkness. But I'm not blinder or crazier than anybody else and I can assure you the city you walk through each day isn't my city or anyone else's. Your city is Soledad like mine can only be called Matías.")

LXVIII

Soledad and Matías were walking at dawn toward the hotel where the blind man lived when they ran into the lost children. They were pretending to be gargoyles on the statue of the Corregidora and were motionless, wearing ferocious faces. Seeing them like that reminded Soledad of the times when she was a little girl and played at disappearing with her father. After going through all the closets, beds and corners, her father would walk by without seeing her. Soledad would breathe slowly and keep as still as a porcelain doll. He'd wonder, "Where has my Sun gone and left the night so dark?" The doll would refuse to answer, her clay lips silent, true to her skill for being a statue. Javier García would make himself smaller, so small he was about to drown in one of his own tears, until Soledad moved, held out a hand and shouted with a smile, "Here I am!" And the world would once again make sense.

"Here they are!" said Matías a second before the children jumped atop him and crushed him with tickles and hugs. The old man let them and laughed while he pretended to threaten them with his cane.

"Little runts, do you think because I can't see I don't know you're about to ambush me? Don't you know the blind walk around with guardian angels at our sides? Isn't that right, Soledad?"

The girl kept silent. The blind man reached out in the air and took a few steps until he found her.

"Well, girl, cat got your tongue?"

But Soledad still didn't answer. Then the man, catching one of the kids playing around him, said to her, "But they're just kids, don't tell me they scare you. Come here, kids, let me introduce you to a friend. Her name is Soledad."

The kids looked at the blind man as if he were crazy while he pointed to a space in the air and they began to laugh. But surprisingly the boy with the defiant chin reached out a hand towards Soledad.

"We've met," he said as if it took effort to formulate a thought. After a pause he added, raising his hand to his chest in a gesture that indicated an intention to introduce himself, "Clarín…"

The children became silent and turned their gaze to where the other was talking and began saying their names: Rabbit, Guille, Charlie, Miguel…

But as Soledad had decided not to utter a word, they turned their faces toward Matías and Clarín.

"I suppose she has to trust you first," the old man said, filling the silence until the girl decided to talk. "Well, later…And you all aren't going to tell me that your ambush was nothing but a…By chance would you like me to tell you a story or a fable? But no…you kids don't like stories."

The children assaulted him again: they pulled on his coat sleeves, they put their hands on his neck and in his armpits and the man had to give in.

"OK, OK, I surrender. But first I have to gather myself."

One of the children took him by the arm and led him to the edge of the fountain to sit down while Clarín took out a bottle of some suspicious liquid from his loose pants where at least one more kid would have fit. He held it out to the blind man. Matías took off the cap and drank a couple sips. "Damn, that tastes like cough syrup," he said, giving it back. "Well, it seems we're finally ready. What story would you like? 'The Musicians Who Refused to Play for the Emperor,' 'The Most Beautiful Man-Made Things,' or 'The City of Impossible Desires'?"

Sitting around the blind man, the children didn't choose any of them. Matías began to explain, "Look, kids, the first is something our friend Thoreau would have described as a little story of civil disobedience. It took place very near here, not long ago, with the workers at the Palace of Fine Arts, and even though it seems the opposite of a fairy tale, it's not. The second is a story about bridges sung by a poet: above overflowing waters that drag along corpses, roofs and branches, two people meet, touch and recognize each other; it is and isn't a love story. And finally the third I like to tell myself when the city becomes a jail and a rat's nest and a labyrinth. What do you say? Have you decided?"

"'The City of Impossible Desires, please,'" asked Soledad and the children turned towards the place she had spoken from. Only the child named Clarín turned to Matías and insistently pulled on his jacket.

"Matías," he said, "tell us…"

Gifts and Countergifts 2
(Of Impossible Desires)

Mexico was a city as fervent as the desire that gave birth to it. This is recounted about its founding: the hunters of a tribe all had the same dream and the same thirst. They saw a woman sleeping in the waters of a lake. They dreamt they raped her and she, without awaking, responded to their violent caresses. They took her again and again but she didn't wake from the dream of water and in reality they didn't possess her. Upon arising, the hunters searched for that lake. They went on a pilgrimage from one place to another but they couldn't find any traces of the dream, and instead their thirst for the woman grew. One day, exhausted, they came to a valley surrounded by mountains and volcanoes. Then they saw her: a woman of water slept, reclining in the bed of the valley. The men ran to meet her, but when they thought they had her in their grasp their hands only touched the crystalline waters. They decided to remain there where a reflection had almost turned their dream into reality. While building the city each remembered the woman: her broad hips, the horizon of her face, her delicate eyelids, and as well the brutality of assaulting her, the violence of oppressing her. Thus tongues of land and mortar penetrated the water, sharpened boats tore through the recently formed canals, and palaces and gardens floated like perennial kisses. The hunters, in waters up to their waists, became fishermen. And with their nets dragged through the lake on nights of a full moon, they tried to catch that silvery woman who shone on the surface of the lake.

Today Mexico City is extinct like the desire that gave birth to it. From the force of trying to possess it, the fishermen and travelers, always thirsty, ended up drinking her. Today visitors stop atop the arid mountains that surround the desert. Only birds of prey, cacti and reptiles sit amidst its burning sands. Then the visitors flee: they discern the body of the woman of water that slept upon the valley floor and they discover a full and unexpected thirst, capable of drying out their souls.

LXIX

One day Soledad saw the blind man leaving the hotel where he lived. His hair was slicked back and despite the heat of the approaching midday, he wore a dark cape with a red lining, like a magician's. Instead of crossing over to the portals to sit at the desk where he earned his living, she saw him go straight ahead with his cane before him, heading towards the Zócalo. He walked along particularly happy for he stopped at each corner and shouted in a loud voice, "The galley goes before the wind." Time after time the phrase achieved its effect because people turned to look at him in surprise and helped him cross the street out of a feeling mixed of pity and respect.

It was the first time Soledad had followed the blind man among the daytime crowds and she was surprised to discover that far from being shut off, the world opened to the circling eye of the cane that went before him. And so crossing through the streets most packed with pedestrians and vendors, people made way so he could pass by. It was truly magical how the cape contributed to the blind man's obvious genteel dignity. Or it was simply a miracle, because how else could one explain the wonder that made Soledad recall Moses parting the waters of the Red Sea. She couldn't help smiling now that the galley Matías Torres majestically sailed down 20 de Noviembre and the street vendors greeted him while the women offered him flowers.

"Hey you old heretic, Matías, are you gong to celebrate the patron saint dressed like a magician?" asked in a fluty voice a man with long hair and no eyebrows selling lottery tickets.

"Like a witch but not bewitched. I mean, which team are you on," the blind old man answered slyly. The lottery vendor smiled at the parry and just let out a whistle that was shortly repeated by a man selling pastries twenty steps down and a young woman watching a stand of nylons and stockings on the next corner.

"Ay, Matías," she said, leaving her stand to help him cross the street, "why don't you write some poems for me? Look at the life of the fancy talker. You more and more loving and me working and working to buy a library for you and you alone…"

"Punish her, my Matías,' said a man selling umbrellas and windbreakers. "That's what women today are like. They offer you the

190

treasures of Solomon and then you have to go take care of them..."

"Shut up, you sore loser. Better you keep an eye on my stand and be left half-blind," said the woman as she took Matías by the arm and walked along a few more steps. "Are you going with the angel? You know, to the gates of Paradise."

"Bratty Lupita, don't joke around..."

"I'm not joking...I swear it's the truth. One has to have eyes to eat...I mean, no offense to those present. And so, are you going to the pealing of the bells?"

"Yes, Lupita, but afterwards I'm free and your wish is my command..."

"Of course. The working girls from the Merced already miss you guys. So...whatever you say."

"After the peal of the bells."

"OK, here we are. I have to go. If not I won't feel like working, but just sitting there to watch..."

The woman gave the blind man a peck on the cheek and then turned around so suddenly that Soledad didn't have time to avoid her. They crashed into each other and while Soledad starting looking again for the shadow of Matías, she lifted her eyes and saw it: the angel literally announcing a kingdom not of this world.

LXX

Immobile, its wings in repose, a white mime face and long hair knotted in a pony tail, the body poured into a sleeveless black leather suit and work boots, the angel had a statuary air, the eyes fixed on a lost point, the static muscles showing an eternity that only moments of happiness, death or photography can offer. Nothing to do with the traffic, uproar, movement of the avenue. Precisely for that reason, the people carried along by that hurried rhythm filled with car horns and shouting stopped a moment to contemplate him. And facing that sudden apparition they remained breathless and in their amazement persisted a reverential attitude towards this encounter that had something sacred about it. Some people renewed their step but turned to look while still going off on their way. Others waited there hopeful, sure of being near a miracle. Still others playfully went up to the angel, passing before it with the complicit and curious gaze of those who then knew themselves out of danger. Someone noticed the hat at the foot of the statue and seeing the coins and folded notes inside it, tossed in some change.

Then the angel began to awake. Its wings of silvery cardboard unfolded toward the heavens and its powerful body completely revived itself with delicate measured movements. For a few moments 20 de Noviembre remained silent, and the halted breath of its red streetlights stopped the pedestrians and cars in plain rapture, as if suddenly some deity had made himself present in that act of unknown beauty which barely lasted a few seconds, the time in which the angel pirouetted before spreading out its arms again and falling backward to reveal a naked glimpse of his perfect body, in that abandonment coming before death or ecstasy. Then it composed itself again, gathered in its wings, took a deep breath and letting out the air returned to its previous immobility. A magic halo remained among the people whose gaze came back to the street. Cars went through the green light that said, "Run for your lives." But for a moment, that moment between the angel's new stillness and the speed the avenue had again assumed, Soledad could have sworn people had seen up close a glimpse of paradise.

Matías waited a few moments until the angel became a man, let down its wings, picked up the hat and a rucksack resting to the side, and came up to him.

"Maestro Matías," the boy said to the blind man with a hug, hoisting the rucksack to his shoulders and banging it into Soledad. Matías tilted his head and then said, "I have my own wings, too…"

"A tail rather," the boy joked while he took Matías by the arm and led him back towards the Cathedral. The chatting and kidding around went on, now duplicated by the presence of the boy who carried wings and a bag on his shoulders like some kind of strange adventurer. Stopped at a light, he took out a washcloth and bottle of baby oil from his bag, poured a bit of the liquid on the cloth and wiped his face to remove the make-up.

"And how's life going, boy?" asked Matías before they started walking again.

"Kind of tough…I've just gone through hell. It was even a struggle to get out of my house. We've talked before about how the street feeds me, but I also feed the street. I have no bosses, my work is direct: I give to them and they give to me. We've talked about rites and payment. But that's not fulfilling. You know, at times people look at me and say, 'What an easy way to earn a living that bastard has.' And me, I fuck myself up for hours standing there with no other rest than changing position...I haven't been making much lately money and people look at me like I'm some dressed-up mannequin: they don't look at me closely nor do I transmit anything...It's sad and tremendously tiring."

Matías looked toward the boy. The disenchanted tone in his voice worried him.

"No, no...take it easy, maestro. I'm not doing so bad. I convinced myself to go on the hunt. Every time I didn't feel like coming to work I would take my wings and put them here in front of me like shields. Then I'd say to myself, 'Jorge, go hunt a mammoth for your family. To feed Helena and the little boy...' I'm not going to tell you it always worked. Sometimes I just preferred smoking a joint, but later I'd tell myself, 'No, Jorge, you're fooling yourself: people don't give anything to you because you're not trying.' A blockage of energy...Then I'd go back with the adherents of the Adoration. You know, prayer purifies. And people are once again responding. Yesterday a woman, an older lady, said a few words while I was acting. They came from within her, she spoke of forgiveness and grace, a complete voyage. And you know...everyone watching felt the old woman's words. No, master, a communion with wine and host until it sticks in your throat."

Matías couldn't see the boy's impetuous gestures, the silent force his body exhaled that made people look at him like some stranger, but he did perceive the emphasis in his voice, the heat of his physical presence in the confided familiarity, the slaps on the back and the frank embrace.

For that reason when Jorge touched his shoulder before crossing the Plaza de la Constitución, he also perceived the danger, his whetted feelings, that tension of the skin turned all muscle and instinct in face of a threat. And then he heard the whistle coming, the warning to make way passing through the air like an arrow that instead of falling grows until it covers several blocks.

Soledad didn't understand what was going on but as soon as that arrow continued extending itself, the vendors from the street stalls scurried toward the doors of the stores, or simply took down with a wonderful ability their foldable screens and canvas back-drops that they ingeniously tied cords around in such a way they were turned into big bags able to be carried on the back like any bundle. Suddenly on the avenue there were only pedestrians and street vendors without merchandise who walked along peering around corners. Something in the air weighed upon one person and another, a nervous sensation that undermines bodies and extends like an instantaneous electric liquid. Jorge and Matías remained expectantly and behind them Soledad peered at the horizon of autos without coming upon any trail. The threatening feeling was so strong that only by having the other two close by did she not run away.

"Here they come," she heard Jorge say, not taking her eyes from a truck with no license plates, armed with men hanging from the running boards who brazenly showed their menacing bare arms, the proud and shameless gesture of those aware of the incredible violent power they possess. They didn't pick anybody up but went down that avenue right near the Plaza de la Constitución, their sinister faces displaying the power acquired when repression and terror are instituted as means of social order and security. When they went by the corner where the boy and blind man stood, one of the men inside the truck—whom Soledad hadn't noticed despite the fierce gesture his teeth laid her bare with—motioned to the driver to stop. The men on the running boards thought it was time to jump into action but from inside the truck came the order, barely escap-ing from the two rows of teeth pressed together: "Quiet!" Soledad found his way of looking around was as obscene and shameless as the fierceness she had discovered in his teeth. She couldn't stop looking at the man. In any other situation she wouldn't have dared; it would have weighed upon her the worry of touching him with her gaze and he, thus recognized, would have shot her with that surging evil which passed through his eyes. Instead, to suppose the man couldn't see her made her feel invulnerable; she could scrutinize him without that decorum which lets us believe we can make others feel uncomfortable.

But the man must have felt those fingers of the gaze because he turned to look towards a point in the air behind the boy. It took Soledad a few seconds to realize he was looking at her. Then she started to shake: it was like running through the labyrinth believing the dragon was unaware of her presence and then discovering the dragon possessed eyes that could strip her with absolute perversity.

"Any problem?" Soledad heard Jorge's fearful voice ask the man in the truck. Beside him Matías kept silent while his hand closed tightly on the handle of his cane, ready to stick by his friend no matter what happened. The men hanging from the running boards remainned literally in suspense, their bodies half in the air, ready to attack.

The man in the truck slowly passed his gaze over the boy and blind man and then that point in the air which seemed unoccupied. When he brought his gaze back to Jorge, the boy holding it the whole time, the man rubbed with a finger one of those teeth in his vile face. "Let's go!" he suddenly ordered and the truck continued around the plaza.

"The bastards from the district council," said the boy as they started walking again. "They're hungrier than usual: they don't let people sell things in the street unless they get their bribe. They don't know what to do with me, because I'm not selling anything...They also want me to give them a cut, but they're crazy. They frighten others by taking away their goods, but what can they take from me? My work is done for the city. They don't know what to do with me."

The blind man kept silent. Leaning on the boy's arm he walked along confidently. It occurred to Soledad, who followed behind, that they made a curious couple with the cape flying behind Matías and the boy with cardboard wings on his shoulders. They finally arrived to the doors of the Cathedral. They crossed through the atrium but instead of heading to the main entrance walked to a little side door leading to the bell towers. The boy put his hands in an opening and agilely opened the lock. The door opened and they began to climb the stairs. Jorge went in front a couple steps so he could help the blind man up; when he offered him his hand, Matías stopped a moment to say, "Each one of us has to complete our own destiny: that's why we're here. But it's silly to risk too much. Remember Virgil's words, Jorge, don't trust the sea just because its surface is calm."

The boy smiled before answering, "Well, it seems rather elegant to call those sons of bitches 'the sea.'"

LXXI

They had finished climbing up and Matías was resting on the top step wiping the sweat from his forehead when a swarthy man with a meticulously trimmed moustache and friendly air came up to them.

"Matías, I didn't think you were coming," he said, helping the blind man up the last step and slapping the boy on the back. "I've reserved for you the Holy Angel, because I know that's the one you like."

"Thanks, Polo," said the boy, standing beneath a large bell facing west. "We'll make it sing like the angels…"

"Roar like the cannons," said Polo with the pride of a father talking about his children, "as this one was cast with the bronze from the cannons of Hernán Cortés. Did I tell you, Matías, the other day I was cleaning it and found the date it was cast? 1792, it looks like."

Soledad watched them move to one of the tower's balconies while Jorge slowly swung back and forth the cord attached to the clapper of the Holy Angel.

A troupe of children came into the belfry. Polo left Matías a moment to welcome them. Soledad recognized a couple of the kids but was surprised they were accompanied by two women wearing aprons and mischievous smiles who more than their mothers looked like older sisters. Finally the girl she had seen in the chapel at the church Christ of the Good Death came, followed closely by that boy with a defiant jawbone who was used to walking at the head of the lost children. Polo, who had sent the women to the eastern tower, looked a moment at the new arrivals.

"Ruth and Clarín," he said after thinking a few seconds, "to the other tower…"

The girl smiled and began walking towards the grand arch of the central nave, but the little boy named Clarín refused to go.

"No, Polo…I'm going with the men," he said as if rage prevented him from speaking.

"It's nothing, nothing…I'm going with the women, too," said the bellman in a stern tone. "I need help with Santa María de la Asunción, I can't do it alone. Go on, wait for me in the other tower."

But before he finished speaking, the boy had disappeared. Polo found him next to Matías and Jorge.

"And your friend?" he asked the blind man as the bell ringer came up to them.

"Soledad? I wanted to invite her but she hasn't been to see me...At times she disappears for days. It's too bad because she would have liked it. Would you believe me if I told you, Clarín, that she reminds me of a bell? You know, you don't have to see a bell to know it's there. Well, Polo, what time are we going to celebrate the patron saint?"

"As soon as the sacristy informs me, we'll begin the peal. I'll give you the signal," and then directing himself to Jorge, he suggested, "And you boy, why don't you get Guadalupe's clapper ready?"

"But don't you only ring that on special occasions?" replied the boy, who had the idea of ringing the Holy Angel.

"And you don't think that the feast day of our Lady of the Assumption, no less than the patron saint of the Cathedral, is enough? Go on, climb up the highest bell tower there. Besides, Matías is well taken care of here," he said winking at Clarín, "now that he has a strong arm to help him."

Just as Soledad heard the last words of the bell ringer she suddenly saw in the center of the tower a spiral staircase that led to the very top. She began to climb the wooden risers. As soon as she saw the flight of stairs, she perceived the secular trace of other souls that had gone up and worn away each of those steps, leaving in the polished impressions of so many ascents and descents vestiges of a pulsating and moving humanity. They were so human that one could feel their flesh groaning as soon brushing against them with each step. But it wasn't sorrow exhaled by those wooden muscles; there was a secret and exultant life for those who knew how to listen for it.

The steps so marked along the length of the centuries led towards the top and Soledad let herself be carried along as if she were penetrating into a mystery, enveloped in that spiral magic that suddenly seemed the destiny of man, and now her own destiny as well. She who had never boarded a boat now felt herself inside one that offered refuge while the menacing sea remained outside. She went up to the prow, the bridge, and from there she discerned the sea she so feared: that city tumultuous with life, a city-lake of concrete vegetation and fishes and frogs of volcanic stone that gently spread out beneath that radiant afternoon sun. She observed the horizon and it seemed she could touch with her hands the buildings before her, as if the air conferred upon her eyes the magic of a maddening closeness. She didn't know why but she thought about desires, that fascination that makes us believe that obtaining them would make us happier and more fulfilled…No, desires could seem near, pretend they were fulfilled or even in fact be realized, but inner ruin was inevitable, that emptiness after grabbing a star by the hand only to discover we are still left with our craving. What always remained was solitude, that feeling of irreparable loss no star or wish can completely satisfy. She knew this now and in some way had begun to accept it. Curious to think that she'd had to live her life exactly as she had done only to end up in that tower and recognize it. She went out onto a balcony. She looked at the panorama before her and understood a will distant from her own extended there beyond her thoughts. And in some way she felt she wasn't the owner of her desires but was inexplicably living her life so this thing which some call destiny could be fulfilled. Although the city unfolding around her wasn't infinite, to look and know it was there in all its tumult, ungraspable except for a few seconds, filled her completely. She recognized she was alone, but instead of scaring her, for the first time it comforted her. Amidst all that sea of uncertainty, an ocean that led her to withdraw into herself, she now held a certainty that was hers alone: her solitude.

Suddenly she heard the doors of the heavens open, countless angels creating in harmony the purest chimes that extended through the air with the force of their metal hearts. She lifted her gaze inside the tower and discovered an immense bell whose metal tongue Jorge rang with a rope. She looked at him a few moments, enraptured by that force flowering in such a resonant sound and followed by a chorus of metallic voices. She descended the spiral staircase and came across other enormous bells that danced giddily, pirouetting around themselves, put in motion by boys who gathered to push them and then carefully retreated, running in another kind of dance so that the weight of the bells upon their return wouldn't strike them. Each one in his place and the Cathedral converted into a giant ship taking off into the heights. Soledad felt an unspeakable emotion fill her throat and burst through her eyes brimming with tears. The sound of the bells penetrated her pores and invaded her with its purifying force. She could see Matías and Clarín pulling together on the rope of the bell Polo had called the Holy Angel. There was excitement in some faces, devotion in others, and in everyone a serene and exultant happiness that poured out in big drops of sweat and brilliant gazes, their eyes opened or closed in ecstasy. It was indescribable, a madness that erupted and dulled the hearing and the soul. A peal of immense bells, hand bells, smaller bells like those from a village church...And on the other side, in the eastern tower the bells were also singing. Soledad thought of Lucía: if she'd been there she would have hung from a bell in order to become one with the movement and the sound. On the other hand, she remained there crying, letting that limpid sound pass through her and feeling a growing lightness.

Down below people stopped to hear the peals. It was such an unusual occurrence that few could resist that call from above and they looked at the towers both perplexed and thankful for those few minutes of reconciliation and calm the city offered them with its habitual generosity. A few drivers stopped on the Zócalo and looked up. And while the call of those bells lasted, even the soldiers at the National Palace lost a little of their square shape, letting the balm of those sounds enrapture their souls and for a moment transport them to another place.

LXXII

A few weeks had gone by since the festival at the Cathedral. Soledad would go visit the bell ringers, contemplate the city, listen to Polo talk to the bells and clean off the soot, repair the clappers, call them by name: Assumption, Domingo de Guzmán, Guadalupe, the Three Hail Mary's. Each bell had its name and its history, its own voice and followers. Apart from the lauds and masses during the week, which the official bell ringer was in charge of, on Saturdays and Sundays multitudes of children came to the Cathedral and walked among the pigeons to touch the bells. There were those who pre-ferred Jesus of Nazareth because its clear voice raised the faces in the Plaza Mayor, seen clearly from the privileged balcony of the eastern tower. Others insisted that Polo let them ring the bell of the patron saint, Asunción, and when they couldn't they stood beneath its shadow and raised their arms to feel that prodigious vibration which remained seconds after its last sound.

There was one bell, in turn, that almost nobody wanted to touch. "The Castigated" the children called it, but Polo, who had tired of looking for its name on the bronze lip, ended up baptizing it as San Felipe Neri and frequently asked Jorge to make it speak.

"It was silent more than ten years. It's right for it to sing and speak, because if not it's going to fall ill," explained Polo as if Jorge were about to refuse.

"Sure," answered the young man. "We all know it's your favorite."

"What favorite? All my bells are equal to me."

"Don't get mad, Polo. I was just joking."

But that wasn't true. When everyone else had gone and he thought he was alone, the bell ringer reproached the Castigated.

"It's your fault. How did it ever occur to you to kill that little boy? If you didn't like him touching you then you should have told me. But to hit him as you swung around—not even if you were a feather. Poor little boy, we didn't even know his name."

Intrigued, Soledad later asked Matías about the event (she preferred just to look at the bell ringer Polo in silence, and not interrupt the man's idyll with his bells).

"Yes," answered the blind man while they sat at the base of the flag-staff in the Plaza Mayor. It was a luminous dawn, with a full and turgent moon pouring over the city's downtown, at those hours turned into a dreamlike stage. "The Castigated killed a boy in 1967. Now how do you know about that bell? Did Polo tell you? And since when did you meet him?"

His face reflected suspicion as he asked her, "You were there the day of the Feast of the Assumption, no?"

She mumbled an unintelligible response.

"OK, OK, no need for some big explanation. The Castigated has remained without its clapper since that occasion. The Green Cross brought the boy down and the little priests condemned the bell to ten years of silence."

"As if it were a person," murmured Soledad as she scrutinized the Cathedral's western tower, from where the Castigated silently looked on.

"They're more than people. Ask Polo who dreams about them and speaks more with them than he does to his own wife and

200

daughter…But that stuff about punishment is nothing new. Valle-Arizpe remarks that the bell which once adorned the central balcony of the National Palace not only was castigated with one hundred years of silence but condemned to exile by Carlos V. That's how it ended up here."

"One hundred years of silence? Well, what did it do?"

"It used to ring by itself, as if it were possessed by the devil. It would ring the fire alarm at dawn and people would wake up in a daze…It would ring another time and the mayor would send people to the firing squad…Finally it rung with final justice and men believed themselves dead…That's why they took its clapper and were going to send it to the Indies. Someone saw it forgotten in a corner of the palace and noticed its crown and the unequalled mastery of its workmanship. So as not to disobey the order they hung it above the main clock, but without its clapper. It remained there silently for centuries until Juárez ordered it melted down. But in the process the metal started rusting. As if the soul of the bell resisted the change in its body…"

"They should have sacrificed a girl to it at the moment of melting," murmured Soledad while she observed the central balcony at the National Palace.

"And how would you know?"

"My father used to tell me stories when I was a little girl. In one a young Oriental woman is thrown into the cauldron so the bell her father is casting by order of the emperor has a true voice and soul, after who knows how many attempts that increasingly compromise the life of the bell maker…The girl, who loves her father above all else, decides to cede her soul to the bell. No other bell in the kingdom had a purer voice or could be heard farther away."

A long silence enveloped the plaza and the moon shone among the clouds in a silvery splendor.

"Matías," Soledad finally asked, "do you really think I'm like a bell?"

The blind man sought out the girl's face. His fixed eyes softly looked at her before he responded. "Yes…but punished. Not by others but by yourself."

Soledad looked at the blind man with ire. How could he know so many things?

"You'll see," went on Matías. "You recognize people by their voice. You can put on rouge and wigs, change your clothes and face, but the voice emerges from within, through the make-up we've fabricated, those people we think we are, and it surfaces and delivers itself without us able to control it. If there's anything authentic in man it's his voice. And yours, Soledad, is resonant and sonorous no matter how hard you try to extinguish it."

Two tears fell down Soledad's face. Matías took her hands in his and said, "Cry...The ancients used to say weeping cleansed the soul and cleared the voice..."

Soledad cried in silence, swallowing her tears. Before she realized it—perhaps because she was crying or perhaps because the moon displayed a seductive brilliance, or because the tears were falling by themselves—they were suddenly surrounded by the lost children, this time accompanied by the boy who posed like an angel on 20 de Noviembre Avenue.

LXXIII

The first to notice them was Matías. "It seems we have some surprises today," he said before kissing Soledad's hands. Then he parted his hair falling over his forehead and settled into his improvised seat. The girl looked behind but still hesitated a moment: before them were the frozen statues of Clarín, Ruth, the other street children, a tall boy with wings who could only be Jorge. Soledad looked above them at the immense reflecting moon and then at the statues of soldiers who watched from the Palace cornices like ghostly gargoyles and she thought she was dreaming. Suddenly, as if hearing a secret music, the statues of the children and the angel began to move measuredly, smoothly. Arms and legs slipped through the air taking pleasure in their own suppleness. Hands sculpted ethereal faces, lips half opened, waiting to be kissed. Twirls, movements more and more vehement, like the fluttering of angels in flight. Matías jumped down from the pedestal and also began to move. His jerky movements were like those of a marionette: in his own way he too was dancing. And the moon continued rising. At one moment its light no longer fell obliquely over the plaza but poured directly in a somnambulant cascade over those bodies, each one dancing to its own delirium. Soledad observed how they then ceased to be bodies and turned into shadows of themselves, and although they brushed against each other, each shadow danced alone. She didn't have to think twice, but jumped down from the pedestal and began moving around, too, a timid flame whose edges fluttered in the night air.

The moon was still high when Jorge noticed a point on the ground that moved with the sinuousness of a rebellious little wind. Without stopping dancing, he observed how the point drew a shadowy face and for a moment thought he could make out the silhouette of a girl.

LXXIV

It seemed to Soledad that Jorge was following her. The boy walked around the Plaza Mayor after coming down from the bell tower and headed toward Madero Street. She hadn't seen him since the luminous night on which she and Matías were talking about the Castigated and suddenly Jorge and the street children had surrounded them. Now it was midnight with a waning moon and the boy walked distractedly along, wandering back and forth as if he were looking upon the ground for some lost object. After stopping to think for a moment, he crossed through the Mercaderes Portals and continued down the same avenue Soledad had taken. The loud music of a recently opened discotheque filled the way. Soledad crossed the street to avoid the crowd of young people pushing and shoving to get in. Jorge on the other hand scurried between them without paying attention to the women who turned to look at him. Perhaps because of his confident gate, his masculine traits and unquestionable grace, or that natural air that granted him the right to be among others, what's certain is that although he wasn't wearing his angel garb, people still made way and followed him with their gaze.

Soledad stopped on the corner of Profesa Street to see where the boy was heading. Hesitating a moment, he crossed Isabel la Católica and began walking directly towards Soledad. She gave a start and pressed herself again the fence guarding the Jesuit church. She waited for the boy to go by and then she followed. The few pedestrians—street sweepers, taxi drivers, indigents, a few daring tourists—let her trail at a distance without losing him. She was amused to find their roles reversed: it was she now who followed his steps in order to discover—she suddenly realized—the "secret life of an angel." Passing before the church San Felipe de Jesús the boy stopped. He went up the steps to a side entrance and knocked on the door. Soledad hurried across the street. As soon as the handle turned a voice said, "Adored shall be the Most Holy Sacrament…"

"Forever and ever," responded the boy. Then opening his shirt, he displayed a kind of medal that Soledad thought she had seen before. Before kissing it, he muttered, "Your yoke is soft, Lord, and your burden light. Give me your grace so that I may carry it with dignity."

The door opened for Jorge. But just as she was about to steal in appeared a face Soledad immediately recognized: that of Pascual, the man she had talked to at the church of Santo Domingo and whom she had met before on Reforma. As if talking to himself, he murmured, "No, Francisca, you can't come in. This is a vigil for men. Nothing promiscuous, no place for evil passions."

Soledad steeped back in consternation. How could that man divine her in the middle of his own madness?

Still amazed, she headed toward Reforma. She hadn't been to visit General Valle for days.

LXXV

She knew him to be alone and unsheltered, mad and nostalgic, and she smiled to think that more and more there was less distance between the general and her. They would discuss the past city and the present, Soledad learned about the art of carrying a carbine, the usefulness of riot police on foot and on horse, about huntsmen and riflemen, walking scouts and mounted scouts, sappers, artillery, lancers. In turn the girl read to him books that she easily snuck out from the San Agustín Library, whose librarian, a friend of Don Matías, confided to the blind man the sudden disappearance of volumes of history that couldn't be explained as simple theft. There was a particular interest in books from the nineteenth century, especially biographies of Maximilian and Miramón.

Matías laughed at his friend Beristáin, a real library rat who knew forward and back its holdings, and told him that as long as people were stealing books there was redemption for the world.

Soledad, ignorant of these discussions, went night after night to San Agustín looking for those books that could give General Valle some peace about the destiny awaiting him. But despite all she searched, flashlight in hand, she found only lithographs and oil paintings that recreated the scene of Maximilian's execution in the Mountain of the Bells, facing the firing squad head on, and as always he was accompanied by the Indian Tomás Mejía and Leandro Valle's intimate friend Miguel Miramón. One dawn she discovered that the painter had carefully executed the face of Miramón and in contrast to most of the paintings which depicted this scene, the artist had even captured the profiles of the soldiers and prisoners who found themselves part of a useless and hopeless encounter, clearly seen in the desolate face of Miguel Miramón who has just turned toward the artist. From there the friend of General Valle looked at the future centuries with the infinite gesture of someone who realizes he is lost in a circle of betrayal. Soledad almost jumped for joy: she hadn't discovered that General Miramón died shot in the back; rather the face in that painting revealed his guilt as a traitor. She decided to show it to her friend Valle.

She climbed upon the pedestal of the statue on Reforma and put an arm around the monument while placing the book before his eyes. There on the sepia pages Leandro Valle recognized his friend aged in years but still faithful to the memory he guarded, when they had bet on a return match for a cock fight "in the hereafter." Nevertheless, after almost revealing a smile, the statue's face fell into shadow, as if layers of stone suddenly covered it. Soledad hurried to say, "But, General Valle, look at Miramón's guilty face. It's the face of someone who knows he's guilty of treason."

The statue began to trill an interlude, "Pica, pica, pica, parakeeta..." Soledad looked at him in confusion and the general felt obliged to answer.

"That face you trust so much is nothing more than the painter's fantasy. Miguel never would have shown himself guilty even if he was. We had different, even opposing, ideals, but the man who acts without deviating from himself can't be accused of treason and disloyalty...I was neither one nor the other, but God—or the

Malignant One, which I believe can offer the same payback—ordained that it should be I who was sentenced to death as a traitor. But that's not my trouble or burden. Treason or loyalty: the coin spins rapidly and inexorably; the hand can be as virtuous and able as slight-of-hand, the right and left can be inverted and interchanged. I had guarded the hope despite stories to the contrary that if Miguel had been killed in the back, the ill fortune of fright and anxiety that pursues some men, he and I could meet again at the end of time."

So close to the general's childish face with her own she could almost hear him breathe, Soledad felt the man's body trembling.

"I imagined so, but I refused to believe it," she heard him murmur.

"General Valle, I don't know what to say. Perhaps I shouldn't have shown you any of this."

The man went back to his little song, "Pica, pica, pica, parakeeta..." The girl understood the general didn't want to talk any more, so she closed the book and started to climb down.

"Wait...How does it go? I almost can't remember, 'Pica, pica, pica parakeeta, pica, pica, pica, the rose...' Damn! Why are the gusts of forgetfulness so willful? Was it parakeeta or parakeeto? If I could at least forget what I don't forget..."

"General, don't despair." Soledad hesitated a moment. "Do you want me to find you a songbook from your time? Certainly that song might be in one..."

"No." The man remained silent a few moments, passing through labyrinths of the past, as if looking for a lost memory. Suddenly he seemed to find it and said, "You smell quite like Señorita Laura Jáuregui...Vanilla with gardenias. Excuse me, Soledad, it's been ages since I've had a woman so near."

Soledad stayed another few minutes beside the man. At those points where her fingertips pressed upon the general's shoulder, or all that long proximity where her leg coincided with his flank, she perceived a torrent of living, titillating energy. The man finally said, "That's enough...Too much compassion is a stain on decorum."

Soledad jumped to the ground and took a moment to compose herself. She looked at the sun rising between the buildings behind the general. Then she added, "No, general, it wasn't compassion. It's also been ages since I've been near a man.."

The general cleared his throat, apparently uncomfortable. But it seemed to Soledad his eyes smiled when on that occasion they said goodbye.

LXXVI

One of her favorite pastimes was to watch Jorge work. It didn't matter if it was during the day nor what he was doing on such as a noisy avenue like 20 de Noviembre. She slipped behind some passerby going in the right direction and so, in their shadow, she cut the distance separating her from the angel. She could contemplate him for hours, as long as he remained static until he received a donation for his art. And she saw him act, move his wings to lift himself into flight, to glide like the open sky surrounding him, and a sort of state of grace radiated from his luminous skin; then the fall, that abandon lifting his jacket and revealing his perfect torso and his downy face lowered toward his abdomen. Soledad didn't tire of admiring him and discerning those glorious moments of being all eyes, of drinking in each of his movements, of touching him with her gaze in openmouthed caresses. And then that almost sorrowful whirlwind she felt churning in her belly, which made her know herself with a thirst that in such a state of want filled her completely.

At times the angel pronounced words, gifts to be touched with the ears, to suspend understanding in a bubble and, in the confusion thus created, encounter an unforeseen and momentarily full meaning. He would say, for example, "skyrocket of a thousand lights, my heart among the clouds," and people would stop to look at his chest and contemplate the sky as if those words were literal. But not only that, people also responded: an old woman, a bike messenger, a girl just out of secretary school thanked him from amidst the crowd, they pressed their hands against his wings, they kissed him.

One day as Soledad stood there on the sidewalk before him and contemplated the boy amidst the incessant traffic of cars and trucks, she observed how the angel waved his hand in the air as if signaling someone. It was so sudden that without understanding what she'd done she raised her own hand and returned the greeting. Jorge returned to his act but Soledad couldn't believe he had seen her. Anyways, she waited for the boy to finish working before going up to him. Then, fearful but above all moved because the boy had perhaps recognized her, she whispered in his ear, "You could see me, right?"

Jorge nodded. He had sat down in the middle of the avenue and Soledad knelt beside him. She watched him take out a bottle of oil to clean off the white-face that gave his face the immobility of a mask. Soledad still couldn't believe what that simple affirmative gesture revealed and so she insisted with a voice full of emotion, "So...when you raised your hand you were really waving to me, isn't that the truth?"

Jorge nodded again. He took off his boots and put them in the rucksack, from which he took out a pair of gray tennis shoes that he put on.

"But now you can't see me..."

The boy shook his head no while he finished tying the shoe-laces.

"Then how did you know I was here?"

Jorge turned his head towards Soledad and answered, "I don't know. I just saw you."

Soledad noticed how a black tear, one of those that Jorge painted on with an eyeliner to look like a *commedia del arte* harlequin, had stayed intact. She had the urge to touch it. She stretched out her hand but stopped just a millimeter from Jorge's skin.

The boy closed his eyes as if he were remembering something or perhaps waiting for the caress. Then he went on.

"Suddenly I saw you. Nobody had given me a cent all morning and I didn't think I could keep still much longer. Then I thought of the air, I let myself fall into the air. I relaxed my body. I was myself air...I was floating. That's when I saw you...It's like how now my eyes are shut and I feel your hand just about to touch me. Why don't you?"

Soledad felt like she'd been discovered and pulled back her arm. But Jorge perceived the movement and managed to stop it.

"I knew you were real," he said in a triumphal tone.

An electric current, a brilliant discharge that nevertheless didn't cease, as if her hands possessed their own lives and had been turned into fountains of light. Her body was like a house and that house, which had been dark before, was illuminated from within. And along with the light, a kind of happiness was invading the rooms and corners, becoming more and more intense. They went up to the Cathedral's bell towers, Soledad not taking her hand from the boy's, Jorge holding onto the air. They went up, challenging all gravity, and their happiness ascended, too, making them lighter. They didn't see Polo, who must have been in the storeroom of the western tower.

When they were face to face, Jorge brought Soledad's hand to his chest and closed his eyes again. They didn't say a single word, their lips spoke a language of skin and instinct, and I have no more ink to write these lines.

It was almost three in the afternoon. Jorge asked her to come ring the Holy Angel with him. Soledad let herself be led along but when Polo let them have the rope of the bell facing 5 de Mayo, she felt afraid and tried to free herself from the boy. He wouldn't let go and with her hands between his own he began to make the clapper move. The spiral of sound broke forth and extended through them as if their own bodies were bells. Soledad didn't think twice when Jorge, impelled by the last peal of the bells, told her, "Make a wish."

Her heart beat feverishly and an agitation that almost took her breath away didn't keep her from obeying. She made her wish. She discovered that, with the last metallic vibration, a tickling happiness incarnated her once again.

LXXVII

> I touched his hand, his five fingers, I touched his chest and his shoulders, his belly and his sex. I touched. I also touched his ass, his legs, his ankles, each toe on his feet. I touched each pore, each hair, each wrinkle and, thus, I touched the center of my own being. I shone. The earth and the bell towers vibrated. A force began to awake. It was the dragon from the labyrinth. I mounted it, the watery scales foam beneath my flanks. I embraced its broad, powerful loins and we sunk into the sky. Only by touching, touching me.
>
> (A knot was untied. It seemed impossible with that sea breaking upon me like one wave within another. And to feel that

everything was due to three simple words born in that exact spot where the body in deep shadow needed thought to clarify and recognize itself. But the most important thing was to say them, watch them tremble, thirsty doves, outside myself: "I desire you," I said and the heat of a flame radiated through all my pores. It was a plenitude coming from within, lavished like a gift or grace. "I desire you," I repeated, unable to believe I'd dared say it. Skin and body unleashed themselves and no longer obeyed me. I turned into a letter that was cracking, a sign finally finding its meaning.)

LXXVIII

Soledad couldn't contain herself, so as soon as the streets cleared she went to meet General Valle about Jorge. She didn't go into details but spoke enthusiastically about his job as a living statue that earned him a living by stopping traffic with his silvery cardboard wings. General Valle, who more and more showed a reticence towards history and instead wanted her to read him Dante's *Divine Comedy*, asking time and again she recite the "Inferno" cantos, seemed to emerge from his dream when he heard Soledad saying the boy was challenging him to a duel of statues. At first it seemed absurd, but then the proposal began to amuse her.

Soledad was so happy that she forgot about the episode of the painting of Miguel Miramón. She looked at the statue of General Valle, she looked at herself and her ardent heart, and she longed for life to stop indefinitely.

"Soledad, perhaps you could tell me," the man on the pedestal began to say without looking at the girl. "I've learned there is a street bearing my name..."

"I know it," answered the girl and without thinking, as if cast under a spell, she went on, "It's an absurd street, nauseating, people buy and use drugs there...lost children (but also those that are found and that are hiding), child prostitutes. Clarín and the others live there on a rooftop. That's where Matías goes walking. There's a boy I've only seen a couple times that people say terrible things about. He also lives on Leandro Valle. Matías told me he's the nephew of the legendary Sope, a killer, drug dealer, rapist, and bandit with connections who was given an ultimatum by an enemy gang. Well, to say ultimatum is a bit vague: according to Matías he was wounded in his family jewels and although he survived, he begged his mother to shoot him.

"The other Sope, the nephew, has proved himself the worthy heir of his renowned uncle. Ever since being a kid he's bossed around other children even bigger than him, he's dealt drugs and robbed stores and houses, and once assaulted a police station. Yeah, he also lives on Leandro Valle."

For a long while Soledad and the general remained silent. A light wind stirred the tree canopies. Soledad felt cold but not guilty when the man searched out her gaze and added with determination, "OK, the time has come. I accept the duel your friend proposes." As he certainly must have used to sink a sword into a man's chest, cleanly, with certitude, even more to help him die well.

LXXIX

They made an appointment for the day of Saint Cirenia the Martyr. For not being a religious man, General Valle knew the book of the saints days forward and back, as if punished in some corner of his life he had undertaken to learn useless things from the almanac with the clear objective of killing time. For that reason he could confirm, "Next Friday, which happens to be All Saints' Day, we will hold our duel." The girl, in turn, seemed to remember her own name. "That's true," she said with her distant gaze looking towards Chapultepec Castle, "we're at the end of October. How time passes. I'd forgotten it was my saint's day. At first papa didn't like to call me Soledad. He used to say that wasn't the name for a girl. So we invented Lucía, a lucent being whose tail was bit and so cried out…But all that time I came to believe my name belonged to no one but me." Perhaps that's why, because someone had reminded her of her past and a kind of bewilderment had overpowered her, perhaps for that reason Soledad climbed up onto the pedestal and kissed the general goodbye. She jumped down and took off submerged in her thoughts, not noticing that the man on the pedestal was left ruminating over his own.

But Jorge didn't dress up as an angel for the duel. As soon as Soledad told him the date of the challenge he ran over to the Matamoros market on Lagunilla Street to look for the appropriate garb. He finally found an old jacket that looked like a frockcoat, pantaloons, and some high riding boots. He also found a sword to hang from his belt and a wide-brimmed hat. The day of the duel he wore that clothing but didn't put on his make-up because he preferred to have a clean face and his hair pulled back. When Soledad saw him—they had made a date to meet at the entrance to the Cathedral at midnight—she was astonished by how fine he looked in his attire. The few people they went by on their way down Reforma looked at the boy with respect. Moreover there was no lack of crazy people who not content with ceding their way to him, bowed ceremoniously as if a noble were passing by. They went on and walking past San Felipe de Jesús, exactly in the spot corresponding to the main altar, Jorge made an intempestive genuflection.

"It's that the Most Holy is displayed," he added when they started walking again. Then Soledad got up the courage to ask, "You're one of those who pray at night, no?"

"Yes...there comes a moment in which believing becomes a necessity. Then you can think your life is miserable, your cat is immortal, the day you own something you will achieve happiness. I've been an adherent of the Adoration for two years...I came looking for a place to sleep because the days you're part of the vigil they give you a bed to rest in between prayers. I thought I was fooling them but it didn't take long for me to realize I was the one tricked—they knew what was going on and let me be. To see them speak, bend forward, pray seemed to me there were no more deluded people in the world. Look, believing that thanks to their prayers the city conquers the darkness each night and is resuscitated at dawn...Seriously, Soledad, there are people in the Adoration that believe that and pray to wash away with their nocturnal vigils the grievances that the world, the press, television commit every day against our Lord God. At first I had to hold it in so I wouldn't burst out laughing in front of them. Besides there were all sorts of personalities, crazy people who spoke to themselves, drunks like myself looking for a soft corner to fall in for the night, those with a bitter look on their face...but as well those who lived in a state of permanent grace, despite the poverty of their clothes or their grime, their sweat or their piss. And I saw them and truth be told I felt superior. But one thing about me, I'm as stubborn as a badger. And I saw that some persisted and that after praying and believing they had saved the world they greeted dawn transfixed. Without realizing it I began to envy them. One day I woke up completely miserable—my child was sick, people on 20 de Noviembre had been giving me almost nothing, I was fighting every day with Helena—and I came to the church. I came to the vigil just for the sake of coming. For the first time I didn't feel myself better than them. In their misery I recognized my own misery and I felt so close that I could hate them and love them like myself. It was as if the doors to heaven had opened for me. I wasn't alone."

Soledad listened to Jorge as they approached Reforma and she couldn't help but look at him with a sense of admiration mixed with mistrust. Was he talking seriously? Could someone who believed himself in his right mind still believe in God nowadays? Obviously there were the armies of Guadalupean worshipers ready to defend their faith like only a Christian, Arab and Aztec joined together could do, but they were almost a case apart, converts to the Lord who needed a pastor to help them put their lives in order, who would let them everyday see in that face in the mirror not those dark forces that return to us in dreams or dictate our deepest appetites, but let them place outside themselves—the devil is always in others—all that we fear about ourselves. When had Soledad stopped believing in the God of Christianity? She had inherited her Catholicism like those empty ritualistic customs that accompany most of the Mexican middle class, however divided or non-existent it seems to be. Lacking a true "inner Christianity," her religious faith was barely enough to celebrate a first communion whose precepts took longer to memorize than to be forgotten in an instant. As a teenager, she finally began to believe that thinking people were doubters. There were also several sacrilegious readings to experience: Nietzsche and Hesse, Villaurrutia and Paz. At last God descended from his throne to hide in the basement of rusty, useless objects.

Meanwhile they'd reached Reforma. As soon as they approached the statue, Soledad proceeded to the introductions.

"General Valle, this is your challenger," she said, pointing to Jorge, who hearing the girl's voice took off his hat and bowed to the monument.

"Pleased to meet you," mumbled the young man.

"The pleasure is all mine," added the man on the pedestal, but Jorge couldn't hear him. Then Soledad intervened: "He says he's also pleased to meet you."

"Ah…I thought I'd be able to hear him. Request, then, that we discuss the details of the duel."

"Let's not speak of minutia or wait any longer: until one is vanquished…or one triumphs, either of which demonstrates both our worthiness. Onward…" responded Valle as if he were haranguing the masses. Soledad looked for a moment at the general's boyish face. It seemed to exude an extraordinary calm and she explained everything to Jorge.

"Shall there be no time limit? But listen, Don Leandro del Valle and the mountain ranges that accompany you," Jorge leaned back lazily, "I do get tired. I pretend to be a statue but I'm not…"

"Go on, Jorge, we'll finalize the details later," interrupted the girl.

"OK, OK, you both win," he said and crossed the avenue to stand next to the silent statue of Don Ignacio Ramírez. He took a deep breath and became perfectly still.

Not even an hour had passed when Soledad shouted she was coming over to see him.

"Is it finally over?"

Instead of answering him, Sol held out the saber.

"Take it. It belongs to you."

"But did you take it from him? Or can he no longer hear you? As they say, did you profane his statue?"

"No, no. It wasn't me. It was him. General Valle himself dropped the sword."

"But then did he win?"

"I suppose so."

"He tricked me."

"I suppose so, too."

"Well, I beat myself by going around challenging real statues."

Jorge held out a hand in the air hoping the girl would take it. But she was too busy observing the statue, as if she were resisting believing what had happened.

"I wanted him to go away but now that he has I can't believe it and wish he'd come back," she finally said.

"Yes, but you can't turn the page back on desires …"

Soledad looked at the boy, who kept his hands in the pockets of his frockcoat. She went up and touched his lips.

"You know," she said to him playfully, "I always wanted a guardian angel, even if he suddenly disguised himself as a…" She paused while looking him over from head to toe, "…or tried to disguise himself as an insurgent or a partisan. And you, what did you want?"

"No, all that stuff about desire is no good…I only take," and he held out both hands to embrace Soledad's hips, "what I have in my hands."

"But to anyone looking you're just touching air."

"You think so?" he asked, beginning to kiss her.

"No, Jorge, here no…"

"But you said he's already gone away," the boy said, gesturing towards General Valle.

"Still, let's get going."

LXXX

From the cathedral's eastern tower the city seemed immersed in a swarm of silence. Dawn spread longingly, endlessly, in that motionless time of dream or desperation. Soledad let out a long yawn and the panorama filled with watery threads. A while earlier Jorge had gone home. For her part, she lay down and stretched out after the duel of the statues. She wished for a real bed to lie in but the big department stores had recently inaugurated a security system whose alarms, once activated, didn't stop ringing until a special team of guards arrived to turn them off. She would have go back to the Recinto Juárez in the National Palace that conserved, among other furniture, the bed that Benemérito had used during his intermittent stays in Mexico City, when the National Palace was the presidential residence. She rested well in that austere brass bed; its mattress—of course much newer than the rest of the furniture— was comfortable despite more than one soldier having slept on it before Soledad. Accustomed as they were to thinking the Palace a kind of doll's house only used for official ceremonies ever since President Cárdenas had moved his residency to that hill in Chapultepec known as Los Pinos, the lieutenant in charge of those

Marian patios could risk taking a little nap and dream of other glories less heroic and more terrestrial: the next drinking game that General Orozco had challenged him to, a few enchiladas at La Poblana, a restaurant behind the Palace, a tumble with the whores on Circunvalación so his equipment wouldn't break down from lack of use...

It wasn't hard to keep the lieutenants and his subordinates from lying down in the bed of President Juárez: a few words, a couple elbows, some hairpulling were enough for the rumor to spread that the wife herself of the Indian president had come to visit her former abode. Soledad smiled at such murmuring and slept peacefully, happy because she'd ended up with what she wanted. Only more recently she'd opted to sleep in other beds, for there were now so many rumors about ghosts running through the Palace at midnight that she was scared she'd run into one of them.

But now she had no other recourse and so strode toward Moneda Street. She banged on the door with the iron knocker until a sleepy soldier stuck his nose out. Not finding anybody the boy closed the door, but she knocked even louder. The soldier grabbed his machine gun and took a few steps out. Soledad crossed over the threshold while the young man looked around in astonishment at the empty street. She went up the staircase towards the room. On a landing she came across a couple soldiers smoking a joint. She was going to keep going when one of them said, "A few kids have disappeared as if by magic. Maybe 'cause they're hungrier than hunger and as skinny and scurvy as shadows. But their grace time ran out. They say they got trapped in those tunnels the commissioner ordered closed the other day when he wanted to take a shortcut to Los Pinos for an appointment with the Prez. You know what they say, Lieutenant: there's another city beneath this one and that's why, despite any traffic or demonstrations, the Prez always gets to events on time."

"Yeah, I've heard that. The other day one of my boys showed me an entrance but the truth is it was really dark, it smelled like hell, and not even if I was Superman or Batman am I going to sniff around where I ain't been ordered."

"I say the same. Bravery for those assholes who want to die young. I've never wanted to be a hero and that's why I'm going to live to be an old man. But the commissioner was in a hurry, you know how life is for cabinet members, and there goes my buddy Epigmenio, his driver, stepping on the accelerator and making that truck twist and turn like a little whore. They come to the alley at Santo Tomás—the current commissioner only likes to look and there's fresh meat everywhere on that street. In the end, they're stuck in traffic and can't reach Fray Servando. Then Poncho, one of his bodyguards who knows downtown inside and out, told them about a subterranean shortcut."

"Poncho? Didn't they fire him last year for causing some scandal around Christmas?" asked the lieutenant.

"No, that was Poncho Rodríguez. I'm talking about Poncho Ramírez, Four Fingers. You know who I'm talking about?"

The lieutenant nodded, not quite remembering.

"So he told them about the shortcut. The commissioner was so nervous about being late he wanted to try it and so he orders my friend Epigmenio to go in where Poncho told them, that road work on Roldán or Santísima Street, wherever it is. In any case they went to a warehouse parking garage and then moved some barricades out of the way and went down a passage black as the mouth of a wolf with only their headlights to guide them. My friend said they were shitting in their pants but nobody was giving up. They finally came to an intersection they only discovered because from far off they could see a light coming from above, from a sewer grate or ventilation duct. Poncho gets out of the car to check their direction, to see if they were going toward the Hill of the Star or Churubusco. My friend Epigmenio says Poncho didn't take more than a few steps before he was lost from sight. They sat their quiet. My friend could hear water flowing nearby. 'What's that asshole looking for if he doesn't know where we are?' the commissioner finally said. 'Poncho...come back you bastard!' shouted the other bodyguard sticking his head out of the truck. He shouldn't have done that. The echo bounced from tunnel to tunnel without stopping. Then my friend felt like they were being looked at."

"Looked at? Who by?"

"He didn't even start searching. You don't know him but when my friend suddenly gets cold, his legs start to shake and so he didn't want the commissioner to notice. But the commissioner must have felt something too or being in a hurry made him anxious because suddenly, not waiting for Poncho to come back, he ordered, 'Let's go, bastard, put it in reverse. Where did you ever come up with taking me down some fucking shortcut, fucking Epigmenio. Tomorrow I'm closing this rat hole.'"

"And the other idiot, Poncho, they left him down there?"

"He came out hours later all scratched and dirty. It could have been worse. But why say anything if you don't know what you're talking about? He finally came out, though. What really seems stuck in there are those kids because the next day they put planks over the entrances throughout the whole neighborhood. And nobody would have known if it hadn't been for one of their sisters, that girl that screws Sope and all the other guys who come in her face. They say she's a nymphomaniac, but where I come from we got another name for that."

The men burst out laughing. Then the lieutenant took a deep drag off the joint they'd almost finished, burning his fingertips.

Soledad felt a chill. No doubt the man was talking about Clarín and the other children. It had been days since she had seen any of them around. She got tremendously cold and a sudden deep shadow overwhelmed her eyes, as if a whirlwind strained within her, threatening to shut off the lights.

She pulled herself together. The men still leaned against the balustrade, smoking another joint. She ran out of the Palace all the way to the Plaza de Santo Domingo. She was going to look for the blind man at the Hotel Río de Janeiro, waking him if necessary. But Matías was sitting in front of the statue of the Corregidora and Marbles rested at his side.

"Soledad…are you there?" he asked the air.

The old man held his hands atop his cane and smiled. Marbles approached the girl and began to lick her hands; Soledad pushed the dog away and confronted the blind man.

"And the children? Why didn't you tell me anything?"

"Ah…you've heard about that," he said, still smiling with a grin that Soledad found insupportable.

"Matías, how could you?'

"As the great Goethe used to say, 'All your ideals haven't separated me from the true being, that is, the nature of good and evil.' I persevere through the shadows but I don't always find the light…"

Soledad was speechless. What had happened to Matías? Had sorrow by some chance utterly driven him mad?

"Come, girl. Sit down. Don't trust appearances. I've had a few drinks. Were you asking about Clarín and the other children? They're fine. All of them. No, Marbles?"

The dog wagged its tail and stretched out again at the foot of the old man. Soledad hesitated a moment but then sat down beside him.

"But…they weren't trapped in the tunnel?"

"Yes…but not for long. Those kids have perseverance. Marvels of living in a state of permanent alert. The thing is they searched for an exit and found what they think is paradise: a warehouse in the Merced full of sacks of pistachios, hazel nuts, gum, cases of rum. They threw themselves a party and when they had enough all they had to do was wait for the market to get bustling in the early morning hours. Then they scurried through the gate left half open by the deliverymen. That simple."

"So they're OK. But why did Ruth go complain at Fine Arts?"

"Ruth made a complaint? I don't understand." The blind man remained pensive a few moments. He finally replied, "Wait, wait: the other day I recounted to them the myth of Pegasus. They loved the story. Clarín said he knew one about the fountain in the Palace. Yes, I remember that Ruth wanted to go up there but the kids didn't want to take her. Because the head of the guards won't let her enter…"

"But he does the kids?"

"Not them either, but they're more clever. You've already met them. What I never would've imagined is the girl wanting to see the Pegasus so much. I only hope she didn't mention anything else."

"Else? There's more?"

"There's always more. But day is starting to break. Let's take advantage of that to get a little sleep. We only came to dream, said the poet. That reminds me—it's the Day of the Dead at the Cathedral. Are you ready for the carnival? Ah, because it is a carnival. You'll see," and he stayed silent as if amidst the darkness he was watching a movie of memories seen several times. After a few minutes, his chin dropped to his chest and he began snoring.

Soledad sat looking at the sky. A rosy brilliance behind her announced the dawn. She remembered her friend Rosa Bianco, that gentle, capricious little girl with whom she made fun of the

Ángeles sisters. Then had come the death of her brother, Lieuteneant Pucheros of the Freedom Fighters, and Rosa went off with her mother to the village where the bells sang, Tin-güin-din. Then she'd had a dream: that before going her friend had cut off her neck, right hand, and little finger. In her dream the little girl Sol looked at herself in the mirror and cried because she knew those scars wouldn't disappear. She let out a cry. She ran to the rooftop of the house of the portals and encountered the panorama of buildings, television antennas, cupolas, the triangle of Tlatelolco, waking amidst the rosy clouds. But she smiled when Lucía shouted at her from inside the vase, "Enough already, she wasn't even called Dawn. Her name was Rosa and it doesn't matter if you remember her each time you see that color. There are other words that begin like that: Rosicrucian, roseal, rosarian, rosary…" Soledad sat there thinking and finally added, "Well, I might also remember if I saw the flower…" Hearing her Lucía choked in rage. As soon as she composed herself, she spit out, "Listen, the dragon told me to take care of you but it didn't tell me you were so stupid and corny. Looks like I'll have to work even harder." As far as Soledad could remember this was the first time she had fought with Lucía. And she didn't let her go until Lucía put down on the night stand a book of myths. They read it together. When Athena castigated Arachne for being a better weaver, Lucía so impugned that argument that Sol became pleased with the punishment. When Psyche broke the prohibition of looking at her divine spouse, Sol reprimanded her while Lucía jumped on the bed. Nevertheless, they agreed on one story: both wanted to be Perseus, to kill Gorgon and mount Pegasus. "There you go, now you're learning," Lucía said with pride.

The sky had cleared. Matías was still asleep beside her but Marbles was no longer there. The plaza was filling with voices and people. The Corregidora above them had stretched out to direct the movement of cars and pigeons. Soledad missed her friend Leandro Valle. She would have liked to talk to him more about Lucía, to confess that at times she missed her. Would Lucía never return? A fat woman carrying a couple cartons of milk was about to sit down on her. Soledad had to jump up and climb onto Matías, who had begun to muse, "Yes, Soledad, today is the Day of the Dead. Let's enjoy ourselves and sing about how we only live to dream…" "Fucking old man. You don't miss an opportunity," said the fat woman, getting up indignantly. Soledad shook the blind man until she woke him again. "Let's go, Matías," she said, "I'll help you to your hotel." The old man staggered along obediently and played the bullfighter with cars as if instead of being blind he was an actor or instead of being asleep he was daydreaming.

LXXXI

That afternoon things acquired their own character again. The cloud of smog that normally invaded the city had turned crystalline and beings and things were born enveloped in a purity so unusual it was blinding. Soledad rubbed her eyes, discovering the city as a lake of light that her gaze drank up, and she thought, "I'm not awake yet." She tried to close her eyes again, to bury herself within the waves of her own blood, to lose herself in the passages of the vase, to submerge herself in her protective penumbra. But then she perceived that she didn't have to press her eyes shut too tightly nor close in upon herself to quiet the exterior world: outside the city put a finger to its lips, waiting. "Something is about to happen. Will I wake up or is it better to go on dreaming?" she asked with the amphibious voice of someone who knows herself asleep. She opened her eyes. Volcanoes, buildings, air, time shone as they let themselves be caressed by the light. In effect, time had stopped to enjoy the freshness of the afternoon. Everything was quiet, including her heart. To be and not to be there. Was that death, our gaze lingering as if we were alive?

At that moment the bells of the cathedral rang unexpectedly. The world was being reborn, the city was resuming its course. At least that's what Soledad thought until she lifted her gaze and discovered that not only the metal bells were moving anxiously: farther up, at the tops of the towers, other bells—immense, stony, majestic—shook out the dust and the dirt in order to wake from a dream centuries long. About to fall, Soledad set her judgment aside, happy to see how those gigantic bells atop the cathedral's towers madly swung back and forth.

Things like that happened frequently in Soledad's city, but people refused to see them: their eyes and souls blinded, they consumed the miracle like a bad drink, their winged feet made them search for refuge in their houses on wheels, to hurry to the bus and the subway, into that turbid air of odors and bad tastes that glazed their gazes and let them lose themselves in any corner of their skin, except the center.

And of course, the thundering sound of the moving stone forced them to put wax in their ears and the steps of the fearful were directed by their own Ithacas.

But on that occasion, instead of departing the people searched out the doors of the cathedral. A river of souls entered as if part of a vast, authentic pilgrimage. "It's the same for the deceased faithful," she heard a bell ringer say. She decided to descend from the bell tower. As soon as she opened the metallic door leading to the atrium a fat old man came up to her, saying with a Spanish accent, "Hey beautiful…Yes, you. Are you alive or have you just died?"

Soledad could only ask, "You noticed me?"

"Well, eyes that open, my queen, aren't deceitful."

"Yes, perhaps. I can't assure you, sir, but I don't believe I've yet died. And you?"

"Good and dead. I sleep here in the cathedral: Antonio López Catalina/6 August 1894-6 January 1983/Beci de Bilbao, Mexico City."

"Ah…"

"Don't be scared, my child."

"No…it's just I don't understand."

"Look, my love, it's getting to be night. Do me a favor."

Soledad looked at him astonished. What could that man ask of her?

"I have a little granddaughter…She comes to cry over me because she loved me in life and didn't see me die. She thinks I don't forgive her. Look for her. Her name is Teresa de Jesús. Tell her…tell her I love her, too."

The girl promised to do so and the man went off thankful. Then it occurred to Soledad that she might find her father among that multitude. Walking against the flow of the crowd she approached the grates of the atrium and leaned upon one of them, scrutinizing the faces of the people who continued to arrive. But far from finding Javier García she spied the lost children at the moment they escaped through the palace of government's Marian door. They carried among them a bundle that slowed their escape and

222

they would have been overtaken by the squad of soldiers that a few moments later came out after them if it hadn't been for Sope and Ruth sticking their heads out of a sewer grate on Moneda Street to take the bundle. A young man who'd also seen the children running from the palace with their cargo explained to her, "In my time it wasn't so easy to get near the seat of government. Just imagine, I was bringing Don Porfirio a little gift, a hellish machine of my own invention. But the militia was watching and following me and the thing ended up exploding in my hands. Right here on Seminario Street."

Soledad looked at the face of the man talking. She just smiled at him but avoided looking at his hands, scared of finding them destroyed and bloody.

"My name is Arnulfo Calderón de la Barca...In case we meet again," he said and began to walk away.

"Mine is Soledad García," she said as if recalling a dream. "My father was called Javier García. Do you know him?"

The man was already lost amidst all the people entering the cathedral. A face returned that seemed unknown to Soledad, although she had seen it only a few seconds earlier.

"Here we all know each other. Your father is going back down the entrance to the underworld in Chapultepec. Do you want me to tell him anything when I see him?"

Soledad became a sea of questions: When will I see him again? Is he happy? Where he is? Does he miss me? The man finally disappeared into the cathedral while Soledad carefully observed herself; she looked at her belly and for the first time she saw the vase as an organic labyrinth where a tiny Lucía, barely as big as an almond, was looking at her with the blind eyes of someone gazing within. The bells rang again madly, to the windward and the leeward, for the cathedral was cutting its lashings and weighing anchor. She looked up: dozens of souls hung from the ropes tied to the clappers and were swinging back and forth like children. They laughed and played, liberated from all guilt and punishment, like Ruth who had obtained the winged horse from the Palace fountain—the bundle the children were carrying was nothing less—and now mounted it with her perfect legs to unleash it into flight. Soledad felt the urge to climb aboard, too, before the cathedral finished weighing anchor, but then the hand of Matías stopped her.

"Take me to 20 de Noviembre Avenue, girl," the old man asked, "where they're arming themselves for the revolution."

"What? What revolution?"

"No, I didn't say revolution. The delegation's trucks are taking away the street vendors. I must have said violence...repression."

Soledad felt the strength of the blind man's hand on her arm but even so she couldn't continue walking. She fell, slipped, stood or simply shut her eyes to calm the vertigo that brought back to her the anguish being unable to find any place she could grasp onto.

They finally reached the avenue. There was little movement except for a few street sweepers, a small group of taxi drivers stopped in front of a restaurant with fluorescent lights, and here and there a passerby hurrying to the subway before it closed.

"Matías, nothing's happening here," the girl finally said.

"You're right, here nothing ever happens," added the blind man while his nose, reddened by that early November, sniffed for a scent in the air. "But anyways, even if nothing has happened here, if they haven't even gotten a scratch, come with me to city hall."

Soledad took the blind man's arm and walked with him across the avenue. It was then she discovered the wet sidewalks and a current of water that flowed toward a sewer grate, as if an unseasonable rain, firemen or street cleaners had cleaned the way. She felt her heart clench just to think that blood could disappear beneath a stream of water, be erased so easily, become transparent.

They walked in silence until Soledad, suddenly feeling better, asked, "Matías, you're going to say I'm crazy but...do you know what the lions at the entrance to the forest in Chapultepec Park are made of?"

LXXXII

"But, Soledad," Matías finally said as he stopped to catch his breath. "I didn't answer your question before because in this country where all lies are truth until the contrary can be proved, everyone knows what the lions at the entrance to Chapultepec are made of. So, Jorge?"

"The lions?" Jorge had also stopped to rest. He was still limping despite having got out of the police station more than a week earlier. "Any kid knows that, right Clarín?"

Clarín and the other children turned to look at the two men.

"Yes, I know…" he said, returning to Matías and taking his hand as they went on.

"Yes, yes, everyone does," commented another child. Soledad didn't know whether it was Rabbit or Miguel. Then another broke in and began pushing Jorge.

"We want to go to the castle," he said, mumbling.

"OK," gave in Matías and took Soledad's arm again. "We promised you a Sunday in Chapultepec Castle and now we have to fulfill it."

They were beginning to walk up the ramp when Clarín stopped by a man taking photos with an old camera. Barely had he taken the plates from the body of the camera sitting on a tripod did he submerge them in a bucket. The images muddily emerged before the eyes of the other children who had also come up with Clarín. Jorge asked Soledad and Matías to wait for them.

"None of that," said the blind man with a resolute voice. "One photo for everyone."

The children jumped around. They took Matías by the hand and all placed themselves before the camera. Soledad understood they were waiting for her. She walked up to the blind man and touched Jorge on the shoulder. The two made room for her just as the photographer snapped the photo. There followed the normal procedure: the plate, a few moments of waiting, the bucket of water. When the photo was finally developed the children looked skinnier than usual, Jorge—who had moved at the last moment—was out of focus and the eyes of Matías were blank. The only figure that turned out well—the photographer frowned—was some girl who must have just been walking by that the camera by chance captured at the last fraction of a second.

LXXXII-bis

Destiny is a father who calls from the Elevated Knight of the castle. I have gone off too far. Father shouts. No matter,

I have to go back. Barely do I arrive, a vehement tug on the ear that is almost a kiss. The closed door: a visage of light for the rattlesnake that carries chance in its tail.

LXXXIII

From the castle's terraces on that somnolent morning they could touch the clouds. It wasn't so early, but the city yawned and resisted waking from its sleep. Soledad looked at it in contemplation as if it were finally her own. Well, it wasn't complete possession; rather, she felt part of the city and she loved it now like a body itself, with its face of a poor little Cinderella, at times washed by the mist; with its body, imperfect but supple and vigorous; with its bad breath and unimaginable guts; with its raptures that made it touch the sky and its efforts to avoid destruction.

In the distance a group of clouds frolicked in the shadows. An elongated figure like a serpent, its belly rather swollen, its head that could well be awaiting a caress or preparing to attack. She smiled at the profile of a leaden dragon that in its own dream floated upon the horizon. To see it in the distance, guarding the basin of the valley where the city extended in its indecipherable labyrinths of streets and lives made her think that perhaps Lucía was right: she had never come out of the vase. It was curious to imagine that this entire city which still hadn't stretched out completely could fit into a simple Chinese vase, and that the dragon was swimming in its skies without causing more suspicion than those of some passerby who looks up and says, "So many clouds. It looks like it's going to rain..." She thought about showing the children the dragon but they were running about playing on the terraces. Jorge and Matías tried their luck with a few tourists who wanted to know the history of the castle. The children interrupted them. In the upper part of the fortress they had found a fountain full of coins.

"It must be a wishing well," said Matías after bidding a formal farewell to the tourists. "I don't recall it. It must be the fountain of the grasshopper..."

"No," went on Jorge. "They said it was farther up and the grasshopper's is here below."

"Aha," nodded Clarín, pointing to the castle tower.

"Ah, then they found the one at the foot of the Elevated Knight."

Soledad looked, and there the tower rose straight up, the solitary guard of a sleeping city, like perennial desire directing life.

"I didn't know there was a wishing well," continued Matías. "So did they finally ask for something?"

The children remained silent. Soledad looked at their hands and pants still wet and added in amazement, as if she still didn't believe it, "They didn't ask for a wish, they took them."

The children thought the old man was going to scold them, but instead he said, "Well done. You have to grab desire by the tail. Where are you going to invite us to eat with those coins?"

It started to rain as they came down from the castle. The children disappeared on the lower ramp, pushed along by the wind. Jorge and Soledad helped Matías to run along. In a burst the raindrops struck them like sudden, cool kisses. Soledad felt that life, even if fleetingly, could be a blessing.

LXXXIV
(Epilogue)

Contrary to what Soledad might have desired, her mother asked for help from the National Center for the Localization of Disappeared and Missing Persons. In various parts of the city they put up flyers with her photo and physical details. Modesta, who brought Carmen the suitcase, the papers and the Leica camera she rescued from the room on the roof, helped her establish one bit of information at the end of the description: "Disappeared June 23, 1985."

Most of the flyers turned yellow or tore away. Among those that survived a little longer, one remained stuck on a lamp post on 20 de Noviembre Avenue. Soledad never saw it but she would have liked the message someone scrawled beneath it:

her body can't contain her

Translator's Acknowledgments

Thanks first of all to Ana Clavel for letting me jump into this vase with her and take a voyage through its labyrinth. Here's to those mezcal nights in Oaxaca with Cué and Cuéllar. Ricardo Vinós captured this tale exactly in his cover image, a true visual translation that conveys so many thousands of words, "una vida y otra vida," as might have said an exile whose work he shared with me on the streets of Tenochtitlán. Lulitas, mi chilanga querida, was ever patient with my endless questions about Mexico City slang, architecture and geography...And finally my thanks and eternal affection to that biggest, greatest city in all of the Americas, with its stories and ghosts, demons and angels. I owe this translation to the memory of all your labyrinths, so ancient and so modern, I've wandered through.

OTHER TITLES FROM ALIFORM PUBLISHING
literature of the Americas
and the world

Master of the Sea
José Sarney (translated by Gregory Rabassa)
ISBN 0-9707652-7-4

> "Sarney gives us his country's maritime lore, as well as a raw picture of a life along its shores." *Los Angeles Times*
> "A unique and absorbing read. Recommended for all literary fiction collections." *Library Journal*

Die, Lady, Die
Alejandro López
ISBN 0-9707652-6-6

> "A story full of madness that combines Almodóvar and Latin pop." *Página 12* (Buenos Aires)
> "A dizzying novel: there is no truth beyond that of the alienating mass media." *Tres Puntos* (Buenos Aires)

Jail
Jesús Zárate (translated by Gregory Rabassa)
ISBN 0-9707652-3-1

> "In its absurd slant, Zárate's approach resembles Beckett's *Waiting for Godot*, in its questioning of cruelty and power, Kafka's *Penal Colony*." *San Francisco Chronicle*
> "This amazing novel assumes nothing about freedom." *Rain Taxi*

Luminous Cities
Eduardo García Aguilar
ISBN 0-9707652-1-5

> "The author juxtaposes scenes of decadence and splendor, vulgarity and exquisiteness, creating a dizzying mosaic of urban life, injecting into this mix a strong dose of surrealism that impregnates his prose with a magic quality." *Américas*

229

Magdalena: A Fable of Immortality
Beatriz Escalante
ISBN   0-9707652-2-3
> "A fable of feminine ambition that alludes as well to other genres and traditions: biblical and Borgesian parables, alchemical treatises, fairy tales."
> *Delaware Review of Latin American Studies*

Mariana
Katherine Vaz
ISBN 0-9707652-9-0
> "*Mariana*'s evocation of life in seventeenth-century Portugal glows with colour." *The Times Literary Supplement* (London)
> "An exquisitely beautiful love story...an insightful exploration of the sort of mysticism that springs from the combination of carnal experience and its forced absence." *Il Giornale* (Rome)

Mexico Madness: Manifesto for a Disenchanted Generation
Eduardo García Aguilar
ISBN   0-9707652-0-7
> "A scathing, sober and meticulous examination of hot-button political and economic issues." *The Midwest Book Review*
> "History, speculation, philosophy and analysis that offers insights into the consequences of a dramatically changing world." *Washington Report on the Hemisphere*

My World Is Not of This Kingdom
João de Melo (translated by Gregory Rabassa)
ISBN 0-9707652-4-X
> "Spectacular...a gem." *The Los Angeles Times Book Review*
> "A chaotic mythological history of the Azores...an insular society in a brutal but pristine and fantastical setting, an Eden soon to be destroyed by politics and greed." *Ruminator*
> "A baroque impasto where language is applied with a palette knife, not a thin brush." *Revista* (Harvard)

<u>also in 2006</u>

Afloat Again, Adrift: Three Voyages on the Waters of North America
Andrew Keith
ISBN 0-9707652-8-2
Outdoorsman Andy Keith relates three trips at unique points of his life by canoe and kayak down the Mississippi River, across the Boundary Waters Wilderness Area to Hudson Bay, and through the Great Lakes to the St. Lawrence Seaway and the Atlantic. This is both a geographical and spiritual journey.